Mind Games

Also by Heather W. Petty

Lock & Mori

LOCK &MORI

MIND GAMES

HEATHER W. PETTY

SIMON & SCHUSTER BFYR

New York London Toronto Sydney New Delhi

SIMON & SCHUSTER BFYR

An imprint of Simon & Schuster Children's Publishing Division
1230 Avenue of the Americas, New York, New York 10020

SIMON & SCHUSTER BFYR is a trademark of Simon & Schuster, Inc.
For information about special discounts for bulk purchases,
please contact Simon & Schuster Special Sales at
1-866-506-1949 or business@simonandschuster.com.
The Simon & Schuster Speakers Bureau can bring authors to your live event.
For more information or to book an event, contact the Simon & Schuster Speakers Bureau at
1-866-248-3049 or visit our website at www.simonspeakers.com.
Book design by Krista Vossen
The text for this book was set in Bembo.
Manufactured in the United States of America
First Edition
10 9 8 7 6 5 4 3 2 1
Library of Congress Cataloging-in-Publication Data:
Names: Petty, Heather, author.
Title: Mind games / Heather W. Petty.
Description: First edition. | New York : Simon & Schuster Books for Young
Readers, [2016] | Series: Lock & Mori [2] | Summary: In modern-day London,
sixteen-year-old Miss James "Mori" Moriarty and classmate Sherlock Holmes
set out to discover who is framing Mori for the Regent's Park killings.
Identifiers: LCCN 2016015587| ISBN 9781481423069 (hardback) |
ISBN 9781481423083 (eBook) Subjects: | CYAC: Mystery and detective stories. |
Characters in literature—Fiction. | Love—Fiction. | London (England)—Fiction. |
England—Fiction. | BISAC: JUVENILE FICTION / Mysteries & Detective
Stories. | JUVENILE FICTION / Law & Crime. | JUVENILE FICTION / Love &
Romance. Classification: LCC PZ7.1.P48 Mi 2016 | DDC [Fic]—dc23
LC record available at https://lccn.loc.gov/2016015587

To my sweet friend Sophie,
who loves all the ones
I name James the best.

I stared down an overconfident Sherlock Holmes, begging him to so much as twitch. He held his weapon in one hand high over his head, the shaft end pointed at the floor between us.

"Ready?" he asked.

I tilted my chin up in a half nod and made a noncommittal noise. "Mhm."

I held my weapon up as well, one hand at each end, just high enough to glare at him from under it. The perfect height to shield the overhead blow that had been his opening gambit all afternoon. He was sweaty, and his cheeks were rosy, partially from his efforts, but mostly out of pure joy.

"Don't forget you're trying to keep me off balance. Use my strength to bolster yours." He offered me perhaps the most arrogant smile he was capable of delivering and added, "Not that you'll get the opportunity."

He was the happiest I'd seen him in weeks, which probably should've concerned me a bit. Was it normal that he seemed to enjoy nothing more than our attacking each other with sticks? Not that I expected much normality from Sherlock

Holmes. But when we'd sneaked out of school before my last class, I hadn't expected him to bring me to a sparring gym.

He'd caught me clumsily practicing my aikido katas in my attic space the week prior and decided that I needed to learn Bartitsu, which he claimed was "the ultimate self-defense art." Evidently, Lock liked to use the word "ultimate" when what he really meant was "antiquated."

True to form, Lock swished his cane in a semicircle through the air above his head and then sliced down toward me with as much power as he could. I released the crook end of my cane just before the crack of the canes' collision echoed through the room. He actually grinned at the sound, the arrogant ass, watching the released end fall down toward the ground, thinking he'd already won. His amusement faded quickly, however, when he realized what was about to happen next.

I used the power of his hit to boost mine as I flipped the cane around, smashing it against his hand so that he dropped his weapon with a satisfying grimace of pain. I kicked my foot out as the cane clattered against the floor, sliding his weapon out of reach, then brought the crook of my cane up under his chin, pushing just high enough to make him uncomfortable.

"You're a quick study," he said, shaking out his hand. His grin had returned, perhaps in response to my own, perhaps in a vain attempt to seem unaffected by the awkward angle of his neck. I pushed my cane slightly higher, forcing him up on his toes.

"You're predictable." I twirled my cane down and used the crook to snag his knee, but I must have moved too slowly. He somehow kept his balance as he hopped toward me. I tried to spin away, but he grasped both of my shoulders, so that my efforts only knocked us off balance, sending us both down into a heap on the practice mats. I should have gotten the worst of it, as he fell on top, but at the last minute, he wrapped his arms around my head to keep me from concussion. Always the gentleman, my Lock—right up until he started shaking with laughter instead of rolling off me apologetically.

I allowed his fun to last exactly ten seconds before I warned, "The very minute you release me, I will kill you."

"That doesn't seem like incentive to move." He pushed up onto his elbows and smiled down at me, so that his cheeks bunched up under his eyes. "Want to go again?"

I focused on his smile rather than the weight of him on me, which set off blaring alarms in my brain. Memories threatened to surface despite my focus, memories of a night two weeks prior, of my father, of me not being able to move, of his cruel eyes staring down. His warm blood on my cheek.

"Must we?" I blurted out with a little too much force. I recovered with a wink.

I saw something like concern flash in Lock's eyes, but obviously not enough to make him move. Or maybe he was testing me again. We hadn't spoken about that night or my father—not since it happened. My choice. He said he'd never ask, that he'd wait until I brought it up, *if* I brought it up. Still, every now and then, it felt like he was deliberately prodding at my brain to see what might spill out.

But I hadn't only trained to fight with sticks since the

night my father almost killed me. I'd sneaked into the back of the gym on the weekend in the middle of a self-defense class—just to observe, or at least that had been my intention. But when the woman running the training saw the bruises on my face, she'd talked me into staying after class. She'd run scenarios with me until after midnight, one of which was almost exactly like my current Sherlock predicament.

I knew how to get out from under him. I wasn't truly stuck.

Still, none of that removed the alarm, the cold turn of my sweat, or the rising feeling that I should lash out at Lock until he let me go—all symptoms of the victimized. I didn't have time to dwell on that, however, because Sherlock looked as though he was about to speak, and if he asked me if I was okay one more time, I was definitely going to turn violent.

I rushed to speak first but kept my voice soft. "You like this Bartitsu stuff a little too much."

I thought he might still ask the question left unsaid, but he seemed to check himself before offering a simple, "I do."

"Because it's ancient?" *I know how to get out of this*, I repeated to myself, though it was needless. The panic had mostly subsided.

"Because it's surprising." He ran his finger down my temple, pushing sweat-plastered hair off my skin and back behind my ear. His expression changed while he did it, and I tried very hard not to let my lips twitch into a grin at how easily he was distracted by me.

"Off." I pushed against his chest, and still he didn't move.

"I would, but I don't want to die."

"Die quick or die bloody." I bent one of my legs to rest my knee at his hip and playfully tilted my head to the side to mask the shift of my body in that direction. "It's up to you."

His finger traced down my jaw to my chin. "How long do I have to decide?"

I smiled to hide the sudden uptick in my breathing. "Ten seconds. Starting now."

At ten, I pushed off with my foot just like I'd trained and twisted my body until I could get my feet under his chest to replace my hands. His eyes went wide just before I kicked out, easily tossing him aside. There was no one there to shield *his* head, though. I might have felt remorse over the hard thudding sound it made against the practice mat, but it wasn't like I hadn't warned him.

He held the side of his head as he sat up. "Not quite bloody. I suppose I should show gratitude for your mercy."

"The very definition of magnanimous, really." I held out my hand in a peace offering, and he stood so easily that I unintentionally pulled him too close. I had to tilt my head back to see his face, and before I could do more than note his amusement, he leaned closer still. Soon, his lips hovered not more than six inches from mine. I cleared my throat and added, "How will you ever show your thanks?"

"I'm going to make it up to you."

"With a groveling apology and gifts?"

He seemed amused, but resigned to my suggestion. "Evidently, but first . . ."

I knew he was going to kiss me. He'd been looking for an

opportunity since the last of the other sparring couples had left the practice room, leaving us alone with our canes. I also knew how I would respond, and I felt heartache scrub away every happiness I'd felt while being with him that day.

I stepped back. "First what?"

He smiled, moving in sync with me. "You have exactly two more steps before you run out of space to ask stupid questions."

I stepped back again. "Don't you think kneeling and begging for forgiveness should come before anything else?"

He didn't answer and didn't look anywhere but at my lips, which I pursed subconsciously. I then somehow managed to affect a bored expression as I took my final step away from Sherlock that, as predicted, would be my last. My back hit the wall and my mind scrambled for something to say—anything that might distract him away from what he was about to do. A question. I still had one more question.

He didn't let me ask it, however. He braced himself against the wall, laying one hand and forearm flat against the concrete by my head. His other arm looped around my waist, pulling me into him. When his lips were almost to mine, my heart sank even further, despite the tease in my voice when I said, "That's not begging."

"It's a form of begging."

He was right. The way he paused before he kissed me, the pleading look in his eyes for this to be the day that I forgave him—for this kiss to be the one that turned everything back to normal. Lock was begging. And it should have worked.

Even without our lips touching, just the closeness of him set my heart fluttering, changed my breathing. He affected me, my Lock, in a way he shouldn't have been able. Not anymore.

Because it was all so temporary.

That was the reminder I gave myself when I turned my face away so that his lips brushed my cheek. "Temporary." The word that I'd kept with me whenever I was with Lock. Ever since the night two weeks ago when Lock had brought the police to my house to save me from my father, I knew we were on our way to being done. We were on separate paths, parallel for now, but still separate, our arms stretched across the gap to keep us connected. But the gap was still there, widening every day that I saw the innocent glint in Sherlock's eyes and felt the black ash of rage staining mine.

I have rescued you, he seemed to say with his every look.

You have only prolonged the inevitable, I countered with mine. Sherlock had stopped my father from killing me. He obviously wasn't sorry for doing that. But he'd made the call to send police my way, not even knowing if I needed rescue. He'd done it because he didn't trust me. He didn't care what would be best for my life or for my brothers'. He just didn't want me to change. That's what he'd said. He'd kept me from killing my father in some vain attempt at preserving what little innocence I still possessed.

And it might have worked. Those first hours after my father's arrest were filled with so many details to recount, detectives to placate, and reporters to dodge, I'd almost forgotten the cold, dark creature I'd become that night. I'd distracted myself with practicalities and left what had happened in a mental drawer to deal with in some distant future, when my world wasn't falling apart.

But I'd had to relive that night over and over in the past two weeks, making statements to this officer and that, my story checked and double-checked before the police would even consider keeping him away from us. My father locked up wasn't the freedom Sherlock had thought it would be. Even though the police had finally hidden him away from me, my father was always with me in my memory, filtering into my day-to-day thoughts in unexpected ways.

That day in the sparring gym with Lock wasn't the first time a memory had exploded from the drawer and taken my composure with it. It wasn't the first time my anger had crawled back, waiting in the shadows to remind me that I couldn't trust Sherlock Holmes anymore. That he'd never trusted me in the first place. That he'd betrayed me when he could have helped, leaving my father lingering out there like a blinking red warning light in the distance—a promise of trouble to come.

But even with all the anger and memory pounding in my head, even though I turned away from his kiss, I couldn't push Sherlock away. *I won't let my father take anything else away from me.* That's how I rationalized it, but I knew better. Things weren't right between us. They might never be right. But he was still my Lock and I still wanted him. It wasn't fair of me, but I did.

So when Sherlock's head bent and I felt his heavy sigh

against my neck, I lifted a hand to cup his cheek. It wouldn't quell his frustration, but maybe, if I could focus only on today, if I could forget his betrayal and my father's violence, maybe then I could keep Lock by my side—before I fell to pieces, locked away my emotions for good, or did something that would guarantee he'd leave me forever. I pressed my cheek to his and held him close. Temporary, I knew. I just wasn't ready to let go yet.

Chapter 2

Sherlock was in rare form on the bus back to Baker Street. Though outwardly calm, his hands twitched and fumbled into one position after another—on his lap, under his crossed arms, gripping his knees—like they were looking for a place to rest. Probably a reflection of his thoughts just then. Did that mean my stillness was a reflection of mine? Were we the perfect picture of awkward and gutted?

Weeks ago, his fidgeting would have annoyed me until I reached out to grab one of his hands. Weeks ago, that would have calmed him completely. And that was the thought that brought back the now-familiar ache to my heart. Because weeks-ago Mori no longer existed—not the way Lock needed her to. And as much as I wanted to reach over and stop his fidgeting, I couldn't do it. I couldn't make him think that things were all right again. I probably shouldn't have been around him at all, but I couldn't stop myself from doing that, either. I was a heap of couldn'ts when it came to Sherlock Holmes.

With his hands draped over the seat backs in front of us, he turned toward me. "I solved it," he said. "That missing rat case."

"Well done. Did you end up going to the house?"

Sherlock shook his head. I'd been down in Lock's lab at school when Martin Banks came in and begged Sherlock to find his girlfriend's missing pet rat. He'd been pet sitting and hadn't latched the cage door all the way after a feeding. I'd wandered off just after Lock had made the poor boy draw a house map and before he'd finished his giant list of questions.

"It was in the box spring of his sister's room, just as I'd predicted."

I shuddered. There would be a thorough check of my own box spring in my future.

"The rat had stolen stuffing from one of his sister's plush bears and made a nest."

I could tell there was more by the rise of Lock's brow and the way he stared past me out the window by my head. A completely unconvincing attempt at nonchalant.

"Go on. Tell us about the beady-eyed monster and your part in keeping it locked in a cage where it belongs."

"There were four babies, just as I'd predicted!"

Total guesswork, I was sure, but Lock was awfully proud.

"Martin seemed so impressed I could solve it without leaving the lab, he completely missed that the clues were all obvious, had he taken even a moment to think about the problem for himself."

I turned slightly toward the window to watch the steady stream of headlights whisking by us. "I'm assuming you still took his money?"

I saw Lock's scowl in my periphery. "He only left half of what he'd offered when he came in."

"Maybe you should stop bragging on the obviousness of the clues." I grinned and flipped through a physics booklet that the teacher had left on my desk in maths class. She was constantly trying to get me interested in the stuff, but I preferred straight maths. Or maybe I just preferred the theoretical over the physical. "How many does that make this month?"

"How many of what?"

"What are you calling them, exactly? Problems? Cases? Have you become the school detective? Shall we hire you a receptionist and find you an office in a seedy part of town?"

Sherlock waved off my mockery, though I didn't miss the small smile that filtered through his false modesty. "Nothing of the sort. I'm finding baubles and a few missing pets."

That wasn't entirely true. Since a reporter had run a piece about the "teen sleuth who saved a girl's life" last week, Lock had been approached by a steady stream of students at school with troubles of their own. I thought he'd turn them all away to keep up with his own studies, but he hadn't. And the gravity of his cases seemed to be escalating.

"What about Riva?"

I shouldn't have brought it up, that case. I'd gone to Lock's lab after drama to remind him that school was over and had gotten stuck waiting as he'd finished testing eighteen different samples of cigarette ash to see if he could tell the brand by scent alone. Riva had stepped into the lab dressed in street clothes, but she didn't say a word, and she wouldn't move her gaze from the worn, industrial linoleum floor. Lock and I had exchanged a look, but neither of us spoke for a bit. After a while, I'd grown tired of the anticipation.

"Do you have something to say?" I had asked. "It doesn't seem like you enjoy the both of us staring at you."

Riva nodded and brought the backs of her fingers to her cheeks. "I need help."

"It's for you," I told Lock, and grabbed my bag to leave.

Riva made an odd noise that still managed to convey the message that she didn't want me to leave her there alone with Lock. I dropped my bag and fell back into my seat.

"My mother is missing," she said.

"Have you informed the police?" Sherlock asked.

At the mere mention of police, Riva's eyes had widened and she'd backed up two steps toward the door. I stood and stepped toward her and put a hand up to stop Lock from asking anything else.

"I'm guessing you haven't," I said. "You're worried that your mum might get into trouble if you tell the police?"

She nodded.

"Can I ask your name?"

"Riva Durand."

"And your age?"

"Fourteen."

I nodded once and turned to Lock. "A parent leaving her child at home for an extended period of time is what police call 'child neglect.' And because Riva is too young to stay by herself, they'll toss her in a group home, where she'll stay until they decide whether to charge the mother or not."

Lock had stared at me for a few seconds.

I lowered my voice. "Or you can help her before anyone else finds out."

Lock frowned, but he pulled a chair over by mine for Riva and then plopped into his rolling chair and glided over to us. "Tell me everything you remember about the day she left."

He hadn't solved this one from the comforts of his lab, but he'd found the girl's mother pretty readily. She had crashed on the couch of a friend, sleeping off the aftereffects of a too-long weekend, and lost track of the days—or some other excuse that really meant she'd wanted to forget she had a daughter to care for. It was the first time one of Lock's cases stayed with me well after it was over. I'd even waited outside Riva's house the next couple of nights to make sure her mother came home, which is when I found out that Riva had younger siblings, just like me, only hers were all under the age of five.

Lock, however, had solved the puzzle, and that was that. And when I found him in his lab the next day at lunch and suggested we do something to make sure it didn't happen again, Lock's only suggestion was to report Riva's mother to the police. Of course it was.

"We already discussed that option and why it is an asinine one."

"That's what the police are for." He'd only realized his mistake after the words had left his mouth, but he couldn't apologize, because he didn't think he was wrong—only wrong to suggest it to *me*, apparently.

14

"We barely got my brothers placed with Mrs. Hudson. What do you think will happen to Riva and her siblings? What if they don't have a friend who still keeps in touch with his fifty-year-old nanny?"

"She's not our nanny," Lock said. "Not anymore."

"Yes, *that* is the important point here."

Sherlock had frowned and gone back to his study of ash. He'd moved on to pipe tobacco since Riva's visit. "Suppose they don't have a way to stay together. Either we are satisfied with doing our part, or we call the police and think they are better off separated and cared for than together and neglected."

I'd stared at him, begging him to take back what he'd said. But he wouldn't. Not even if I'd reminded him that if he'd been as flippant with me, my brothers would be in the system at that moment. That if I were Riva's age, if I were even one year younger, I would have been in a group home instead of free to stay at my own house, because his precious law decided that being sixteen meant I could take care of myself as long as I had a suitable place to live, but being fourteen meant Riva couldn't.

I would never remind him of any of that, though. It would've been a waste of time. No, he wouldn't even think of anything but those ridiculous piles of ash. So I'd said, "If you'd use your giant brain for something that matters for once." And then I'd stormed out of the lab, sure I was done with his pathetic law-and-order ideals for good. But he'd shown up outside each of my afternoon classes and followed me onto the bus home, until I no longer had the energy to ignore him.

We'd only just resolved everything two days ago, and I was bringing it up again. For what? To make him see how much what he did could matter to a person?

"It's not just pets and baubles," I said. "Finding someone's guardian hardly equates to a bauble."

Sherlock scowled out the bus window. "That puzzle barely took me a day to work out."

"She now knows where her mother is."

"Wasn't it you who suggested we needed to do more?"

I sighed and bit back all the things I wanted to say. I wasn't about to rehash our argument over something so stupid. Instead, I decided to start a new one. "I thought it was all about the puzzle for you."

Sherlock looked back at me, and I kept my eyes on my booklet. When he spoke, his tone was softer than I expected. "We could still call the police."

I shouldn't have been surprised, really. But sometimes that boy was so clueless, I had to wonder whether he had any thoughts in his head at all. "The police."

"I just mean—"

"After everything you've witnessed." He had nothing to say to that, so we stared at each other while the bus slowed and came to a stop. I stood, rolling my booklet into a tube as I stomped down the steps and off onto the street. He chased after me and fell into rhythm with my stride. Then he reached for my hand, which I let him hold without realizing until it was too late to pull it back without looking like a pouty child.

"Can you really not see past your father's version of the law to what it is supposed to be?" he asked.

I scowled. "The law is not absolute. Laws are ever wavering, affected by the good and bad of those in position to create and enforce them, which leaves some citizens more subject to the law than others."

"Are you speaking of wealth?"

"Of course. Wealth, race, gender, disability, orientation—anything that breeds prejudice also breeds injustice."

"And the law is the only thing that can fight those injustices. Do you really think corruption and prejudice will *lessen* without the authority of law?"

"Are you so afraid we would all become monsters without the law?"

"Not all."

"Who then?"

He looked at me, then away. *Me?* Was he afraid of what *I* would become? I studied his profile for a few moments, then glanced down at our still-clutched hands. I tried to slide mine free, but he held fast. He was right to be worried for me. He was wrong that the law would stop me, however. It never would.

But I had to know what he really thought. "Are you such a believer in the law? Or are you just afraid of who *I* might become outside of it?"

"You . . ." Lock paused just long enough to let me think I was right. Then his expression went blank. Was he actually afraid of me? I'd never even considered the idea, but it was possible. Probable, even. He'd seen me at my most vulnerable and most dark—all within the span of a single day. I'd have to wonder if he *wasn't* afraid of me, really.

"I don't know," he said at last. "Am I afraid of what you might be? Or am I afraid of what I know for certain *I* would be without the constraints of law?" He looked me straight in the eyes and asked, "Am I more afraid of you or myself?"

I hadn't expected him to say that, and I could tell by the sudden furrow of his brow that he hadn't expected to say it either. But he quickly recovered. "So, let us say that you are right, and there is no justice in the world. Then all we have is the law!"

"What is the point of law without justice?"

"It is still the law. It is a contract between the people in a community on how to live together peacefully."

"But without justice, the law is empty. Why follow something that has no benefit?"

Sherlock tightened his grip on my hand. He didn't say anything else until we crossed to Baker Street. "It still applies, whether it benefits you or not."

I shook the hair back from my face and gazed up at the starless sky. "Then should I say that the law does not apply to me, because I choose not to accept it?"

"We are to be anarchists then?"

I sighed. "Anarchy is chaos, as is the law. They belong together. Anything that arbitrary is useless. . . . Do not smile at me, Sherlock Holmes."

He didn't even try to heed my words. "I can't help it."

"You can. You choose not to." I bumped his side with my

arm and he started to laugh, but the sound of it died away sooner than was natural. We took only one more step before we stopped walking.

My house was surrounded by people, with two cars in front—one dark sedan and one gray police car with blue flashing lights. Officers were coming in and out of the front door. We started running up the street, and when I got a little closer, I saw a blond woman standing at the bottom of the steps, her arms protectively surrounding my younger brothers, Michael and Sean. Freddie, the oldest of my brothers, stood just in front of them, his arms crossed to face down the uniformed officer who was peering at him over his notebook.

"This is a restricted area," an officer said as I ducked under some police tape that formed a lazy barrier around the cars and our stoop. But his slight smirk told me that he knew exactly who I was.

"This is *my* house," I said. I instantly labeled him as one of my father's. It was a little game I had played in the long hours spent at the police station giving statements. I sorted every officer I came into contact with as "father's," "not father's," or "worthless regardless of loyalties."

I started forward and he reached out to block me again, but Lock intervened and I left him behind to explain things. The officer facing Freddie was almost sneering when I finally reached them.

"You say she's your auntie?" the officer asked. "She'll have to prove it."

"Not to you," the woman said, her American accent bringing

a smile to my lips. She turned to wink at me and a flood of relief washed away a few of the knots in my brain that I hadn't realized were plaguing me. "I'm late, aren't I?"

Alice.

In the days after my father was jailed, I'd had to fight through an exhausting pile of government forms and rules and protocols to keep my brothers together and out of a facility. Mrs. Hudson immediately filed to take them in herself and was granted interim care of the boys, which would last only eight weeks. I'd had no idea what we'd do beyond that. And apparently I wouldn't need to know.

"Aunt Alice!" I said. I managed to return Michael's and Seanie's questioning stares with a quick nod that seemed to put them somewhat at ease. Michael even reached over to take Alice's hand, which made me desperate to ruffle his hair. Instead, I placed myself between Fred and Officer Sneery, who seemed to be eyeing everyone's reactions a little too closely. "I didn't think you'd make it until next month or I would've told the boys their auntie was coming."

"They were surprised," she said, smiling at Seanie, who looked immediately at the ground. "But Mrs. Hudson helped introduce me. And Fred here even remembered me from way back."

Alice, of course, wasn't our aunt. Our mother's sister could've lived out of the country or around the block for all we heard from her, which was never. Alice had been Mother's best friend and biggest fan when they were young. She was also the only member of my mother's con-artist crew to escape death at my father's hand.

Alice turned back to the officer. "I have my papers in order and filed with Tri-borough Children's Services. These children are now in my temporary care pending a full care order. So, if you'll please vacate our house."

The officer cleared his throat and leaned between us. "I heard these kids' aunt lives in Australia."

"You should be careful who you listen to, Officer"—I made a point of tracing his silver nametag with a hovering finger—"Parsons, is it?"

"You must be the liar," he said, looking rather pleased with himself as he sketched a word across his notebook. "Or, I meant to say, *daughter*. Slip of the tongue."

"Clever, our officer Parsons. Isn't he clever, Aunt Alice?"

"Ever so," Alice said in her most sardonic American accent.

A flash went off behind us and my heart sank. Someone had called the press. Still, I kept my voice light, even as I shifted my body to keep Freddie out of their view. "So what's all this? Did you miss us?"

"We got a tip—," he started, but his words were drowned out by shouting.

"Free Moriarty! Free the innocent! Free Moriarty!"

"Send him to prison where he belongs! Clean up our police force!"

"Free Moriarty!"

Our protesters were back, both sides. One bald man calling for my father's hanging in the town square and one tiny, curly-haired, red-lipped woman shouting the others down. She was our very own version of Sally Alexander, only instead of throwing paper packets of flour at Miss World candidates, our Sally had been screaming vulgarities at me and my family every day since my father had been incarcerated.

Perhaps she didn't deserve such a distinguished nickname, but there was something about her I liked. Maybe it was the way she jabbed at the police with her bony elbows to get them off her whenever they tried to take her away for disturbing the public decorum of Baker Street. Or the way she plied them with baked goods and a Thermos of tea the next time she saw them, like she'd known them forever. She was on the side of a monster, but she allowed no one to dampen her efforts to be heard. She would not be silenced. How could I fail to respect that?

"Find the real Regent's Park killer! Give us back our sergeant! Free Moriarty!"

Her counterpart looked like nobody, and even though his message was the more righteous of the two, something about him was entirely off-putting. He always lifted his nose a bit when he looked at us, like he could smell our father's genetic code wafting off our skin. He was a bit of a git, really.

"Toss away the key! No tolerance for police corruption!"

Still, he said all the right things.

A heavy hand landed on my shoulder from behind. "Inspector wants to see you."

The hand was gone before I could see who'd touched me, but when I turned, Sherlock stood pointed nose to bulbous nose with what had to be London's tallest, widest constable.

With a smile in his voice, but not at his lips, Lock said, "I must insist that you do not touch her. But do lead the way to the inspector. I'm fascinated to hear what he has to say."

The giant constable's shoulders rolled back to better puff out his massive chest, but he didn't retaliate further than that. With his eyes still on Lock, he lifted one sausage-like finger toward me and said, "Not you. Just that one there."

"Oh, what to do?" Lock lamented, not backing down one inch himself. "She's a minor, so I'm afraid she must be accompanied by her guardian"—he gestured toward Alice—"who is rather busy at the moment caring for three young boys kept out of their house for reasons no one has shared with us yet."

The constable huffed and then started toward the house without another word. Sherlock shrugged at me and took my hand, and then we both followed along behind him.

Chapter 3

Detective Inspector Mallory sat at the head of our kitchen table, one long, slim leg draped over the other like he'd been invited for tea. As we approached, he took a gulp from a tiny cup without acknowledging Sherlock and me, then shuffled through the papers within the manila folder splayed open in front of him. Mallory cleared his throat and the two officers who had been snooping through our kitchen drawers and cabinets filed out of the room, leaving us alone with him—the DI who had pulled me out from under my father's strangling hands.

I should, perhaps, have been grateful for that at least, but I couldn't seem to rid myself of past images of him and Detective Sergeant Day standing on our stoop and doing nothing to rescue us from the drunken monster inside the house, of their overly cheerful waves as they abandoned me and my brothers to deal with the monster on our own, of the way their eyes couldn't seem to find the welts and bruises on my brothers' faces. And if those weren't enough reasons to despise the man, I could still clearly remember the dismissal in his eyes when I'd sat up in my hospital bed and accused my father of killing all those people in Regent's Park, including my best friend, Sadie. I remembered each word he spoke, when the inspector looked me straight in my battered face, just hours after he'd stopped my father from killing me, and said, "Being an angry drunk does not make one a killer, Miss Moriarty."

Mallory kept us standing there in the silence for what felt like minutes, and when he did speak, his voice was quiet and calm. "Miss Moriarty."

My tone wasn't as gentle. "Mallory." I wanted to add a few dozen questions about who the hell he thought he was and why the hell he was in my house, but his continued silence could only mean that he wanted me to explode. I wasn't about to do anything to fulfill that man's wants.

Mallory sighed and flipped over a page from one half of the folder to the other. "Do you have the sword that killed those people in the park?"

"That's what all this is about? You're looking for my father's weapon?"

When Mallory didn't answer, Sherlock spoke up. "The officer outside said you'd received a tip. Is that why you're here? Someone said the missing weapon is here in the house?"

I'd made several stupid mistakes in my dealings with my father and his crimes, but none were as dumb as throwing the weapon he used to kill all those people into the lake in Regent's Park. I'd thought at the time I was breaking his serial killer ritual, stealing his weapon away to make everyone safer. But it didn't stop him at all, and only aided his fight against the charges in the end. My father had kept what could have become the figurative smoking gun in his closet, and I had no one but myself to blame that it was no longer there as proof of his guilt.

"A tip," I said, suddenly very sure who had instigated our night's chaos. "Was it an actual call? Or did one of my father's loyal officers suddenly get a hunch?"

Mallory flipped another page but did not look up. It was almost as if he thought I wasn't worth the effort. "Your answer, please."

"Don't you think I have the right to know why there are strangers snooping through all my private things before I subject myself to your questions?"

"No." He hit his fist against the table hard enough to make his teacup rattle in the saucer. Then he cleared his throat and softened his tone again. "You gave up those rights when you accused a police detective of being a serial murderer and then chose to remain living in his house."

"I am sixteen, which you know gives me every right to choose to live on my own, and this is *my* house."

"*This* is still a crime scene, if you told the truth—"

"I did."

Mallory continued on as if I hadn't spoken. "—so, no, Miss Moriarty, you have no rights here. And I will ask my question once more. Do you or do you not have the sword that was used to kill citizens in Regent's Park?"

I stared at the top of his head until he finally looked up at me, then I said, "I do not."

Mallory nodded. "I see. Well, it has yet to be found. I

suppose it will be a key piece of evidence in determining who actually committed those crimes."

I crossed my arms. "As if you don't know."

Mallory stared at me silently.

"So, we're pretending now that you didn't stop him from killing his own daughter?"

"He was slashed across the face and chest. Some might think he had no choice but to protect himself."

Lock's hand came to rest on my shoulder, which was the only thing that kept me from screaming my next words. "I told you he did that to himself."

"Yes. Using a knife that had your prints on it." Mallory turned away from my glare and back to his papers. "You seem to think that it's a small thing to make such giant accusations against a policeman. It is not. The Westminster Police Borough is a brotherhood, Miss Moriarty. When one of our own succeeds, we all triumph. When a brother falls, we all mourn. When one of our own sins"—he looked up to meet my eyes again—"we are all stained."

"Then your hands are bloody, Detective Inspector Mallory, first with the blood and bruises of three innocent boys you failed to protect from the fists of your *brother-in-arms*."

Mallory flinched, and I slammed my hand down on the table, drawing his eyes back to mine, and Lock's hand back to my shoulder.

"Second, with the blood of the five from the park." I lowered my voice and held out my hand to show him my clean palm. "You and I can share the stain of a girl who was strangled for bringing my brothers a pie. But, make no mistake, if you claim that man as your *brother*, your hands are stained, Inspector. They may never come clean."

Mallory opened his mouth to speak, but I turned and stormed from the kitchen before he could, shouting behind me, "You won't find what you're looking for here, so get the hell out of my house."

But my words were overrun by a bright-eyed uniformed officer who dashed through the front door and into the kitchen shouting, "Guv! We found something!"

A herd of officers converged on the entry and followed Mallory out the front door, leaving Lock and me to stare after them.

"What could they find?" he asked.

I shrugged. "Nothing out there but the rubbish bins."

"Bins that have been on the street for how many hours?"

I didn't know, but everything was too quiet for a beat, and then I heard Alice shout, "Kid, stay behind me!"

I was out the door before Sherlock and almost ran into the backs of two officers who stood guard on the bottom step. And while they wouldn't let me pass, there was just enough space between them to see what an officer had dug from our trash.

It was a hand. A severed hand, mottled gray and slightly puffy with rot, stuffed into a large, clear zipper bag.

Someone from the crowd screamed, and Alice tried her best to hide my brothers out of view as a wave of flashes and camera lights overtook the front of our house. The world around us went to chaos, but still all the officers turned to look at me—the girl with a severed hand in her rubbish.

Sherlock moved faster than the officers, grabbing me around my middle and practically carrying me into the house. When we reached the kitchen, he was full of assurances that what they found had nothing to do with me, that it was probably all a mistake, but I knew he couldn't protect me from what came next. I still ended up sitting in my kitchen, with Lock and Alice on either side of me while the inspector retook his seat at the head of the table.

After a very long pause, Mallory closed the manila file folder, looked up at me, and said, "You're going to have to come to the station."

Sherlock stood in protest, but I kept my eyes fixed on Mallory. I couldn't tell what he was thinking, whether he was feeling triumphant or skeptical or bored, for that matter. I didn't know what to think or feel myself. I could think of only one person who might try to call in a tip and give the police something to find when they got here, but he'd been in a jail cell for two weeks. And while my mind traced every possible way my father could have tossed this mess in my lap, my silence was making it look as though I were acquiescing to Mallory's request.

"For what possible reason?" Alice, bless her, spoke up in my stead. "There's n—"

"A body part was found when searching the house."

"Outside the house," Alice countered.

"In her rubbish bags."

Sherlock slammed shut the lower cabinet door beneath the

sink. "Not her bags." He stared at the white bag in his hand and then set it on top of Mallory's folder. "You of course noted that the bag the hand came out of was green, like those found in the park bins, not the white with red stripe provided by the City of London."

"That doesn't necessarily mean—"

"And that the other items in the bag were clearly take-away containers, bags, and other rubbish from the zoo, shops, and restaurants in the park. You at least saw the smashed coffee cup that literally said 'Feeding time at the zoo' on it."

When Mallory said nothing, Lock wandered behind him, to the far side of the table, then sat down in the chair directly across from me. His grin was subtle, but infectious. "Her bins have been left out front for hours now. Anyone in the city could have dropped that bag in there."

Mallory swept the empty bag off his folder and started to speak, but my Lock wasn't done. "Most important, however, you wouldn't have had to watch Miss Moriarty grow up to know that she's much too intelligent to cut off someone's hand and drop it into her own rubbish bin, when there are public bins literally every thirty feet across the city."

Mallory pressed his lips together. "Perhaps not."

Alice cleared her throat, bringing our attention back to her. "And the press will want to know why a detective inspector as bright as you would bring a teenage girl to a police station when she is clearly being framed. Do you have an answer for that, Mr. Mallory?"

He apparently didn't, as his chin dropped to his chest. Then, without a word, he pushed back from the table and stormed from the kitchen. I followed him out and stood in the kitchen doorway to watch him call off his dogs. The officers slowly streamed out the front door under my watch, none of them bothering to say a word in my direction. Not that I would have answered. My mind was working too fast trying to figure out answers to the most important questions: What the hell was a severed hand doing in my rubbish bin? Who the hell put it there? And why?

My father was the obvious answer to all three, but then I got stuck on the how of it. My father. Two weeks behind bars and I was still not free of him. I closed my eyes against the surge of rage that burned through me and felt my jaw clench. I didn't, however, realize I was trembling until Sherlock slid his fingers between mine and squeezed my hand.

"Almost over," he said.

I'd only meant to free myself from his touch, but I jerked my hand from his with enough force that the final uniformed officer to leave paused and looked over at us on his way out. I took a deep, shaky breath before I turned away from Lock and headed up the stairs. I paused on the center landing. "Distract my brothers while I check their rooms?"

I saw Lock nod in my periphery.

At the top of the stairs, I walked straight to the end of the hall first, where the two youngest shared a room. It looked reasonably in order. The dresser drawers weren't all fully shut, and the bedclothes were a bit mussed, but nothing had been seriously disturbed. I straightened things a bit and headed to Fred's room next, which was in a similar state to Michael and Sean's, except for the bed. It was perfectly made, even though Freddie hadn't properly made his bed one day in his entire life. The answer to how his bed had come to its present state wasn't all that hard to ascertain. A blue envelope was placed on the very center of his quilt, addressed: *To my son.*

I snatched up the letter and pocketed it. I wasn't sure I wouldn't explode were I to read it just then. So I pulled Freddie's bedclothes free of their ridiculous corners and then headed downstairs.

About halfway down, I stopped on the landing once more and nodded at Sherlock, who jumped up from his spot reclining on the bottom stair and ran up to meet me. Alice stood in the kitchen doorway, tugging at her bottom lip and staring at the now-shut front door as if it were about to swing open and attack her. My brothers followed Lock up the steps and started pelting me with questions like, "Did you see what they found in the bins? No one would show us," and, "Is it true dad killed people with a sword?" and, of course, "They didn't take any of our stuff, did they?"

The last was Seanie, and I could have kissed that boy for giving me a way to escape what was bound to be well more than a hundred questions to answer that night.

"You'd better go check your rooms for missing things." A trio of wide eyes was the only response I got before they all stomped up the stairs in a race of desperation. I called after them, "Check everything twice!"

"Well and truly distracted," Lock said, leaning against the wall. "Am I next?"

I nodded, but with a smile. "You might as well go. I'm just going to tidy up—"

My mobile rang as I was speaking, and I answered it without thinking.

"Junior."

"Detective Day."

I'd successfully avoided calls from Detective Sergeant Day for more than a week now. And truthfully, the very last thing I needed that night was to be forced to speak to yet another policeman. I'd heard too much from DS Day since he'd tackled my father to the ground and cuffed his bloodstained hands behind his back. He mostly phoned with messages from my dad, but never forced the issue or acted upset when I summarily ended the calls. He seemed to feel guilty about having to contact me at all, leaving me to decide if he was still a subservient accomplice of the now-disgraced DS Moriarty, or if he was just acting as message boy out of habit.

But that night he was all business. "He wants to see you. Tomorrow morning at seven."

I glanced at Lock, who was frowning.

"No," I said. "In fact, you tell him that my answer isn't just 'no,' it's 'never.'"

That seemed to brighten Sherlock's mood. He'd obviously surmised what I was saying no to. This wasn't the first summons I'd received to meet with my father, and while I'd refused every one, Lock still acted relieved when I did, as if he expected me to trot down to the jail at any moment.

I turned my back to Lock and lowered my voice.

"And you can also relay that his sneaky little mission was thwarted. I won't let my brothers hear even one more word from that pathetic old man. Do we understand each other?"

DS Day, just as thick as he ever was, asked, "Well, are you going to see him or not?"

I paused to consider the various blistering ways I could answer that question, but decided to just end the call.

I suddenly didn't want to be in the house anymore. After so many nights by myself in that place, it felt stuffy now that there were five extra bodies. Noisy. I should've made sure my brothers weren't torturing Alice on her first night. I should've welcomed Alice and found out all that had happened and what we'd do next. I should've thought of a way to send Sherlock home peacefully. But all I could think was that I wanted out.

So when Lock stopped me from going upstairs with a hand on my wrist, I barely kept myself from slapping it away. "Come downstairs," he said. "I'll make us some tea."

I looked from his hand to the door, then shook my head and pulled my hand free. "I have to go."

I'd pushed out the front door before Lock or Alice could stop me, though they both called my name. Had I given it any thought, I might have realized that while the police cars and tape were gone, the crowd of onlookers, protesters, and press wouldn't be so easily dissuaded. Thankfully, there were only a handful left, and only one cameraman quick enough to snap a few pictures before I started to run. Whether by luck, surprise, or laziness, no one seemed to follow me, and soon I blended into the busy sidewalk, though I didn't slow my pace. Running meant leaving everything behind just that much faster. Running meant finally being able to breathe.

Chapter 4

I ran toward Regent's Park, which, despite everything, was still my place of escape. I crossed the bridge and got away from the crowds of people on the street, but I was left with the same nagging parade of questions about all the chaos at home, now with added hows. Like, how I was going to deal with Alice's and Lock's questions about my dramatic runaway stunt. How I was going to survive another onslaught of police and press. And how I was going to figure out who was putting spare body parts in our rubbish.

A soft breeze blew around me, chilling my skin and my thoughts. I plodded on, trying my best to blend in with all the others who walked by on their way to a night performance at the amphitheater or home from the zoo, whining kids in tow. My feet took me to the bandstand first, like they always did. It used to be my place to hide from the world; now I came like a pilgrim paying homage to a religious shrine. Perhaps to ask for forgiveness.

I rubbed my thumb over the surface of Sadie's locket—the one her grandmother had given her before she'd left America, which now hung around my neck. When Sadie had first shown me the insides, it held pictures of her and her grandmother, both at age fifteen, looking like twins through time. But when I'd received it via delivery two days ago, it had a picture of me on one side and Sadie on the other, both of us with daisies in our hair from the day we'd competed to see who could give out two bouquets of flowers first, one piece at a time. She'd won, which is why I had flowers behind both my ears. The locket had come with a note that said, "I understand yours is the face that replaced mine. I'm glad she had a friend like you."

A friend like me. Would Sadie's nana still be glad, I wondered, if she fully understood how I'd put her granddaughter in harm's way?

I sometimes made myself stay at the bandstand, staring at the willow where my father had dropped Sadie's body onto the muddy tree roots. It was a silly practice, but some days forcing myself to be there felt like a kind of remedy for my daily frustrations, where an injection of pain was the prescription. Wasn't that the purpose of penance? To burn away the guilt with pain?

Still, the very last thing I needed that night was another dose of poison, so I purposely kept to the path that led toward the boat rentals. In the time since I'd lost my bandstand safe haven to Sadie's memory, I'd taken to sitting by the fountain planter where Todd White had died, sometimes reaching up to touch the medallion that once hid my mother's getaway cache, as though a bit of stone could hold the residue of her.

But it was too public of a place for that night. I wandered—aimlessly, I thought—until I was unwittingly following the path where Lock had led me to our first crime scene, back when we thought it would all be just a bit of fun to make guesses about a killing in the park.

And then I was in the trees, in the almost complete dark, kneeling down by the clover carving that marked the place where my father had stabbed Mr. Patel with my mother's aikido sword. My father had killed three times at least before he got around to Mr. Patel, but his death was the one I lived with day in and day out. In part, perhaps, because his was what started me down the path to discovering what a monster my father truly was. In part, because his was the only murder that seemed to matter to the people at my school.

It was getting harder and harder to face school. My family notoriety resulted in this odd mix of sympathy, scorn, and fear on the faces of the students passing by me in the halls. Drama class was another mix altogether. Lily Patel and her pack of hyena-beasties couldn't quite force themselves to hate me outright when my face still showed signs that the man who killed her father had tried to do the same to me. But now that the swelling and cuts and bruises had healed enough for me to cover them in generous amounts of makeup, Lily's friends had started turning every class into either a proper and overt shunning or a minefield of not-so-subtle, passive-aggressive commentary on my family tree, accompanied by nasty looks.

Neither fazed me much, but there was a bit of fun in calculating which they'd choose as I walked the theater aisle to the stage. The odds tilted decidedly toward commentary. Perhaps they were merely bad at shunning.

I would have preferred a bit of shunning last Friday, after being hounded all the way to school by an unyielding reporter, who actually believed I'd give her quotes for a profile about me. Instead, Friday's drama class was another opportunity for the hyenas to loosen their jaws. I was privileged to overhear how a person with even a shred of decency would have at least transferred schools by now instead of making herself a daily reminder of their poor Lily's loss.

I offered the girls my thinnest smile to thank them for their wise words and then wandered into the circle of chairs on the stage, taking my usual seat, directly across from Lily Patel.

Lily was her own minefield. She didn't seem all that bothered by my presence, despite her friends' keening. She never spoke to me or about me, never joined the shunning sessions. Instead, she just studied me. Openly. Like I was as unfathomable as a Pollock painting. I preferred her stares to the dramatics of her friends, really, because she didn't avert her eyes, even when I stared back.

We'd been studying each other every day of the six since I'd returned to school, sometimes through an entire class session. And the oddest thing was starting to happen, for me at least. I was beginning to feel like I knew her. Perhaps it was Lock's influence, but with so much time on my hands and so little interest in Miss Francis's end-of-term puttering about, I felt like I spent the span of every class taking in Lily Patel to the very last detail.

At first it was just general things, like the fact that she had the same necklace in both silver and gold, which she would match to the metal of her earrings. She always wore a bronze cross tied around her neck with a black ribbon no matter what other jewelry she wore. She mostly hid the cross under her uniform shirt, so that I only got glimpses here and there. She wore her uniform perfectly, without a button undone or hem unaligned, but she changed out her handbag every other day, and I had yet to see a repeat.

It was probably cheating, but I learned she was a vegetarian by listening in on a post-lunch conversation in the hall. Not particularly health conscious about it, though, as her bag was filled with empty bottles of Thai coffee and crinkled-up pastry wrappers that afternoon in drama.

Last Thursday I learned that Lily played cello, when she brought the instrument into class. She'd probably done it dozens of times before, but it took her hefting the giant behemoth case down the theater aisle for me to notice that those papers she studied during free time in class were actually music scores for orchestra. Her heart didn't seem to be in it, however. Her attention was mostly distracted to the stage, even when there was nothing there but lights and dust and our empty circle of chairs. Her heart didn't seem to be with Watson anymore either, though that guess was based more on his desperation than any behavior from her.

So I knew that much about Lily Patel. All those ridiculously useless facts, and that her father had been murdered right where I sat in Regent's Park.

I touched my fingers to the clover leaf her father had undoubtedly carved into the tree trunk to note where he hid his money, and I let myself wonder briefly if Lily knew what had been hidden there. What would they have done with the money, had they known where it came from? Would it be life-changing money for them? Or would they rather have denied its existence to sustain their memory of Mr. Patel as it was, without Sorte Juntos, the criminal organization he and my mother had been members of?

I pulled my hand free from the carving before my thoughts circled back to my father, and instead let myself imagine what it must have been like to run something like Sorte Juntos. To be my mother. To pull the puppet strings of a team, guiding them in and out of some of the most secure places in London. To take whatever she wanted to take. To be above and beyond the rules and the law and any kind of morality. To be free.

Mum had lived that life. So had Alice. And somehow they both ended up living incredibly mundane lives as adults, one in a row house, the other on a farm. Not for the first time I wondered how someone with that kind of freedom and power could willingly decide to step into a cage-like marriage with my father. But those were the kinds of thoughts I was trying to avoid.

Footsteps brought me back to the present and to the realization that I could have been followed by a reporter and, more distressingly, that I was sitting on the spot where my father had killed a man. But before I could do more than stand, the light from a flashlight shone full in my face.

"You." A female voice, but I couldn't tell if the tone held surprise or accusation.

I shielded my eyes and started imagining worst-case scenarios, starting with a morning full of headlines about how a serial killer's daughter was caught visiting his crime scenes hours after police had searched her house.

"What are you doing?"

I had no answer for that, so I turned my face away from the light and stepped toward the shrubs where Lock and I had hidden on the first night of our little game. The beam of light dropped from my head to my feet and my accuser said, "Wait."

I kept walking until she said my name.

"Mori, wait."

I hazarded a look and was surprised to see Lily Patel staring at me with the same expression she wore in drama, like she couldn't decide what to think, but just the sight of me made her sad.

"Why are you here?" she asked.

She was holding flowers and an unopened can of beer, which seemed an odd combination, but I knew I had no right to ask anything. So I glanced toward the shrubbery again and took one more step. "I'll go."

"Stay. I really want to know why," she said, no trace of anger in her voice. "Why are you here?"

I looked over at where the clover carving was. I could barely make out one edge of it now that the light had moved, but the shape of it, the way the leaves pointed, all of it matched the image on my mother's coin exactly. I thought I didn't know why I was there, but that wasn't true. There was a reason—a reason I wasn't sure I should tell Lily.

I hadn't told anyone about the picture of my mother and the other members of Sorte Juntos, or how she factored into the crimes. First, because I wouldn't allow my father to hide behind her death. But mostly, I didn't want pictures of my mom sprawled across the news sites. As a more practical reason, I also didn't want Alice's involvement to be discovered.

Lily would surely take anything damning to my father directly to the prosecutor, so telling her the story was out. But for some reason, I didn't want to lie to her either. A stupid, stupid want, really.

"My mother," I said, after a tremendous pause.

"What about her?"

"She knew your dad. They were friends."

Lily dropped her flashlight but didn't make a move to pick it back up again, so it was left to rock on the ground, casting an odd, shifting light all around us. "What kind of friends?" She paused, but not long enough for me to answer. "Is that why?"

I shook my head, though I kind of wanted to be able to tell her that it was all as easy as an affair and a jealous husband lashing out. Only that lie would make it seem as though her father had done something wrong, and that wasn't the case. "I don't know why, but they were just friends. Not what you're thinking."

"How long have you known this?" She stepped toward

me, tapping the flashlight with her shoe. And when the light shifted, I could see tears shining in her eyes. "How long?" she repeated, when I remained mute.

"The memorial. There was a picture of your dad in a group of people at a party. My mom was part of that group."

A sparkling tear dripped down her cheek and she sank to sit in the dirt. It was my opportunity to leave, but I no longer wanted to. And when I couldn't tolerate the awkwardness of her silent tears and my looming over her, I sat down as well.

Almost as soon as I did, Lily said the very last thing I ever expected to hear that night. "Sorte Juntos."

We stared at each other for a while, saying nothing— gauging each other while my mind spun, trying to sort out how in the world she would know those words. She'd spoken them like a password, like some kind of spy-code call that begged for a proper response. I could think of only one, so I slid my hand into my pocket and dropped my mother's gold coin, clover-side up, into the dirt in front of the flashlight. I heard a soft rustling and then Lily dropped an identical coin next to mine. And when our eyes met again, she looked like she was about to smile.

"You took the picture from the memorial."

I nodded. "How much do you know?"

Lily set the flowers down next to the flashlight and then hugged the black beer can to her chest as she studied me. "What kind of question is that?"

"Did you always know about the group?"

She shook her head, but didn't elaborate.

44

"Do you know what they did?"

"Are you trying to figure out if I approve of our parents stealing millions of pounds from banks and jewelers?" Lily shrugged. "There are worse ways to make money, I suppose. What was your mom's job in the crew?"

"I don't know much about it."

Lily seemed to suspect the lie, but that didn't stop her from saying, "My dad opened the doors and safes."

"Impressive."

She sat up a little higher at the compliment to her dad. "I think so too."

"How long have you known he could do it?"

Her expression darkened. "Not long."

I thought about pushing her, but I didn't want her to stop talking. She didn't know my mother like Alice did, but maybe she knew more about Sorte Juntos than Alice was willing to tell me. There was so much I still didn't know.

After a moment she continued, "My dad was just a locksmith, but we always had money for schools and trips. We also owned our house, which had a locked basement where Dad spent most of his time."

"You were suspicious?"

"Not really. I thought maybe he had habits I didn't want to know about. But one night last fall, he came home drunk, ranting about how 'It wasn't what *she* wanted. It wasn't how *she* wanted to go.' So I took him to the basement door and made him tell me how to open it so he wouldn't wake my mom. But it changed everything, that night."

A hollow expression filtered across Lily's face, one I knew well. The emotions attached to that memory were being burned out of her as she remembered them. Because he was gone now, she wasn't allowed to hate him for that night anymore. Just another way death leaves its mark on survivors.

Her father's comments pointed to the truth that my father had asked for money to help sustain my mother's life and to the reason Mr. Patel and the others from Sorte Juntos had said no—because they knew and respected my mother's wishes better than my father ever had.

"Which one was your mom?" Lily asked. "The one with blue hair or the other?"

"Why?"

"That picture you took, that was from the basement. I was the one who put it on the table at the memorial. He had a whole line of them up on the wall above his workbench down there. I kept them when I cleaned up. I could bring them. Next time."

I wanted to see the lot of them, of course, but her offer felt more like the start of a bargaining session than generosity, and I was in no mood to make a deal, nor was I ready to make a date for "next time."

"Do you often come here?" I asked.

Lily nodded and looked down at the bouquet she'd left next to the flashlight. "Mom refuses to do anything with his ashes"—she choked a bit on the word but recovered quickly. "There's no other place to visit."

I had one of those—a place to visit—but I'd never been to

it. I hadn't even gone to the graveside part of Mum's service. It wasn't like standing on a patch of grass by a granite slab of rock was going to provide some great balm to my soul.

Lily stood and meticulously balanced the bouquet up against the tree. She next opened the beer and said, "He had cases of this stuff imported from India. Kalyani Black Label. He said when he could find it in the UK it never tasted the same as the stuff he ordered direct."

She carefully took a sip, then winced at the taste. "Three cases left in his basement. Thought he wouldn't want it to go to waste." It was an odd thing to say before pouring the liquid out slowly over the ground until all that was left was a puddle of foam.

When she was done, she came to sit next to me, facing the tree and the mess she'd made. "This is better than interned ashes anyway," she said. "If his spirit's anywhere, it's probably here."

I didn't believe in spirits, but if they existed, I could believe one's spirit would more likely stay where its blood had spilled than with a pile of ashes in a ceramic vase.

"I still hate her for it, my mom. She keeps his ashes in an urn in her room, hoarding them for herself, like she keeps everything else of his. She hasn't even taken his clothes to charity yet. Hasn't packed them up."

"My father was like that too."

"But you found the coin?"

"Mum gave that to me before. But I have a few other things of hers. I sneaked in when he was out and took some."

"Weren't you afraid he'd notice?" she asked, turning to look at me.

"He did."

"What happened?"

"He tried to burn everything else that he had of hers and then hit me when I tried to stop him." There was no reason not to tell her. It's not like she hadn't seen evidence of his violence on my face. Still, I surprised myself with the confession.

"Did he hit you a lot?"

"Twice."

"Then just that time and . . . the night he was caught?"

I nodded, then watched in my periphery as she tried to formulate her next question. I knew she probably wanted to know what had happened that night, and I could have told her the same lies I'd told the police in rigorous detail, but in the end I decided to change the subject entirely.

"I'm sorry he killed your dad."

Lily didn't respond for so long, I started to contemplate how best to leave the clearing without her. I even picked up my coin from the ground and stuffed it back in my pocket. That broke her silent spell, but she left her coin in the dirt.

"Do you know why he did it?"

"Does it matter?" We both stared at the beer foam floating above the dirt.

"Yes?"

"Because he's a monster. A violent, angry bastard who doesn't deserve his next breath, much less the luxuries he's getting in a jail cell."

Lily gave in to a wicked grin. It faded quickly, but it made me like her more. "Do you really believe that?"

I nodded, and she slid her arm around mine, scooting closer. It was an odd gesture, like it was supposed to mean something. I supposed the fact that we were both facing the flowers and beer foam was designed to be fraught with meaning as well. But I didn't feel it.

"Your statement to police. You're not going to take it back because he's your dad or anything, yeah?"

I turned my head to look fully into her eyes, so that even in the soft glow of her flashlight, she could see me clearly. "If you believe nothing else I say, know for certain that I will make sure he pays fully for what he has done."

She told me that she'd be at her dad's clearing every other night from then on, then she held my arm more tightly. It reminded me of how Sadie would hug my arm and rest her cheek on my shoulder when she wanted to do something she knew I wouldn't like. I wondered what Lily wanted from me. I couldn't imagine we'd ever be actual friends, but I supposed, when it came to my father, we wanted the same thing. That was apparently enough for Lily Patel. For now.

Chapter 5

I knew that I'd eventually have to face Lock and all his questions about why I'd gone running out of the house for no apparent reason. I even thought that I might find him camped out on our front stairs when I came home that night. I hardly expected to see him the next morning sitting between Michael and Freddie at the breakfast table, messing around between bites of porridge like he was just another part of the family.

"Mine next!" Seanie shouted, practically launching himself across the table to shove a spoonful of porridge at Lock's face. Almost the entire spice cabinet was spread out in front of them to play "Guess What's in My Porridge," a game the boys had invented with Mrs. Hudson the last time we were housebound because of the press.

Sherlock had a perfect record, which Sean was desperate to shatter. But Lock didn't seem all that afraid when he leaned forward to taste from Seanie's spoon. "Let's see," he said, then he sat back thoughtfully, moving the food around his mouth a bit before swallowing. "Currants, nutmeg, and . . ."

Sean's face lit up like he was about to win a prize at a carnival, but it was short lived.

"Pepper? Did you really put black pepper in this?"

Sean's hope fizzled, but he still managed to smile. "I was sure I'd get you with that one."

"You should've used the white pepper," I said, walking to the stove to serve up my own breakfast. "He probably saw it in the bowl."

Sean looked from his bowl back to Sherlock. "No fair!"

Lock held his hands up. "If you didn't want me to use my eyes, you should've insisted on a blindfold."

The boys all laughed, and I slid into the chair at the head of the table, choosing to focus intently on my porridge rather than face Lock.

It got strangely quiet for about thirty seconds, and then Lock said, "Last one done has to clean all the breakfast dishes!"

The boys all scraped the bottoms of their bowls into their mouths and ran from the room at record speeds, leaving Lock to gather their dishes. For the briefest of moments I thought he might just wash them in silence—at least let me finish my breakfast. But I was more amused than irritated when he said my name. Lock had no room in that mind of his to worry about other people's breakfasts.

"Something about last night has me worried." He rolled up his sleeves and turned on the water to fill the sink, like he had just said something about parliament or the weather.

Right to the point, then. I swallowed my bite of porridge and said, "It was nothing."

Sherlock shut the water off and turned to face me, leaning back against the sink. "You told Mallory you thought your father had orchestrated the search last night. Why?"

I stared at him for a few seconds, trying to figure out if he was purposefully not asking about why I ran out on him or if he just wasn't bothered by it. I must have paused too long, however, because he tilted his head a bit and asked, "What?"

I shook my head. "Nothing."

Lock shrugged, but the corner of his mouth twitched a bit as he turned back to the sink, and then I knew. He chose not to ask. It could have been out of fear of my reaction or response. Or possibly he was waiting for a better time and place than first thing in the morning and in my kitchen. But I suspected that maybe, just maybe, he didn't ask because he understood why I left without me having to say. That was one of the better aspects of my Lock. He couldn't be bothered to allow me a peaceful breakfast, but he could give me space to breathe without my having to explain.

I was still smiling into my porridge when he asked, "Why *did* you think it was your father?"

"Isn't it obvious? He wants me to go see him for some reason, so he unleashes his police *brothers* on me and then has Day call thinking I'll give in just to yell at him. He could have been the one who notified the press as well—start to stir doubts among the public and push suspicion of his crimes onto someone else."

Sherlock shook his head. "The call from DS Day is what bothers me about the whole thing. It's not like your father's never seen you get mad about something before. He'd have to know that you'd hardly relent to a meeting when you're that angry."

"There's also this." I pulled the letter to Freddie out of the pocket of my uniform skirt and placed it on the table. I still hadn't opened it. Somehow even *me* knowing what it said felt like letting my father win.

"What's that?"

"A letter from my dad to Fred. I found it on his bed last night after the police left. If he didn't orchestrate the search to get at me, he definitely could have done it to have the letter delivered."

"So an officer did your dad a favor?" He grabbed it off the table and flipped it over in his hand. "Can I open it?"

"Do what you want with it. Just make sure Freddie doesn't see."

He tore open the envelope. After a few seconds he shook his head and slid the note over to me. "I don't think this is why either. Take a look."

"I'd rather not."

Lock pulled it back. "It's just your father's delusional fantasies, really. He goes on about how he was wrongly accused and will be out soon to come rescue them from you. Not enough here to warrant using a huge card like a search of your house to deliver it. Maybe if it had instructions for a meeting or something equally practical. But even then, there are so many less intrusive ways he could have gotten this to Freddie."

"My father isn't known for his subtlety."

Sherlock shook his head again and reread the letter.

"Why does it matter?" I asked. "Either my father orchestrated it or Mallory was looking for an excuse. . . ."

But that wasn't it, and I knew it too. Even before Sherlock said, "There's a third possibility. A more concerning possibility."

"The tip had to have been called in by someone else."

Lock brought the tips of his fingers together. "Because of the hand."

"Because of the hand," I echoed. Had I really forgotten that gory little detail overnight? Someone had planted a severed hand in my bin. Someone who wished me to be accused of something. I wanted to blame my father for this as well. He definitely could have had someone set the entire thing up on his behalf, and I could think of a million reasons why. Perhaps he wanted people to think I was just as criminal as he was. Maybe he just wanted to scare me. Or it could've been some foolish attempt to make our house look targeted and not a good place for the boys to live. Only he couldn't have known that Alice was coming, and until last night the boys had been living with Mrs. Hudson.

Sherlock took my bowl and walked to the sink with it but turned before he put it in the water. "Your father is most likely not the culprit here."

"Maybe not."

"And that is more concerning. If we don't know who it is, we don't know why he did it."

"And?"

He lifted my spoon into the air and said, "And we don't know what he'll do next."

It was a dramatic gesture that was lost on me, because I was still stuck on all the myriad reasons why it could and could not be my father. So much so that I got up from the table and started to leave the kitchen without a word. Lock met me at the doorway, which he half blocked with one shoulder.

When I looked at him, he reached up to push a lock of hair back behind my ear and asked, "It was really nothing?"

The quiet tone of his voice made me want to reassure him, but I didn't have the words. Instead, I nodded, then smiled a little as an afterthought. "I'll have the boys bring down their school bags."

I peered out the window to find a handful of reporters wandering about the pavement in front of our house. The days after my father tried to kill me, our sidewalk was a circus of movement that quickly became an impenetrable wall of people holding objects whenever my brothers and I showed our faces. Notebooks, cameras, microphones, and digital recorders were all thrust at us anytime we left the house or returned home. An explosion of flashes and whirs took in our every expression, sigh, and mutter.

That's when Mrs. Hudson first offered for us to stay with her. We hid ourselves away at her house and had everything delivered, including our school makeup work, which was smuggled in by a ridiculously costumed Lock. We lived like that for three days until the next giant parliament corruption scandal stole the media's attention away. That's also when I'd decided to move back to our house. As much as I wanted to stay with my brothers, being in a stranger's house felt like I

was letting my father and the chaos of the press and protesters drive me away from my home. And that day, despite their
diminished numbers, it felt like they were doing it again.

"Not this time," I whispered as I let the curtain drop back
into place. We'd only just gotten our house back as a family,
and I was determined to make that last. This time I wasn't
going to let them make us hide.

All five of us stood at the door, Sherlock and me flanking
my brothers, our arms around their backs like we could create
a shield from what was about to happen.

"Okay, remember the rules."

"No speaking, just walking," Freddie said.

"Holding hands until we're past the crowd," Michael said.

Sean was last but loudest. "No one left behind!"

The boys all laughed, and Lock took my hand from
Michael's shoulder and squeezed it just before I opened the
door. "Never boring with you."

"Is that a compliment?" I asked, but I wasn't sure he heard.
The very moment the door opened a crack, the onslaught
began.

"Is it true they never found the murder weapon?"

"Do police really think it's still hidden in your house?"

"Are any of you planning to testify?"

"What about reports that the murder weapon could prove
your father's innocence?"

We kept our heads down and took the stairs as a group, but
the wall of people wouldn't budge when we got to the bottom,
and I felt Michael start to tremble into my side. I sighed. I knew

of one sure way they'd let the boys through, but it definitely came with a cost. Lock seemed to read my mind.

"Get them on their way and come back for me?" I said into Lock's ear.

He didn't look very pleased with the request, but he pulled my brothers close to him as I climbed up to the door. "If you promise to let my brothers go to school without following them, I will make a statement."

The sudden hush was almost more frightening than the cacophony that followed. The wave surged toward me, leaving a nice opening for Sherlock and the boys to escape. Only Freddie glanced back as they ran up the street. I waited a few long seconds to make sure they'd gotten away clean before speaking.

"We have no contact with Detective Moriarty and, by law, he is not allowed to contact us. If you want answers to your questions about him, ask Detective Inspector Mallory of the Westminster Borough."

I jetted down the steps as quickly as I could, and through what was left of the opening my brothers had taken, but I wasn't quick enough. The questions started before I could reach the sidewalk, and I had to bat away cameras and outstretched hands holding phones and other recording devices just to take a single step forward.

"What did the police find at your house last night?"

"Tell us about the murder weapon! What does it mean that it can't be found?"

"Do you believe your father's innocent?"

After only about ten steps, I was ready to run into the

house and never come out again, but just as I had decided to give up, a hand reached out and grabbed my wrist, yanking me through the crowd and to the open door of a black cab. I dived in and crawled to the far side of the backseat, and then we took off all in the space of a few seconds. The silence was glorious. Not that it was all that silent. My panting breaths and the murmurs of talk radio plus normal traffic sounds filled the cabin of our taxi, but it still felt like silence.

After a few beats, my eyes met Lock's and we both laughed a little. "Thanks."

His smile filled his voice when he asked, "What in the world did you say?"

"To ask Mallory their questions and leave us alone."

Lock raised his brow. "I'm sure that went over well."

"And my brothers?"

"In the first taxi I flagged down, on their way to school. This is the second."

"Two cabs on Baker Street this early?" I asked.

Lock leaned forward suddenly and asked the driver to turn up his radio.

"Sources report police searched the home of the now confined Detective Sergeant Moriarty, looking for the weapon he is accused of using to stab five men to death in Regent's Park. There is no confirmation that the weapon was found, but pictures are circulating on Internet news sites of officers retrieving an object from the rubbish bins in front of the house and taking it away as evidence. We'll report more on this as word comes in."

I stared from the radio to Lock, who was still pitched forward, like some answer was right in front of us.

"I sent my brothers to school," I said, pushing my fingers through my hair. "Everyone will know by the time they get there."

We spent the rest of our cab ride in silence only to face down another handful of reporters awaiting our arrival at the school. There weren't enough of them to truly block our way, and their questions were easily ignored, but once inside the school, I was forced to walk a different kind of gauntlet.

"Why would she come to school?"

"I barely made it inside from all those reporters. Does she think of no one but herself?"

"I wish she'd just move away."

The third time someone asked why Sherlock Holmes would be walking with a girl like me, I pulled him into a less-populated side hall and said, "Just go to your class."

I was pretty sure his pause was going to be followed by a long argument about why he wasn't going to leave me to walk the rest of the halls alone, but instead he just said, "No." He reached for my hand, but I pulled away.

"Not this time. Just, for me, go to your class."

Lock pinched the bridge of his nose and then grasped his hands behind his back before he leaned in close to me. I fought the instinct to step back, but only because a group of girls walked by just then, and I didn't want to give them any more reason to stare at us. Lock didn't seem to notice or care about the girls, however. He stared into my eyes for a few seconds, then shifted so that his lips were at my ear.

"I know you're still angry with me," he said quietly. "But just for today, let me hold your hand and walk next to you. I promise I won't lend it any significance. I promise I won't think that this makes anything better. Just for today, for me, let me stay by your side?" I didn't answer, so he straightened and said, "I've got much more important things to ponder than the passive-aggressive, ill-informed mutterings of our school-mates. Please help me drown out the noise for a bit?"

He held out his hand, and I studied his face as I laid mine over his. But all he did was smile and exhale in relief. "That's better."

Holding Lock's hand didn't do much to drown out the voices for me, of course. But when the comments got more vicious and the commenters more bold, he wove his fingers through mine and patted out an odd rhythm with his thumb against my skin.

"I actually felt bad for her when her face was a mess. Now I guess we know there's more to *that* story."

"Wonder how many of those bruises were real?"

"How can she even face Lily Patel?"

As if her name had summoned her, Lily Patel came around the corner, buffered by her friends, who worried and kvetched around her until she held up her hand and said, "Enough."

We both paused just long enough to exchange a neutral look. Before we could be led away by our friends, Lily said, "Wait." She looked right at me, then, and pulled the hand-bag that was hanging from her elbow up onto her shoulder. She'd exchanged it for a new one again, I noticed. "Did they find the weapon?" She didn't sound angry, just curious.

I shook my head.

Lily scrunched her face a bit. "Didn't think they would."

She walked on, her scandalized posse in tow, but that small interaction seemed to quiet the gauntlet. Lock and I walked toward my chemistry class in near silence. No more comments. No more whispers. In fact, I didn't hear so much as my name again until we were mere steps from the classroom.

"Moriarty!"

A flash went off in my face the moment I turned. The strobe kept flickering as the paparazzo's shutter ticked off as many shots as he could before Sherlock pulled me into his arms and back-stepped me into the room. A wave of whispers erupted from inside, and my chem professor stormed past us, shouting, "Out! Get out now!"

Lock and I stood in that embrace much longer than we needed to—well past when we heard a couple of other teachers join my professor, and even after the paparazzo's shouts about his rights faded to nothing as he was taken to the nearest exit. I probably should've felt embarrassed as I extricated myself from Sherlock to answer the vibrating phone in my pocket. But I didn't have time to think on such things.

It was a text message. From Alice.

"Who is it?" Lock asked.

"Not even one class for me today," I said.

You need to come home, the text read. Followed quickly by, *Immediately*.

Chapter 6

Getting home involved squeezing through the side gate at school to avoid any lingering press and paying another taxi fare. I left Lock at school, tasking him with gathering my schoolwork for me, but really I didn't want his day to be ruined just because mine was about to be. Sadly, there was no side door to our house, which left me no choice but to push through the fog of camera flashes, shouted questions, and picket signs proclaiming both my father's guilt and innocence. It wasn't until I stood on the top step near our door that I noticed the crowd of bullies was actually significantly smaller than it had been earlier in the morning.

"Please let that be a good sign," I whispered as I opened the front door only as wide as it took to slip inside.

With the door closed, the entry of our house felt like a sanctuary. I leaned my head back against the wood, my hand still on the handle, and took a deep breath. I'd been more than stupid that day. None of us should have left the house for at least a day or two. The sighting of us, even doing something as plain as going to school, only meant one more day of this nonstory playing out as news.

I heard a hiss of pain coming from the kitchen and peeked around the corner just as Alice said, "Sorry."

She winced in sympathy as she dabbed a cotton swab along the corner of Freddie's mouth. Sean and Fred were lined up for triage at our kitchen table, which was covered in first-aid supplies like a clinic. Sean held a pack of frozen peas across his hand, but probably should have had another one for the blooming bruise under his eye. Freddie was definitely worse off. He had a gash along his cheekbone, a bruise on his jaw, and he was spitting blood into a paper cup. He lifted his hand up to scratch his head, and I saw cuts and bruises across the knuckles as well as a tear in his jacket.

I blew out a long exhale, which made both Fred and Sean look up at me, then down at the floor guiltily. I walked in and knelt down in front of Sean to meet his eyes. "Are you all right?"

He nodded and even managed to smile a little when I rested my hand against his hair.

"I'm sorry," I said. "I never should've made us go to school."

"We didn't make it to school," Sean said.

Freddie glared at both of us. "It would've been fine if Seanie hadn't mouthed off."

"I didn't!"

"I said that's enough with the blaming," Alice said. "You both did right in protecting each other and that's the end of it."

I lifted the peas to Sean's cheek and reached for Freddie's hand to bring it up into the light. One of his knuckles looked more swollen than the others. "Move your fingers?"

He wiggled them and winced, but said, "It's fine." He pulled his hand from my grasp and down into his lap, then hissed again as Alice went at his cheek gash with a new swab.

I leaned my head down until Freddie looked at me. "I'm sorry."

He shrugged and then winced away from Alice.

"You'll want to take care of Michael," she said, still entirely focused on Freddie's face. "He's locked himself in the bathroom upstairs."

"Is he hurt?" I asked.

Freddie shook his head. "Don't know what's wrong with him."

Seanie nudged Fred, who scowled but didn't say anything more. Seanie moved the peas to his hand and said, "He's afraid of a van."

"Press vans," Freddie said.

"He says it's not."

Freddie elbowed Sean for speaking, then scowled and muttered, "He's such a baby."

Alice and I exchanged glances. Freddie was probably right about the van, but something was off. He was being uncharacteristically bitter as it was, but he was never, ever hard on Michael like that. I ran up the stairs to the bathroom, lifted my hand to knock, then changed my mind and sat down in the hall, leaning back against the wall by the door.

The strangled whimpers and sniffles coming from Michael echoed around the bathroom and broke my heart a little. He always was the softest of us—the one we all tried to protect at every turn. I sometimes wondered how he had survived all the months of our father's abuse with his sanity intact. Perhaps it was because of Freddie, who either stepped up to take the brunt of it or hid Michael away. I had hoped that Michael wouldn't have to hide as much once Dad was in jail.

"I believe you," I said, loud enough for Michael to hear.

The noises from inside the bathroom stopped altogether, and then I heard him shuffle closer, heard the latch tap against its casing as he leaned back against the door. Someone knocked at the front door downstairs, and Alice cried, "Who is it?"

"Grocery," was the muffled reply.

"Who's at the door?" Michael asked, a shade of panic in his voice.

"Alice called for grocery service," I said. "You don't have to go to school for a while. We don't even have to leave the house."

"How long?" he asked, then hiccupped and blew his nose into some tissue.

"Until it all dies down," I promised, though I wasn't sure how long that would take. I wasn't sure what Dad would do next. He definitely wouldn't be happy about Alice being our guardian. And there was still the severed hand in our bin. So many things that could all go so wrong. But for now I supposed I could promise Michael anything I wanted.

"You really believe me? About the van?" It sounded like he was speaking right up against the corner of the door and doorjamb. The image of that made me smile.

"You've never made up a story like that in your life. I believe you."

I heard the lock click and stayed very still as Michael pushed open the door a few inches. Our eyes met and he brushed a wad of tissues under his nose before crawling out next to me. His little eyes were puffy and red, and his cheek looked swollen, like maybe he hadn't been spared a knock or two during Fred and Sean's street brawl. I lifted my arm up, and Michael's expression crumpled as he crawled under. He didn't fit on my lap anymore, but he still tucked the top of his head under my chin.

"Tell me about the van?"

His voice was muffled, like he had the wad of tissues right in front of his mouth while he spoke. "It was black and followed us all the way home from school."

"Do you think it was a van from the news station?"

"It wasn't!" He sat up in a panic, and the anguish in his eyes nearly killed me. "You said you believed me!"

I tried on my most reassuring grin. "I do. But I need to know why you think it wasn't. Tell me what happened."

Michael took his time to think things through, as he always did. "There were only two people in the van," he started. "They hadn't any cameras. They just stared at us while we were walking. And when I ran ahead, they followed me and pulled along the side of the road in front of us so I'd have to walk by them."

I waited for him to gather his next thoughts.

"And I recognized one of them."

"From the people gathered out front?"

Michael shook his head. "He was the one who said Alice wasn't our auntie last night."

Officer Parsons. Now that was interesting.

"You're sure that officer was in the van?"

"He was wearing different clothes and he was driving."

My anger must have bled through into my expression, because Michael curled up to hide again, tucking his head back under my chin. "You're not in trouble," I said. "I'm just . . . upset."

Michael didn't move for a while, and I let him be still. I probably couldn't have said much of anything to Michael right then anyway. My mind was too busy trying to connect the dots between what had already happened and what it could all mean. If our father was planning something and having my brothers followed, I had to find out what it was before they went back to school.

"What happened at the school?" I asked.

Michael's head dropped down.

"What is it? You can tell me."

He shook his head so that his hair tickled my chin.

"I should probably know, don't you think?"

I felt his body sag a little, and then, in his quietest voice, Michael said, "Freddie said we shouldn't have the taxi take us all the way to school or everyone would stare at us. So we got out a block away and walked, but these older kids from our neighborhood were waiting for us at the school gates."

"And then what?"

Michael covered his face with his hands, muffling his voice

67

further. "They called you a killer. Said Dad was going to prison in your place, which wasn't right."

"And so Seanie got mad?" I smiled a little, thinking about my youngest brother attacking the group of older boys to protect me. It would be like him.

"He said some things, but that's not why the fight started."

"Was it Freddie, then?"

Michael dropped his hands and leaned back to look up at me. "It wasn't them."

I waited while Michael looked from the floor and back to me several times. Then, with the softest glint of mischief in his eyes, he said, "I slapped Toby Parker."

I immediately laughed, though I knew I shouldn't. "Did you? For my honor?"

Michael was trying not to laugh with me but failed. "Then I told him to watch his trash mouth, and then he slapped me back and Freddie punched him in the eye. By then all the boys joined in and Freddie had to fight them off so we could run away."

"Well," I said, through a few more eruptions of laughter that I couldn't control. "I feel properly avenged."

Michael blushed and covered his mouth with the back of his hand.

"You ready to go downstairs?" I asked him.

He stood slowly, but stopped after taking only the first step down and looked back at me.

"Aren't you coming?"

I nodded. "Let me make a quick call first."

I pulled out my phone and wandered into my room as Michael went down, searching through my call history for the number.

"Junior," DS Day said once the call connected.

I felt my lip curl. "Set it up."

"What now?"

"Set it up. I'll meet him."

It was silent on the other end of the call, which wasn't what I'd expected, and then DS Day asked, "What's the catch?"

I sighed. "Set it up or don't. But make it soon, before I change my mind."

"Right."

"And you'll need to find a way to get me out of here unseen. There are cameras everywhere thanks to his little stunt."

"His what?"

I growled internally, wondering just how my father put up with a lackey who was dense as concrete. "Just call me when you have a time. Better yet—send me a text. I don't want to hear your voice."

I ended the call and dropped my phone on the bed, trying to convince myself that this was the right move. I was giving my father what he thought he wanted. But Michael said he saw Officer Parsons following them home from school in a van, and I believed him. I also knew without a doubt that Parsons was one of my father's men, which meant Dad had a plan. I just needed to figure out how to make him tell me those plans so I could stop him.

I changed out of my uniform and washed my face, and on my way down the stairs, I heard Alice shout, "I arranged a whole week off for you three!" A cheer erupted from the kitchen. Alice was standing in the doorway. She slid her mobile into the back pocket of her jeans. "Your makeup homework packets will be here in the afternoon tomorrow!" she cried just as enthusiastically. There was no cheer for that.

The lack of response didn't faze Alice. Her smile was still wide when she turned toward me. "Mail managed to get here before all the chaos, and these came for you." She handed me two envelopes. "Your snack is out on the back patio."

She winked at me, which made it seem like she was up to something. I even heard her say, "Adorable," from inside the kitchen, but I was too tired to question, so I wandered to the French doors. Through the glass, I saw a trifold room partition standing in the middle of the small space. It had a light wood frame with pink lacy curtains that were getting soaked in the May drizzle. I found Sherlock on the other side of the curtain, staring at his tablet under a giant umbrella in one of two deck chairs that looked almost exactly like the ones for hire at Regent's Park. Between the chairs, one of the little tables from what was now Alice's room held two sandwiches, two packets of crisps, and two bottles of fizzy water.

"Why?" I asked, gesturing around us. I actually had quite a few questions, like why he wasn't at school and why all this stuff was out here, and why there was so much food when we'd only just eaten porridge an hour or so ago. But in the end "Why?" seemed to embody all of that in a word.

Lock glanced up from his tablet to where I stood in the rain and, without a word, reached out to pull me under the umbrella. He didn't answer at first, and his cheeks went slightly pink as he quickly went back to reading his tablet. "I know you hate being stuck in the house."

I pressed my lips together and bit down on them to keep from smiling, which only made Lock furiously swipe through pages of something on the screen. I sat down and traded my mobile and letters for one of the bottles of water. "How did you get in?"

"Pretended to be grocery delivery."

I twisted the top off and waited for the bubbles to settle before I asked, "By actually delivering groceries?"

Lock nodded and read with a diligence notable even for him, but I watched as the soft pink skirting his cheeks darkened to a nice rose color.

I should have left him alone or at least said thank you, but it was so much more fun to torment him. "Alice thinks you're adorable."

"Yes. She said."

I took a long drink to suppress my next smile when he scowled toward the French doors and Alice beyond, I was sure. But then my phone rang and the name that flashed across the screen stole away all my amusement. He was supposed to send a text.

"What?" I answered.

DS Day got right to the point. "Tomorrow at seven a.m."

I glanced at Lock and said, "I'll be there." I frowned a little at the slight rise in Sherlock's brow—a sure indicator that he was going to ask questions I didn't want to answer.

"I'll pick you up, so don't be late."

I hung up and dropped my phone onto the table, then waited for the inevitable interrogation.

"Who was that?"

I paused to consider lying but thought better of it. "Detective Day."

"Are you going to see him, then?"

I knew he meant my dad, but I feigned ignorance. "Yes, he's coming to the house tomorrow."

Lock stared down at the screen. "For what?"

"More questions from Mallory, I suppose. He's taking me to the station."

A lie and a truth, but Lock didn't comment on either. I picked up one of the letters and ripped it open, expecting something from the school or maybe a letter from my grandmother, full of gossip about the village where she lives and pretense that she didn't know what was happening to us. Instead, I found a white card with the words THANK YOU embossed in silver across the front. I opened it and the entire inside was covered, corner to corner, with a highly detailed drawing. A drawing of me.

Only it wasn't quite me. The girl in the picture was wearing an elaborate medieval-looking gown and had long, flowing hair that was braided and curled down her back. She stood at the edge of a body of water of some sort, with a giant willow tree behind her, and held a sword out in front of her that she seemed to be passing along, hilt-first, to a dark, scaly hand that jutted out of the lake.

The scene was framed by tree trunks and branches that wove together to form an oval frame, and in the foreground, peeking around the trees to watch the woman, was a man, dressed much more modern, in jeans and a T-shirt. He had dark hair and a balding patch at his crown. The illustration showed only the back of his head and body, but the back pockets of his jeans bulged out like they both had wallets in them. A rubbish bin was to his right, like the bins at the park, and he held what looked like an aluminum can in his right hand. To his left stood a woman in full period dress, complete with ornate side hair buns and tiara, who was leaning in to whisper in his ear.

The picture was as beautiful as it was eerie. It was so intricate, I thought at first it had been printed onto the card, but when I moved my thumb, I realized I had smudged the lines a bit. The scene had been drawn onto the card. In pencil. Someone had created an odd, fantasy version of me, throwing my father's sword into the Regent's Park lake while someone looked on. Perhaps the artist had drawn himself?

"What's that?" Lock asked.

I ignored him and lifted the card to get a better look at the envelope. "No postal mark."

Lock took the card from me and studied it while I opened the second letter. This one was postmarked Camden High Street, which was just north of the park. The minute I ripped down the side, the smell got my attention. The thing reeked like some kind of chemical—like the glue Freddie used to put together his models. The smell only got worse when I slid the paper out and unfolded it.

Like a clichéd scene from an ancient crime show, this letter was a message made up of cutout letters that had been pasted on the page like a collage:

ADMIT YOUR CRIMES OR A WITNESS WILL COME FORWARD.

If I was meant to feel afraid or intimidated, it was a colossal failure, because I almost instantly started to laugh. "Honestly. What kind of dramatics are these?"

Lock sat up and pulled the letter from my hands. He grinned at first. "Clever." But his amusement quickly faded. He just kept looking back and forth between the drawing and the collage, painting them both with his gaze like I'd seen him do at a crime scene once.

"It could still be my father. He does love to cause a scene."

Lock shook his head and held out the collage. "A woman did this one."

"A woman?"

He looked between the items once more. "Both might have been done by a woman, but not the same woman."

I grabbed the message back from him, sure that I'd see that he was just guessing. But he wasn't. Not this time. He'd seen what I didn't even look for—where the letters had come from.

"*Cosmopolitan*," I said, like we were playing a game of "Tell Me When You See It."

Lock smiled, because I'd found the first clue. "*Glamour*," he added.

Take a Break magazine, *ELLE*—every letter had been taken from a magazine's title page. The word "witness" was a blaring clue all on its own. The letters all seemed to come from *Women's Fitness* magazine, like she'd just taken the bright pink *F* off and replaced it with the gray *W* from "Women's."

Lock was staring at me when I looked up.

"It could still be from him. He could have asked someone else to do it," I said.

He shook his head. "She has to be in her forties at least. She probably has a son."

"The model glue."

Lock looked pleased at first, possibly that he didn't have to explain to me all that he'd found, but then he frowned and looked at the drawing. "I think we should be very careful from now on."

"Of a woman in her forties who owns a stack of cut-up magazines?"

"Of *two* women," he corrected. "And possibly this man, who witnessed your crime. And of a fourth unknown figure who dropped a rotting body part in your bin. We don't know what any of them want. Not really."

Four people playing games with my life, according to Sherlock, but he had failed to mention the fifth. My father. And I knew exactly what he wanted. He wanted me dead.

Chapter 7

I'd been to the West End Central Station a few times—enough to know that guests weren't often allowed to bypass the front desk when they visited. So when Detective Day sneaked us in on the level of the holding cells, I had to wonder if maybe mine wasn't an approved visit. It was fitting, though, to start my first meet up with my father in a hallway filled with holding-cell doors on both sides, the rustling footsteps, groans, and snores of strangers echoing out at me.

Day was quiet as we walked, though that wasn't the blessing it should have been, as it only gave me too much time to ponder things, like what I was even doing there? To show my father I wasn't afraid of him? I wasn't. Not really. I was afraid of me—afraid I'd launch myself at him and make an ass out of myself, that he'd somehow take the upper hand while we spoke, that I'd give him what he wanted and get nothing back, leaving him to return to his cell with a self-satisfied smile that I'd be unable to scratch from his face.

I'd arranged the meeting to make him tell me what he was planning, but the closer I got to the room where Day had stowed my father, the more my confidence waned. I knew he wanted me out of the way so he could get out and reclaim my brothers as his sons. But did I really expect he would tell me how he planned to accomplish that? It was more likely he would leave me to guess. And if I guessed wrong, if I planned wrong, then we would all be in danger. Somehow, I had to get him talking, get him angry and make him tell me something.

And I always could get him angry.

One of the cell doors behind us slammed open and two officers came out, dragging a shackled prisoner between them. Watching the prisoner struggle to keep up with the officers' strides, when he had a chain between his ankles restricting his movements to a short trot, was almost painfully frustrating, even as a mere observer. And something about that made me feel strangely better.

I suddenly found myself fantasizing about my father's trip from his cell to where he and I would meet. I was actually smiling when we turned the corner, imagining how humiliated he would feel to engage in a silly little trot like that in front of his fellow officers. I could envision him being pushed out from one of the cells right in front of me, so that I could smirk along with them.

But that wasn't to be. We made our way through card-locked double doors and then stood in front of a door marked INTERVIEW 3.

DS Day put his hand on the door handle and looked back at me over his shoulder. "You ready?"

I met his eyes without answering, and he quickly looked

down like the submissive dog he was, then opened the door for me.

Stepping into my father's interview room was perhaps the most surreal of the collection of moments I'd had all week. I thought I'd been transported back in time, or to an alternate universe where he'd never been caught, where I'd become someone who visited my father at work, where the police invited their daughters to observe interviews and we were still waiting for the criminal to be brought into the room.

Literally nothing was as I'd expected. Where I'd thought to see a prison uniform, my father was dressed in street clothes, a suit jacket flung over the back of his chair. I'd thought to see him chained, at the very least to have his hands cuffed to the bar on the table. More than mere free hands, though, he was shoveling the last bits of breakfast into his mouth with one hand while the other grasped a mug that, when I was prodded closer, smelled more like whiskey than coffee. He even laughed, a sound I hadn't heard in more than a year.

In all the scenarios I'd imagined for that day's visit, not one included my entering to see my father distracted by his own storytelling in a room full of his friends, cheering him on as he finished a proper English breakfast. But something was off. A glance at DS Day provided my first clue. He seemed as stunned as I was, which shouldn't have been the case if he'd set up this little meeting. So I started to look closer.

Dad's wrists were my next clue. When he brought his drink up to his mouth, his shirtsleeve material pulled too far back along his forearm, telling me two things. First, he'd been shackled until very recently, going by the remaining impressions of handcuffs at his wrists. Second, he wasn't wearing his own clothes. The shirt was too small for my dad, short in the sleeve and narrow in the shoulders, which probably explained why he wasn't wearing the jacket.

"You're here," my father said, as if I was the help coming to clear away his tray.

I tried my very best not to grin at all his dramatics, and I didn't flinch away from his gaze, which swept over me in one quick, studying movement. "I didn't realize we'd have such an audience," I said. "Perhaps I should come another time?"

DS Day made a gesture with his head, but the other officers seemed wary to leave. They kept glancing between my father and me, as though they could predict what would happen just by judging the space between us. Finally, one of them tapped the other's arm with the back of his hand, and they started for the door, only stopping short to drop a warning for DS Day. "Something happens and it's your arse."

Day nodded and stayed behind after the officers were gone. I stood next to the interview table, watching him fidget by the door.

"Out," my father barked, coming closer to his true self.

Day jumped a little at the command, but he still managed to sound authoritative when he said, "Recording's off, but I'll be watching. Not so much as shaking hands. I mean it."

My father smiled and gripped his hands around the bar atop the interview table as some kind of consoling gesture that meant nothing. I knew this visit would end with one of us being dragged out of the room; I just wasn't sure yet who it would be.

Once DS Day left us alone, I sat across from my father before he could offer the seat to me. I stared him down, waiting to see what he wanted from our little chat. His first question wasn't unexpected, but I wasn't focused on what he actually said, only which words were chosen and what they implied.

"How are my sons?" *Ownership, prioritized concern for their welfare. Both false.*

"My brothers are no longer your concern." I watched him dampen a flare of anger at my words and decided to push the button again. "I wasn't lying when I said you won't see them, so you might as well strip them from your mind."

He shifted his position and cleared his throat. "I hear Alice is playing at being an adult. How long until she takes off on you?" *Attempt at making me feel insecure, insult to the only adult left in my life who could help me.*

"How we are living is also none of your concern. Neither is Alice."

He leaned back in his chair and tried very hard to force an easy grin, something he might have known would never work if he were even slightly human. "How did you find the flighty bitch? I looked three months with no real leads."

"None of your business."

My father shifted his position in the chair again, this time laying his hands flat on the tabletop in front of him. He was already losing composure, which disappointed, really. His next smile crinkled the line of stitches along his cheek. That one movement made it so that I couldn't seem to look away. And staring at the stitches brought my memories all back in a flash. My helplessness under his weight, the delight in his eyes as he opened the gash on his own cheek, the warmth of the blood dripping onto my face.

"If you're not going to tell me about my home, maybe I'll petition to have Fred come for visitation." A blatant threat, an ineffectual one at that, but the idea that he'd use Freddie to try to force me to talk, that he'd actually spoken the name of my brother aloud from his disgusting mouth—with those few words, my father had stirred up just enough anger to burn away my memories.

I sighed out the last of my panic and said, "Non-molestation order." I'd applied for an NMO for me and my brothers from my hospital bed the day after my father's arrest. It was standard practice in attempted murder cases, according to the child services counselor they'd sent out. She was also how I'd discovered that while I couldn't become guardian to my brothers, I legally didn't need a guardian at age sixteen, and I had the legal right to continue occupying my house. I knew my father was aware of every step I'd taken through the legal system as well, so all of this ridiculous fronting was just more boring drivel from the man. And I was done listening.

I rolled my eyes to stare at the door DS Day had passed through just minutes before. "I thought this would be more interesting than it is." I stood up, and my father slammed his hands on the table.

"Sit."

I crossed my arms, still standing. I thought perhaps he'd

finally lost the last of his restraint, but he managed to compose himself once again.

"I've a story to tell you." He gestured at the chair. "Sit. Please."

"Pass."

I turned toward the door and he said, "It's about your mother."

I heard the slightest edge of desperation in his voice and pursed my lips to stop a smile before looking at him from over my shoulder. "Do you think there's anything you can tell me that Alice can't? She was Mum's best friend."

"That bitch will never know what I know about my wife. I can tell you the real reason we got married."

I turned back to face him, studying his features skeptically. "Still a pass. I don't think you know all that much about my mother, least of all her reasons for doing anything."

This time I made it close enough to the door to rest my hand on the handle before he said something that stopped me. "She killed a man."

He was lying. I knew for sure he was lying, but I couldn't seem to leave the room, despite how much I was internally yelling at myself to just go. I managed to create a neutral expression before I faced him again, not that it tempered the triumph blaring at me from his every feature.

"That's something Alice knows nothing about," he taunted.

"Because she knows better than to believe something so stupidly false."

His expression then was more than triumphant. It was outright victory. Whether what he was about to say was truth or a lie, he believed it. I, of course, still could have left, but he knew I wouldn't, and that made me want to slap him as hard as I could. So I resigned myself to listening to more of his arrogance, newly determined to glean something more out of our meeting than pathetic power plays and his blathering on.

But I wasn't going to make it entirely easy on him.

"Why would that matter at all? She's dead and gone."

My father only gestured at the chair across from him. His turn to play games with me, it seemed.

I sat and said, "I'll listen."

"We'd met long before that dance, your mom and me."

He watched me carefully after he spoke, like I was supposed to express some kind of shock at this, his first revelation. When I didn't, he said, "Thought I'd be meeting a whore that day, not a con." And he was at it again. Apparently not even Saint Emily Moriarty was safe from his skewed implications. "That's how domestics usually go. We get called to an hourly motel to deal with screams from a lady and sounds of a fight, and it's a pimp rolling his tart, nine out of ten.

"But that night it was Em." A darkness slipped over his expression. "She was beaten bloody. Makeup smeared across her cheeks, her hair wild and jutting up in spots like it'd been yanked. And some of the blood was dried, like she'd been bleeding for hours before I got there. But I didn't notice any of that at first, on account of her hands."

His expression cleared, and I thought he was just excited to tell me the next bit, but he seemed somehow proud as well. "Her hands were coated red, like she had gloves on, but it was all blood on her hands, and none of it her own." Definitely pride. He was proud of Mum for coating her hands in someone else's blood.

I couldn't decide if I should act repulsed or fascinated, so I kept my expression neutral, which seemed to irritate my father. I wondered, though, if he knew my real reaction to his little story, would he understand it? Because under my neutrality, I wasn't scared or horrified or anything close to what he might have wanted. I was angry.

I didn't believe *my* mother could ever have been involved in something like that, but I believed Emily was there. I was sure he saw the scene exactly as he described, but it still seemed like a story about a stranger. The mother I knew wasn't the kind to go to an hourly motel, much less allow herself to be beaten there and bathe her hands in blood.

And that was why I was angry. There was a time when I wished to know all her secrets. But in the months since Mum had died, I felt like I'd lost track of her completely. She'd somehow become all these different people, most of whom I didn't know at all. She was this lofty sainted thing to my brothers, more concept "Mother" than actual being on most days. She was a Robin Hood–esque folk hero in the stories Alice had told me. Dad had always painted her as some tragic victim, an abused angel worth destroying everything to avenge. And now I was supposed to believe she was also a battered grifter who killed men in cheap hotels.

Maybe I could have laughed off all those versions of my mother, maybe I could have even forgiven my father for constructing this latest portrayal, but I was losing track of what I knew about her—of who she was before all the pictures and stories and secrets. I wasn't even sure I remembered my version at all. And I wanted my mum back.

Dad went on with his story about a con gone wrong, and how Emily had to fight for her life and freedom from an angry mark. In the end she'd had no choice but to kill him. That much had been obvious from the beginning of his fairy tale. None of the details mattered, though he seemed to be embellishing the story as much as possible. Especially the parts where he turned himself into Prince Charming, dirty-cop version, who let her run off instead of forcing her to go through the physical exams, evidence collection, and statements that the police would demand from her in order to prove self-defense.

They were supposed to meet at a café on the corner later that night, to make sure they had their stories straight, but she'd never showed.

"Never did ask her why," my father reminisced.

I let out a gruntish laugh. "Because she was smart enough to realize that you'd end up using it to get something from her."

The monster returned with a sharp glare. My father clenched his fists and banged one on the table before he came back to himself and realized what he was doing. When he'd calmed down, he said, "We found each other. Your mom and I were meant to find each other again."

I could guess the rest of his story. He saw her at the Tea Dance. She agreed to go out with him to keep him quiet about the dead mark and realized too late what he was. Maybe she even let herself fall in love with him for a time. But I was absolutely sure that it was the threat of jail that made her leave the safety of Alice's farm and take us back to him when she was pregnant with Freddie. She probably didn't yet know what he would become, but she knew she couldn't protect us from him if she were behind bars.

"I barely recognized her, what with her face all healed and all dressed up to play to those pensioners like she—"

"Why am I here?"

"I'm not done with my story." His words came out a little clipped.

"Why tell me this story? What is it that you actually want?"

"She was all dressed up," he started again, but I was done. I stood up and he yelled, "Sit!"

I let loose a hiccup of angry laughter and glared at him with clenched fists. "This isn't fun anymore. Rot in here. Die in here. I'm done with you."

He sat back in his chair, trying to play at calm with a pose that every feature on his face was betraying. "You'll be back."

I laughed again. "You seem pretty confident for a disgraced ex-copper who's about to shack up with all the criminals he's sent to jail."

He smiled. "Won't happen."

"You can live your delusions without me."

"You're why it won't happen. Not if you want to see those boys again."

That threat wasn't entirely unexpected, but it made me

wonder if I could still push the right buttons to make him tell me something useful after all. I leaned over the table to meet his eyes fully. "I'm why you want to stay in this cage until your last breath."

He stood, forcing me up as well, but I didn't move my gaze from his, not even when he stepped out from behind the table to get closer to me. "You'll be my salvation, daughter dear. You'll help me live out the rest of my life—"

"—Trapped, just like you trapped Mum?"

He charged me then, pushing me back into the corner under the camera where Day could no longer see us. He held me there, his arm like a steel bar against my neck. I leaned as far back into the corner as I could and took a deep breath, one I'd practiced taking over and over at home, and then I met my father's gaze, watched him startle at my lack of fear.

"I can get to them anywhere," he said, finally saying what he'd brought me here to say. "From out there, from in here, it don't matter where I am. You'll never see those boys again if you don't help get me out of here." When I still didn't give in to my fear, he released the pressure on my neck and tried to act unfazed. "You'll even come when I call like an obedient little thing."

"Are you sure that's what you want?"

He was still intent on proving he was in charge, apparently, as he moved his face so close to mine that I could smell his breakfast whiskey and feel spit on my cheek as he spoke. "You'll say I was with you when those thieves were killed, got it?"

"This filthy brick-and-mortar cage is the only thing keeping you alive." I kept my tone perfectly balanced and as soft as I could to keep anyone who might have been listening in from hearing my words. I watched something spark behind my father's eyes as he took in my threat. Was it simply fear? I wondered. Was this what he looked like afraid? "Do you really think I'd help you get anywhere near my brothers? I told you that they're no longer your concern. And don't think for a moment I can't stop your little plans."

"You won't see it coming."

"I've already stopped Freddie from seeing your pathetic little note. I know Parsons followed my brothers home from school in a black van. And I know about that threat you had sent to me in the mail."

His expression was equal parts surprise and confusion, so that he suddenly appeared more pathetic old man than monstrous killer. "What threat? You don't know what you're talking about."

He didn't know about the threatening letter. Lock had been right after all.

"I know this. You in here means I leave you alone. But the minute you become a danger to my brothers, I will kill you myself."

"Big words from a little bitch," he spit.

"Think of it as payback for all the years you forced this bitch's mum to live with a pathetic bully like you."

The look he gave me next I'd seen only once before. I'd flipped a switch, it seemed. He came at me again, and I didn't

88

know if it was his slowed reflexes or all my training that did it, but I somehow anticipated what he was going to do. I knew where he'd plant his foot, that he'd push my shoulder back with his left hand and throw a fist at me with his right, and I knew exactly how to move my hands to stop him. I felt my feet slide a few inches apart to my most stable stance, just like Lock had taught me, then my hands were in the air, guiding his fist, my body taking the force of his push and using it to turn me away, so that his fist hit the wall.

It was a perfectly executed defense. I'd even managed to push us out of the dark corner. I looked up and the camera was pointed right at us. DS Day had to be on his way.

My dad cradled his injured knuckles to his chest and bore his gaze into my eyes. "Now that you know what your mom was, know this: You are all the worst sides of her."

I jerked my chin away, staring back up at the camera.

"She was rotten on the inside until she met me. I cleaned her up." He tilted his head, forcing his face back into my view. "Who do you think will do that for you?"

I didn't flinch away from him again, but I had nothing left to say either. I just glared back at him. There was nothing I wanted more in the world just then than for him to stop talking. I just wanted him to stop.

"You better get really good at lying, little girl. You think someone'll love you if they know the truth about who you are? Who you come from? You think anyone would want to be near you if they knew you've got killing in your blood?"

I opened my mouth to answer, but before I could say

anything, the door burst open, spilling the three detectives and a uniformed officer into the cramped space. They tried to separate us, but my father had grabbed on to my arm and wouldn't let go.

"You'll end up just like her!" he shouted as they yanked him back.

"Are you all right?" DS Day's face came between mine and Father's, and then DS Moriarty was on the floor with the officers, who'd seemed like his friends just minutes before, forcing shackles onto his wrists again.

"Fine." I waved Day away from me with the word and moved out of the room without looking back. "Restroom," I said, when I heard him following me up the stairs.

I ran ahead and quickly escaped into the nearest ladies' room, but barely made it into a stall before everything crashed over me. I'd let him do it to me again. He was behind bars and I was free, and still he was the ogre growling and I was the little girl putting on airs. I tried to tell myself he was as wrong about me as he was wrong about everything else, but all I could see in my mind was the blank look on Lock's face when he'd pictured who I'd be without the law.

Am I more afraid of you or myself? he'd asked.

I couldn't see anything but Lock's fear as he asked the question, even as my father's voice came back to haunt me with another. *You think someone'll love you if they know the truth about who you are?*

"No," I whispered aloud. "I don't expect he will."

I swiped a few tears from my cheeks and tried to focus on

the fact that my brothers were safe at home. None of them would be hiding away when I got there, waiting for me to patch up their wounds. And my father would be stuck in a cage for the rest of his life.

That had to be enough for now.

Chapter 8

I was still shaky when I ventured from the ladies' room and out into the echoing hall. I expected to be confronted by a harried DS Day but instead came face-to-face with the calm, disinterested gaze of Detective Inspector Mallory, who stood awkwardly in the middle of the hall with his hands pulled behind his back. He was even flanked by two uniformed policemen, making him look every bit the prisoner he deserved to be.

"Were you crying, Miss Moriarty?"

"What do you want?"

"You are being detained." He nodded to the officers, who started toward me from either side.

I backed up until I was against the ladies' room door. "What are you talking about?"

Mallory didn't answer, so when one officer reached for me, I made my sidestep as natural as possible, then walked forward, out of reach of the second, but all without seeming to dodge them. When I was mere inches from Mallory, I quietly said, "Call them off. I'll go with you, but I won't be manhandled over another of my father's stupid games."

Mallory was just as quiet when he said, "This has nothing to do with your father." He released his arms from behind his back and held a sword in front of me. My mother's aikido sword, or at least an exact copy. "We got a tip from someone claiming that you threw this in the Regent's Park lake."

It took everything in me not to react, but I perhaps allowed too much of a pause before I said, "That's ridiculous."

"Not completely ridiculous. We found it right where the witness said it would be."

"And by 'witness,' you obviously mean my father."

"Do you blame him for everything?" Mallory motioned to his goons and then turned down another hall that held more interview rooms.

As soon as I sat at the interview table, Mallory joined me, placing the sword on the table between us. He cleared his throat and one of the officers came in, glaring at me and placing a file folder in front of Mallory. Mallory waved him out. I waited patiently, even when the inspector took an obviously long time to peruse the papers in the folder. He finally looked up, but the minute he opened his mouth, I pressed call on my mobile, holding it to my ear before he could object.

"Yes, Aunt Alice? The police are attempting to question me without my legal guardian present."

"What happened?" Alice asked. "Where are you?"

"I understand. That's what I thought you'd say. I'll just stay here at the West End station until you come for me."

"I'll be there in twenty minutes."

"Of course I won't answer their questions until you get here."

I hung up, placing the phone in front of me. Mallory tried his best not to reveal his irritation, but I watched his jaw clench and unclench, and his lips flattened when he reached to snatch my mobile off the table. He left without a word, leaving me to sit at the interview table, with nothing to do but think. The very last thing I wanted just then.

Because if I thought honestly about all that had happened in the past twenty-four hours, I'd have to admit that Mallory was right to say that my father wasn't to blame for everything—at least he was right about the sword. My father had been in a drunken sleep when I took the sword from his room and disposed of it. There was no way he could have seen me in the park. Someone could have told him, I supposed, but there was no way he would sit on information like that and use it sparingly to torture me. No, if my father knew what I'd done, he'd have spilled it immediately to free himself and have me locked up.

That meant Sherlock was right as well, and his concerns were justified. My father was still after me. I believed that completely. He wanted to free himself and get his sons back, and I was in his way. But the drawing and letter—my father knew nothing about those. Lock's deductions about who sent them might not turn out to be accurate, but he was right that my father wasn't the only one targeting me. Those letters could have come from anyone. And that meant sitting in a room alone with my swirling thoughts was the most useless thing I could do.

But I was left to wait for Mallory and Alice. We lived all of ten minutes from the station by cab. Thankfully, before I could come up with a list of reasons for why she might be late, Alice burst into the room, looking completely wild—jacket falling off one shoulder like she could barely be troubled to put it fully on, hair a scattered mess, cheeks rosy, and eyes full of fire and brimstone. I probably should've checked my smile, but something about her ferocity just then made me like her more than I ever had before. Maybe I understood a little why my mother had kept her close for so many years. Alice grabbed my hand and said, "Let's go."

I stood to follow her out, but Mallory and his goons were blocking the doorway.

"We need to question her," the DI said, in a tone that made me think this wasn't the first or even second time he'd said it.

"As I already explained, you do not have my permission."

"We can hold her until you give it."

Alice let go of my hand and turned to fully face down the three men, her hands clenched into fists at her sides. "Do not let my accent fool you into thinking that I don't know the law. Now I will take this child with me, and you will move out of my way."

"Let's all just have a seat." Mallory's voice was practically dripping with his most pacifying tone. "You wouldn't want the press to find out that you're failing to cooperate fully with the police."

Alice crossed her arms. "Then charge her. Charge and process her right now, and I will call the press myself. I'll let them know how you plan to persecute a child in a completely transparent and feeble attempt to take the blame off your police force for failing to notice one of your own was a serial killer." When Mallory didn't respond, Alice continued. "It won't be that hard to get them to listen, there are a half dozen loitering about in front of our house right now. I'd only have to clear my throat to gather them, and my message would be broadcast live."

Mallory narrowed his eyes. "We received a tip that someone watched Mori wipe down the sword and throw it in the Regent's Park lake. I am fully justified in conducting a police interview, so take a seat."

Alice leaned forward a little and lowered her voice. "Maybe I'll add in how you personally knew that James Moriarty was hitting his young sons and did nothing to stop him. I'm sure Seanie's cute little face will play well on the evening news, don't you think?"

Mallory and Alice stared each other down for a while, and just when I thought we were never getting out of there, Mallory stepped aside, pushing his officers out of the way as well. Alice grabbed my hand again and pulled me just to the doorway. She looked up at Mallory. "These kids have had to deal with enough of your bullshit. Don't come after them for this trifling nonsense again."

And then she stormed down the hall, dragging me behind her. She asked me only two questions while we waited at the curb for our cab to arrive.

"Did you do it?"

I nodded.

"Why?"

"I thought I was protecting the woman with blue hair in my photo. I thought maybe without his sword, he'd at least refrain from killing her for a day."

Her silence felt like an intake of breath, like it was readying for a longer reply. But instead of releasing words, she wove her fingers through mine and held on tightly.

Chapter 9

Alice was quiet most of the way home, and I didn't make a noise either. I thought maybe she was scared, that she'd used up all her bravado to face down Mallory. And I was to blame for being sloppy when I'd tossed the sword with so many people in the park. But around the halfway point, Alice reached for my hand again. When we rounded the next corner, she knocked on the Plexiglas barrier and said, "Let us off here, please."

She dragged me from the cab and took my arm as we walked down the street, blending in with all the other pedestrians. "I want spinach salad for dinner, the kind with bits of egg and tomato on it that goes all wilty under a hot bacon dressing."

"You want spinach salad," I said.

She smiled widely at me and winked. "Police stations make me crave bacon."

Alice was the worst shopper. The produce was clearly laid out to the right of the entrance, but she went left. I thought maybe she was the kind of shopper who had to wander the aisles and look at everything before picking out what she actually came to the store to purchase. But I didn't feel like following her around, so I gathered what we'd need all on my own, only catching glimpses of Alice as she stood before the aisles, pausing to tilt her head, like she was trying to decide what she wanted from the shelves before walking along them. At the second-to-last aisle, she smiled, then looked over at me and winked before disappearing down the rabbit hole.

The crash I heard soon after made me jump enough to drop the apple I was about to add to my basket. Alice's over-loud, "Oh no!" sent me hurrying to the aisle just in time to watch an older man offering his hand to a downtrodden Alice, who was sprawled on the tile, surrounded by a puddle of liquid, shards of glass, and an assortment of colored olives.

Her defeated expression was such a contrast to the bright smile I'd seen only seconds before, I almost thought I'd had a weird apple-checking lapse in time, somehow.

"I'm so, so sorry. I just can't imagine how this happened," Alice said.

"Careful, now," the man said. Alice rested her hand in his and rose up from the ruin, with as much grace as a princess drifting down from her carriage. Her eyes shone up into his as though he were her balding savior prince, rescuing her from a band of outlaws rather than a mess of her own creation. He reacted in kind, standing a little taller. He pushed his thumbs into the tiny pockets of his vest and rolled back his shoulders a bit at her attention. "Mind the glass, won't you," he said valiantly. "Are you injured anywhere?"

"I've a better question." It was perhaps only the sound of my voice that brought the two of them to their senses. "What are you even doing in this aisle? We are supposed to be shopping for spinach."

Alice pointed to a puddle that had been hidden behind her. "Oil for dressing," she said pitifully. Her whole countenance drooped then, so that you'd think she was confessing to some grand crime. "What do I do now?"

We definitely had at least four kinds of oil at home. I started to say, "Let's just pay for this mess and go—"

But before I could finish, Alice's prince spoke up. "You just let me worry about all this."

I half expected Alice to give in and laugh that it had all been a prank, but her eyes shone with actual tears.

"I can't let you—," she started, but he didn't let *her* finish either.

"Never mind this. I'll take care of everything. You just run along home to those children you care for. Don't give this another thought."

Her eyes still shone, but her expression changed to pure gratitude. She thanked the man perhaps one hundred times on our way out of the store, tears threatening the entire time—tears of thankfulness, I was left to presume.

By the time we reached the corner, Alice's smile was almost wicked. I tried very, very hard to say nothing, but when she winked at me, I lost all restraint.

"On purpose? Really?"

Alice draped an arm around my shoulders, and I pushed it off. "Don't be like that. It's just a little fun."

I stared at her for a few seconds, then turned and crossed the street against the light. She followed, almost getting hit by a horn-blaring MINI Cooper.

I knew I was overreacting—that my level of frustration with her was more about my mood than her actions—but she was wasting time that I didn't have. Time I could have spent trying to figure out who was sending me threatening letters in the mail.

Alice caught up finally just as a strange female voice called out, "Jamie? Jamie Moriarty!"

I started walking faster, but Alice slowed her pace.

"Miss Jamie Moriarty?"

The reporters who'd followed us around after my father had been arrested all assumed I didn't go by James, but none, it seemed, had done enough homework to know what name I actually used in my day-to-day life, which made it extremely easy to ignore them.

"Back off," Alice said. She then lowered her voice to make a few vague threats, I was sure.

I didn't stay close enough to hear. I raced ahead and almost made it home before Alice's arm looped around my shoulders. I didn't throw her arm off this time. "Thanks," I said. "For Mallory and the reporter."

"At the market," she started, but I waved her off.

"I'm just in a bad mood today." I started to walk again, thinking she'd let it go, but she held my arm to stop me. It was apparently time for some kind of talk. I supposed we were overdue for one. We hadn't had time to talk about how long she was willing to stay, or to come up with a plan about how to handle all that had happened in the past two days. I'd not even showed her around the house yet.

But she surprised me by saying, "It's lesson time."

"Lesson? What lesson?"

She leaned in close. "I've been in London more than a week, you know."

I didn't know. "Why didn't you find us earlier?"

She stuffed her hands into her pockets and took long, slow steps down the sidewalk. "I needed to make sure my paperwork was ironclad before I threw myself into the chaos. There's only one man for that job, and he lives near Hyde Park."

"So you spent a week drumming up a false identity?"

Alice looked at me like I'd insulted her. "If all I needed was a license or passport, I'd have done that myself. I needed the whole paper trail, going back to the day I was born—into the loving arms of Em's parents, of course. I had to prove I was your full-fledged auntie, or I expected they'd have laughed me out of the offices."

She turned toward me, taking her next steps backward. And then she stopped walking and leaned back against a lamppost. "And that kind of work means Meeger papers." I opened my mouth to speak, but she interrupted. "Not like you're thinking. M-E-E-ger. No one knows his real name, but his forgeries are so flawless he got the nickname Meeger, after Han van Meegeren, a genius art forger back in the day."

"And these Meeger papers fooled Tri-borough Children's Services?"

Alice scowled. "All that money, and they didn't even check it closely at all. They flipped through to make sure all the forms were there, rubber-stamped it, and sent me on my way."

"Why are you telling me all this?"

"Two reasons. First, I know you went to see your father today, and I'm sure he threatened to challenge my legitimacy as your guardian."

Not technically, but I was sure it was only a matter of time. "And?"

"And I want you to know that we are rock solid. As far as anyone can prove, I am your aunt Alice and legitimate legal guardian. I don't want you worrying about how to protect me or how to fight that man. He'll lose this battle for sure."

I felt my expression soften just a bit. "The second reason?"

"Is your lesson." She turned to face forward and then started walking again. "I've decided to teach you how to be one of us."

"One of you?"

"That first week, I stayed at a little bed-and-breakfast around the corner from that market. The man I was flirting with there? He stalks me every time I'm there. I've been chatting him up a little, answering his questions as I wander the aisles, and today I decided to give him what he's wanted from me all along." She stopped and turned to meet my eyes. "He wanted me to be frail and in trouble, so he could play the hero."

I didn't answer, so Alice grasped a lock of my hair and tugged it affectionately. My mother used to do that to me, and I wasn't sure how I felt about this woman co-opting the gesture, but I tried not to obsess over it.

"I was only giving him what he wanted. Trust me."

I studied her face for a few seconds. "To what end?"

"I'm not sure yet what the end will be. This is what we call 'priming the mark.'"

"So you're just setting him up?"

"Maybe. Maybe not. But now I have him, in case I need something later on."

There was something a little pathetic about that, using people so shamelessly. Pathetic, perhaps, but there was sincerity in it too. At least con artists didn't pretend to themselves.

"Conning someone isn't about getting something for nothing. When you do it right, the mark never knows they were conned. You give them what they want, and they give you a favor in return."

"And by favor, you mean money."

"Not always." Alice was trying to play coy, but I could tell how much fun she was having with her lesson. I wondered how many others had been privy to this curriculum of hers. "There may come a time when one of us is in trouble. That man is primed to help us however we need. He won't forget me and my eyes shining with grateful tears. He'll think about it all night, smiling every time he does."

I released a grunt of a laugh. "Where do you get the ego?"

"Learned from the best. This was all Emily. Your mom taught me everything I know, not the other way around."

I tried not to frown, but I didn't want to hear any more

stories about my mom that day. "Not the mom I knew."

"Just because you didn't know this part doesn't mean it wasn't still her." Alice's smile widened. "Grifting's an art. It takes a brilliant mind, fearlessness, and inner strength that few people can even aspire to. It's how she survived when she had nothing and no one. It's how she saved me. It's also how she got stuck with a bunch of losers like Sorte Juntos to feed and care for. Hell, it's even how she got stuck with that oaf, so don't—"

"What do you mean by that?" I asked, even though I knew already. My dad had spilled it all. And Alice was right. Emily got stuck with a monster because of her conning. I couldn't help but wonder if that was why she'd given it up. Maybe she'd finally had to pay a price she wasn't willing to pay. Maybe it was because of us.

Alice glared at a fire hydrant, though I was pretty sure she was mostly angry with herself. She hadn't meant to tell me as much as he had. It was like she had appointed herself keeper of all my mother's secrets. "Nothing," she said. She didn't speak again until we turned onto Baker Street, and then she grabbed the grocery bags from my hands and said, "Don't be surprised when we get home."

"Surprised?"

"There will be men stationed out in front of the house for a while."

"Men? What kind of men?"

Alice paused, like she was trying to figure out how to say something. "I've called in a few favors."

"What does that mean?"

"They're men who owe me."

"Owe you?" I'd barely asked when Alice's own words came back to me. *But now I have him, in case I need something later on.* "Wait. Are they marks?"

Alice glanced at all the people on the street around us and scrunched up her lips at me in a reprimand.

I lowered my voice, but I was by no means done talking. "You brought men from who knows where, and you expect they will protect us from whom? From the policemen my father will send? From the actual criminals he may know? What are you thinking here?"

She didn't answer me, but she didn't seem guilty or upset, either.

"Have you thought about what will happen if they find out you've been conning them?"

When Alice finally looked at me, a bit of the defiance she'd shown Mallory was back. "I'm not counting on them to play soldier or cop. They're just window dressing for now, all about appearances. *He's* shown his players and we're showing him ours."

"And if *he* calls your bluff?"

Alice raised a single brow. "If we need soldiers, I'll make a different call."

When we got home, two men stood on either side of our stoop, staring straight ahead like playacting soldiers and acknowledging Alice with a nod as she passed by. They took their jobs very seriously, it seemed. But something was off. I thought maybe it was that I'd expected to feel crowded by their added presence, but once I started up the steps, it was like they weren't even there.

I didn't realize what was missing until I reached the top step. The noise. I looked behind us and the two men standing guard were the only people on the street in front of our house. No flashes or camera lights, no whirring, buzzing, or clicks. But more important, there were no questions. Not one reporter was left. And that realization alone made me turn toward a confused Alice and say, "Thank you."

"What's this? Are you playing psychological warfare with me? I get a scolding followed by gratitude?"

I shook my head and glanced back down at the men.

Alice looked at me, wary. "Okay. You're welcome." She pushed my hair behind my shoulder and then rested her hand there. She smiled first, which made me grin, and she didn't let go of my shoulder until we were in the house and heading toward our rooms.

Chapter 10

A violin ringtone whined from my phone the minute I lay on my bed. The Offenbach Barcarolle. Lock was calling, though he should've been in class just then. I toyed with the idea of ignoring it and texting him some kind of lecture about his education, but I wanted to talk to him more than I wanted to play with him.

"Yes, I went to see my father today, but I don't want to talk about that or about them finding the sword or his—"

"They found the sword? Wait, never mind." I could perfectly picture his dismissive hand gesture. "I want to talk about the letter. It definitely wasn't from your dad."

"I know."

"Yes, but now I have an address.... *You* know?"

"An address?"

"You first. How do you know?"

"I brought it up when I saw my father today and he had no idea what I was talking about. Now you. You have an address?"

"Can I come over? It's better if I show you in person."

I smiled. "You mean that you can draw out the explanation and make yourself look more clever if you show me in person?"

Lock didn't laugh with me, but I could picture the rise of his brow as he said, "You are devastating for my ego."

"Someone must balance all the adoration you get from my brothers. Very well. Come over *after* school." I was so entirely sure of his expression just then, I added, "Don't scowl, and go back to class."

"I'll be there at lunch," he quipped back, and promptly ended our call.

I couldn't nap after my phone call with Lock, despite my exhaustion. Lying in my quiet room, I couldn't keep my thoughts from spinning until I sat up, dizzy and desperate for a distraction. I turned to maths first, timing how long it took me to solve problem sets, first in my head and then written out, to calculate how much time I wasted showing proof of work to my instructors. But for no known reason, instead of walking the steps of the equations, my thoughts kept replaying my earlier conversation with my father and, specifically, the way my father had threatened me to help get him out.

From out there, from in here, it don't matter where I am. You'll never see those boys again if you don't help get me out of here.

He couldn't have honestly expected that to work, which made me want to know why he'd said it—why he had wanted to see me at all. It felt like a waste of time for both of us.

Tired of hearing his voice in my head, I tossed aside my books and ran up the attic steps. If maths wouldn't work, I would lose myself in training.

Aikido and Bartitsu are similar in that they are both about balance and focused power. But where Bartitsu is about disturbing your opponent's equilibrium and taking advantage of every slipup, aikido is about using the force of your enemy's attack to add to your own. Aikido is all about power, using everything you can steal from your enemy and exerting as little of your own as possible.

I had to wonder if that was why Mum chose aikido over all the other martial arts she could have learned. It was the perfect grifter's art—if you do it right, you don't even look like you're fighting.

That morning I focused on the sword forms. I made it through maybe fifteen minutes of ever-shifting stances before I lost my balance to a misstep and tripped back over a stack of attic stuff, falling hard onto the plywood floor. A few old photo albums fell to one side of me and a metal box to the other. The box opened in the process, spilling out wads of tissue paper and something hard that clattered across the attic boards and plopped into the insulation.

I pushed the tissue paper back into the bottom half of the box, but one of the bundles was heavier than I expected. I unwrapped it and found a pile of fifty-pound notes in the center. Another heavy bundle had twenty-pound notes, then fifty-pound again, and the rest of the box was filled with torn, empty tissue sheets shaped like they had once held bundles of cash. In all, it seemed there had originally been thirteen bundles. From what I could calculate, the box had once held perhaps £50,000.

I crawled across the floor to retrieve the escaped object and found it was a bright silver multitool/utility knife. But when I pulled open the tools, where I expected to see blades, there were long, thin metal picks with odd shapes at the tips. It took me a minute to work it out, but in the end, I grinned and whispered, "Lock pick."

I dropped the tool into the box with a clang, then felt around for the lid. It was heavier than it should have been, because of an ornate metal piece affixed to the top of it that was pewter and in the shape of a Celtic cross, with a circle that intersected the upright and crossbar. It had vines winding up the sides to weave through the pattern on the circle. All of that was odd enough, but it seemed like a ridiculously ornate box in which to hide money and a lock-pick tool.

With the box back in place, I flipped open one of the photo albums, which turned out to be a scrapbook. When I fanned through the pages, some old newspaper clippings fell out. The first had a picture of my dad holding his hand up, as if to block the press from taking pictures of him and a woman with curly hair who stood next to him. POLICE FIND KILLER, NO JUSTICE, read the headline. I skimmed the first paragraph, and apparently when he was just a constable, my father had managed to find the man who had murdered a child, but he was already dead. I vaguely remembered the case from my childhood, something about a boy's body being found in a dumpster.

Another of the escaped clippings was about a girl who'd been drowned in an ornamental fountain at Hyde Park—the

Joy of Life Fountain, just for some cruel irony. I flipped through a few more pages until I found a picture of a boy who looked to be about Seanie's age. The accompanying clipping was mostly about Inspector Mallory, or Sergeant Mallory, as he was back then.

I started turning pages at random, wondering why in the world my mother would put so much effort into compiling something like this for my father. She didn't seem the type to scrapbook at all, really. It seemed so out of character for her, but apparently this was just one more thing I didn't know about Emily Moriarty. "Were you really that bored with your life?" I asked aloud, brushing my fingers over a program from the promotion ceremony where my father became a detective sergeant.

I closed the book with a shake of my head and reached for the photo albums that had once rested on top of it. Somehow, my little trip down memory lane had sapped all my energy. Even the slight effort it took to restack everything made me feel exhausted. Another escape abandoned, I went down the attic steps and headed toward my room, but my way was blocked by Freddie. He sat in the hall, leaning against my bedroom door, spinning his mobile phone on his knee like a top.

I stared at him for a solid minute with no reaction before I lowered myself to sit on the bottom of the attic steps. "Say it quickly. It's been a hard day and I need a bath."

"Because of Dad?" His words were more blurted accusation than question, punctuated by his gaze, which had become a lot more unflinching in the weeks that Dad had been locked up.

"Why would it have anything to do with that coward?"

Freddie scowled so that I almost felt like I was looking at a different person for the second time in just two days. He had never, ever looked at me like I was the enemy. Not in his entire life.

"I know you saw him today, and don't lie, because Lock told me that's where you went."

"When did he tell you that?"

"This morning, when you left without telling us where you were going, Alice sent me over to see if you were with him."

I made an irritated face and said, "Lock knows nothing about my day." I stood and reached for my doorknob, but Freddie was quicker, blocking my hand with his.

"He knew what I had for breakfast and that I'd bickered with Alice just by looking at me. He knows plenty."

I met Freddie's stare with my own, which usually made him back off immediately, but he was more determined that day. He stood and entered my room. I released a heavy sigh and followed him in. I sat cross-legged on my bed, patting the space in front of me, but Freddie ignored my invitation.

"I just need to tell you some things," he said, staring at the floor.

I gestured to my bed again. "Come on, then. You want to talk? Face me and talk." It was something our mother had said a lot. I thought maybe it had been a mistake to evoke a memory of Mum like that, but Freddie either didn't mind or didn't notice. He scrambled up to sit facing me, taking the challenge more defiantly than I'd expected. "You can't let him get us. No matter what."

I studied his face for a bit, finding new details among all the old features I knew so well. He had a new scar across his forehead from his final beating from Dad, and his jawline had thinned a bit, despite the weight he'd put on from the hearty dinners at Mrs. Hudson's. And though his face was still healing from the recent fight he'd had, he looked healthy. I felt a part of me relax, releasing a tension I maybe didn't realize I'd been harboring.

"Why would you say this to me?" I asked.

Freddie traced a stitched seam on my quilt as it made a path around one of his knees. "Scared," he mumbled.

"Scared of what?"

"Of things going back like they were."

I felt an ache in my chest as I watched Freddie wince away from his own truth, but I figured there had to be more to it than that. "And?"

"That you won't be here to help."

I was left a little speechless. "I'll be here." I only realized what an untrustworthy promise that was after I'd said it. Freddie knew it too, but not for the same reasons I had.

"Not if he has us taken away from you. Not if he kills you."

"He won't." I tapped under his chin to force him to look me in the eye. "No matter what happens, he won't kill me. And as long as I'm alive, I won't let him keep you from me either."

Something relaxed in Fred's expression, but not completely.

I couldn't blame him for not trusting me. He'd seen the welts and bruises on my face and neck. Despite the way Lock and I had tried to cover all that had happened that night, our dad was in jail for murder and for my attempted murder. Fred knew it had almost happened before. That was why his next expression was more wary than I wished, and why his voice was small when he asked, "Swear?"

"Swear. You've seen me training, right?" I nodded defiantly, despite the lingering fear in my brother's eyes that made the ache in my chest intensify until it felt like I'd been stabbed. "You trust Lock, then? Because he's been training me as well."

That brightened Freddie's expression more than it should have. "Oh yeah? In what?"

"Hitting people with sticks." I smirked a little, which made Freddie laugh. "I'm not all that sure it'll help any, but he, of course, finds it highly important."

Finally, a glint of the old Freddie came out as he sing-songed, "'Cause he's your boyfriend."

I shook my head and rolled my eyes. "Nope."

"Liar. I saw you two kissing. You should just admit it."

I tickled him under his chin and did my worst impression of Freddie's teasing tone. "You should go study something and get out of my room."

He started humming some childish kissing rhyme, and I chased him out into the hall before locking my door and falling back on my bed. Freddie had managed to clear my mind in a way nothing else could, reminding me yet again how much I needed those three brats. And I wouldn't have them for long—not if our father really did weasel his way out of his cell. They couldn't be here if he got out of jail—not in London, not in England. It was too dangerous. But they couldn't leave yet, not while my dad had easy access to the authorities and enough media attention to start an international manhunt.

We needed to keep our passports somewhere easy to grab, and we needed a plan, which meant convincing Alice to leave. If anything were to happen to me or if Alice was to lose custody, she needed to take my brothers to the countryside and then to America as quickly as possible. Even if that meant leaving me behind to ensure that he'd never threaten any of us ever again.

Chapter 11

Lock rushed into my room almost exactly at noon, one hand clutching his tablet, the other holding his mobile to his ear. He immediately started pacing the floor as though I weren't there at all.

"How long can it physically take to accept a tip on an actual tip hotline?" he asked his reflection in my full-length mirror. Then he spun in place and paced back to my window.

I watched him for three full laps of my tiny room before saying, "I thought I said *after* school."

He pointed at me with his tablet hand. "I wasn't scowling earlier."

"Liar."

I could tell he was trying not to smile, but then he was distracted by someone on the line. "Yes, this is about the jewelry store that was robbed last week," he said. "The thief is a woman."

His expression went from being pleased with himself to irritated in the blink of an eye. "No, I was not there. I saw a picture from the crime scene that leaked on the Internet and . . . No, this isn't a prank call. Just listen, because . . ."

He looked at me in exasperation and I mouthed: *Who are you talking to?*

Police, he mouthed back.

I rolled my eyes, and fell back onto my pillow. He'd seen a picture on the Internet and solved a jewelry heist. Of course he had.

"Yes, I am aware of the penalties for impeding a police investigation. I'm just trying to tell you that there are three too many pearls on the floor for the piece that was stolen, which means the thief broke one of her own pieces of jewelry while trying to leave." He pointed one finger at the ceiling and said, "A piece she was wearing."

With his finger still up in the air, he smiled widely at me. He was so impressed with his own cleverness, my Lock, and I surprised myself by returning his smile. Only he would count pearls.

He looked horrified in the next moment and ended the call so quickly I could barely suppress my laughter. I lost it completely after seeing the sad puppy look he wore when he lifted his head.

"Aw, what happened?" I asked.

"They asked for my name." He came over to sit with me on the bed, completely defeated. I sat up and patted his back. "They want me to come in for questioning."

I failed again to check my laughter, and Lock frowned. "It's not funny. He said no one could know that unless they were there."

I pressed my lips together, which didn't help at all. "Of course he did."

"You're still laughing."

"It's still funny."

Lock waved me off and held his head high. "Doesn't matter. At least now they know it's a woman."

"Or a young teen sleuth calling in false tips to make it seem like a woman did it." My eyes went wide and I pointed at him accusingly. "Maybe it *was* you! Why aren't you wearing your pearls today?"

Lock wanted to laugh so much. I could see it despite his attempt at a glare, which was a giant failure. "I cannot believe you just said that."

I winked and he lunged at me in revenge. I deflected as much as I could, but somehow in his quest to keep me from bashing his head repeatedly with my pillow, he was able to grab both my wrists and push them behind my back. We looked up at the same time, bringing our faces close. The laughter stopped when our eyes met, leaving us both breathless. I felt his soft huffing breaths on my lips, which made me hyperaware when his gaze dropped down to stare at them.

I turned my head and bit at my bottom lip, which was tingling in an anticipation that only made me feel that much more guilty. After a moment Lock freed my hands and whispered, "Sorry," as we awkwardly disentangled ourselves.

Had he been someone else—if we were a different couple—I wondered if he would have asked me why I kept acting like that, or how long it would take me to forgive him, or if I ever would. He might have pointed out that he'd only done what he needed to do to save my life, and I would have called him a liar, reminding him that involving the police was a calculated decision as was every choice he'd made.

Were we a normal couple, all these missed moments might have ended with arguments or excuses. Or maybe we'd have ended things entirely by now. But we were Lock and Mori, so he gave an apology that he didn't mean, and I changed the subject, despite the ache in my chest. "You found an address," I said. I walked over to the mirror to straighten my hair and clothes and tried my best to avoid looking at him in the reflection.

"Yes. For a clinic in the West End. Two of the letters in your collage came from an advertisement on the back of the cover page, where the mailing label was pasted."

"You took the letter apart? Does this mean you're on the case?"

Sherlock still sounded distracted when he said, "*We* are on the case."

"And I suppose that means we're going to the clinic."

"Of course. And if you're lucky, I'll tell you all about my new case at school." Lock didn't wait for my response. He was already out in the hall when he said, "It's a missing mobile phone, which seems dull, of course. But the only suspect claims to be in love with the victim. . . ."

Lock said something about the suspect's father working for a mobile company, and then he was too far down the stairs for me to hear. I was left to stare at my own reflection in the mirror.

I brought my fingers up to my lips as my forced grin faded and tried not to think about how much I still wanted him to kiss me.

"So, as you see, there's too much data to figure out what really happened," Sherlock said. We were sitting on the bus, heading to the clinic, but his mind was definitely wrapped up in this phone riddle.

"Or not enough," I offered.

Lock ignored me and started poking at his tablet with a little more force than was called for. A boy two years younger than us was being accused of stealing a mobile from a girl in his class—a girl he'd been in love with since grade school, according to the boy. He could barely utter full sentences when she was in his immediate vicinity. Stealing from her wasn't likely. More to the point, his father did indeed work for a mobile company, which made his stealing an outdated phone, of all things, completely unbelievable. He should have been at the very bottom of any suspect list.

Still, when the classroom was searched, the phone was found in the boy's book bag. Lock had been wrestling with the puzzle when he'd been distracted by the pearls. "But I wanted to know what you thought. The boy's pretty desperate."

"Why? He just returned her phone, right?"

"They're threatening to expel him."

"That seems a bit extreme."

"I thought so too, but he's more worried that the girl will hate him and that he won't be able to see her anymore if his parents make him transfer schools."

Neither of us spoke for a few seconds, and then Lock muttered, "Too many possibilities."

It was the exact opposite of my case, the one we were supposed to be focusing on that day. But he wouldn't be able to, not as long as this problem was in front of him, so I decided to help.

"Who benefits?"

Lock looked insulted at the question. "Do you not think I've already tried to ferret out a motive?"

"And there's none?"

"The girl is well liked but not popular enough to have enemies."

"Every girl has an enemy, and it's almost always another girl."

"I thought men were the enemy," he said as a tease.

I narrowed my eyes. "Well, who exactly do you think teaches little girls to see other little girls as the enemy, when in fact it's all just a lie to make sure we never consolidate our talents and rise to power?"

I watched Lock's expression brighten and I changed the subject before he said something annoying, like how lovely I looked when I ranted about the patriarchy. "In the absence of a motive, have you considered it was an accident?"

"Someone accidentally stole the pho— Oh, you mean that our boy was accidentally framed. That it was put in the wrong bag. Yes. Yes, of course."

"And?"

"Three others have his same bag on that level of the school

building, none of whom I can say with any certainty were in the classroom that day."

"What if someone picked it up thinking it was his own and was too embarrassed to return it?"

"And slipped it into our boy's bag, knowing he'd return it to the girl he liked? The SIM card was removed and the content on the phone was wiped clean, which is an odd step if it was all a mistake."

"Someone wanted to destroy something on the phone, then. For sure."

"Agreed, but here we are at too many possibilities. The girl claims there were hundreds of pictures and videos on the thing. She'd upgraded the memory as much as was possible and kept having to delete stuff to make it work right."

"Too many possibilities," I said, falling back into my thoughts.

Lock did as well, for a time, then he asked, "Do you ever wonder what you'll do in future?"

I paused to stare out the window. "Before or after the feminine revolution?"

"After university."

"Doctorate in maths and most likely an academic career. Why?"

"Not sure I'll go to university. Not for a degree program anyway. Maybe just to take classes that sound interesting."

It was a surprisingly impractical and whimsical plan for someone as clever as Sherlock, but I didn't respond. There was a time when I'd had a clear plan for my life. I'd rattled it off so easily to Lock—my future academic career. Just then, however, none of it seemed real. I couldn't believe I'd ever actually be at university, taking classes and following a degree path like everyone else. I couldn't really see past the summer and into our final year at school. I couldn't even predict what would happen tomorrow. All I could think to do was focus on my sworn promise to Freddie—survive this mess and be there to help. It suddenly felt like the most pathetic of goals, even more pathetic than Lock's trolling university classes on his whims. At least he'd be doing what he wanted.

"This work," he said. "I think I'll keep doing this."

"Why not become a proper police detective, then? Or a criminologist."

He shook his head. "Too limiting. Besides, one Holmes working for the government is enough." He paused and fought off a frown. "My mother says that a lot."

I perhaps should have asked how his mother was doing, but I was sure he'd bring it up on his own if he wanted to talk about her.

"Well then, not-police-detective, show me how you discovered this address we're traveling toward."

As it turned out, Sherlock was only half certain that the address he'd discovered in my threatening letter was the UltraCare Clinic in West End. There were two letters that still had a piece of the label attached, one showing "Ult" and "17A" of the address label and the other showing "dish Sq." Lock decided this could only be 17A Cavendish Square, the main-floor office in an old white-brick building of medical offices. It wasn't until we reached the place that I realized we also had no idea what we were even looking for there. That didn't seem to stem Lock's excitement, however. His eyes were alight, as if he were about to climb to the top of the building and jump off it.

The interior of the office was a stark modern contrast to the outside. The front desk was clear acrylic with a slab of polished wood on top. It stood in front of the only bright purple accent wall in a sea of black-and-white scrolling wallpaper. But there was no one seated behind the desk, so I pulled Sherlock to sit with me on the purple chairs that lined every other wall in the entry area.

"Shouldn't we wait by the desk?" he asked, glancing around to take in every detail of the place, I was sure.

"To ask what, exactly? Have any of their magazines gone missing and who do they think stole them?"

He picked up one of the magazines laid out on a side table between our chairs and the next grouping of seats. "I have a theory," he said. He slid a finger under the address label on the front and popped it off into his hand.

"Are they all that easy?" I asked, picking up my own magazine. But this one's label didn't budge, and when I tried to force it, the page started to tear.

"No, but I believe the letters with the address label on the back came from this magazine." He opened the front page, and I instantly recognized three of the letters along the bottom. "The labels for this magazine all come off that easily."

"So your theory is that the person who sent the threat is

willing to go through the time and effort to cut out letters to make the message, but is too lazy to remove the label that might point us to him or her?"

"Definitely a her."

I shook my head.

"And no. My theory is that she left the label on purpose."

"Why?" I challenged.

"That's the question we're here to answer." Sherlock glanced around the room again. There were two older men sitting in the chairs closest to the front desk, and a woman with a sleeping toddler on her lap sitting in the chair farthest away. "What exactly did she want us to see here?"

The front door to the clinic opened just then, and a woman entered. I recognized her almost instantly as one of the regulars from the park. She was a graying blond-haired woman wearing at least seven bags, which had always made her appear to be a globular being from afar. She had four satchels that crisscrossed her body like she was the world's most ambitious courier, and three others draped around her front and back. And, because evidently she had more to carry, she held a large plastic sack in each hand, so that she was forced to push into the room awkwardly and disentangle the sack handles from her wrist before she could write her name on the clinic sign-in sheet.

Just as she'd finished adjusting her bags so that she could squeeze into one of the chairs, the door from the clinic back rooms opened into reception. I immediately sank lower on the chair, so that Lock's body could hide me a little.

"What is it?" he asked.

I pretended to scratch the place between my temple and forehead so I could shield my face with my hand and pointed toward the desk where an impatient, fidgety woman stood— our local Sally Alexander, warrior for justice, or at least her approximation of the ideal. She looked somehow smaller without her picket signs and bright red lipstick. "She's not exactly a fan of mine."

Lock sat up straighter in his chair. "Well, this just got interesting."

"For you. I think for me it's time to leave." The very last thing I wanted to do was get into some kind of public confrontation with the woman.

"Not so fast," Lock said. "I'm almost sure there's more to see."

He was right, not that either of us could have predicted what happened next. The door from the clinic rooms opened again, and this time the woman who came through was perhaps the last person I expected to see—Mrs. Patel, Lily's mother. At first I didn't recognize her, wearing lavender scrubs with her hair pulled up in a tight bun. I'd only ever seen her the once, at Mr. Patel's funeral. But something about her expression caught my eye, and then everything clicked into place. She looked weary, like someone who had already hiked to the top of a mountain that day. It was the same look she'd worn at her husband's memorial.

"Thought I'd never get out of here," Sally said.

"I'm so sorry for the wait, Mrs. Greeves. The doctor had

a few difficult patients this morning that threw his schedule off." Mrs. Patel attempted a placating smile, but I was pretty sure there was no smile that would have placated our Sally, or whatever her name really was.

"If you're sorry, don't let it happen again. Just because I'm old doesn't mean I don't have places to go."

"Yes, of course," Mrs. Patel said. "Completely our fault."

Lock nudged me as the two of them started in on paperwork at the front desk. "Do these two know each other?" he asked, motioning between Mrs. Greeves and the woman from the park.

"How would I know?"

"Watch this." He gestured toward Mrs. Greeves, who asked a question about something on the paperwork and then, when Mrs. Patel's head was down, Greeves reached behind her back to make an okay sign with her fingers. As if on cue, the woman from the park slid a magazine off the table next to her, rolled it up, and slid it into a satchel at her hip. Lock and I exchanged a glance and then went back to watching them with renewed interest.

By the time Mrs. Greeves left, the woman from the park had managed to hide away a second magazine into one of the bags tied at her wrist and a third down the front of her shirt.

Lock kept a lookout until Mrs. Patel disappeared into the back of the clinic once more, and then he grabbed the hand I'd been using to hide and pulled me toward the front door. The woman from the park must have concluded her business as well, because she beelined for the door right as we did, and might have beat us through if she hadn't paused to look behind her, right at me, as it turned out.

"I know you," she said, blocking our retreat.

I offered up a half smile and a nod, hoping either she'd move or Lock would push past, but neither happened. Lock just looked from the woman to me and asked, "You say you know her? From where?"

"Does it really matter?" I asked, in what I had meant to be a whisper but that came out sounding like an exasperated growl.

"Vivianne," the woman said. Then her expression darkened and she said, "Ninianne."

I turned to Lock, hoping he'd finally help to get us out of there, but he only stared at the woman as if he were studying her. I said, "You must have me confused with—"

"Nimue," she hissed.

And I was almost sure she was about to lunge at me when Mrs. Patel's warm voice called out, "Lady Constance! I saved up some more magazines for you. Just like I promised." We all turned toward the reception desk, where Mrs. Patel held out a thick stack of worn magazines. "Here you are!"

There was a bit of an awkward pause, where we all just stared at the magazines, but then Constance lunged toward the desk instead of at me, giving me ample time to drag Sherlock through the door and out onto the street. He guided me down an alley between the clinic and the next building, and then we watched as the Lady Constance ambled past, muttering to herself.

When she was a safe distance from us, I said, "Those were King Arthur references. Is she our artist then?"

"No. Her hands tremor. I doubt she could keep it at bay long enough to do that kind of detailed work."

I frowned, at first angry with myself for failing to notice such an obvious clue, but then at Lock, who whispered, "Nimue," with bright eyes.

I attempted to refocus him away from his amusement. "The artist, Sherlock."

"Yes, well, it's possible she was the one who told the story to our artist, yes? The drawing showed a woman in ornate costume, whispering something into a man's ear. Perhaps he's the artist, and she was the whispering witness. Though she apparently told an embellished version."

"So we've learned nothing."

"Not nothing!" Lock protested. "We know where the magazines come from, and who has access to them. We know the witness and that she's seen our artist. We have found our key . . . or sword, as it were." Lock pressed his lips together to stifle his laugh, but it didn't work. He was laughing unchecked before we'd even reached the bus stop. He started to speak again once we got there, but I held up a hand.

"Don't say it."

"It's just so perfect!"

"Do not," I warned, but Lock could not be stopped.

"Nimue! She's named you as the Lady of the Lake! It's brilliant. I suppose that makes you Merlin's betrayer, as well. Should I be afraid, then?"

I invited him to stop talking with my glare, and this time it seemed to work for a while. That is, until we actually boarded the bus and he leaned closer to me and said, "Nimue's not all bad. She did give Excalibur to Arthur." Just the tone of his voice told me he wasn't anywhere near done.

"Truly, Lock, if you say it, I will be forced to injure you."

He never did take my threats seriously.

"The sword that later killed him, if we're being technical."

I reached through my crossed arms to pinch his side as hard as I could, but he only laughed through the pain. So I scooted closer to the window and turned as much of my back to Lock as I could—partly to hide my grin, of course. And when he finally stopped laughing, I looked over my shoulder and said, "It wasn't Excalibur that killed Arthur. It was the sword Clarent."

Chapter 12

I went to school early the next day, but never did make it to any of my morning classes. I hadn't intended to hide away in Lock's lab, but not even the loud bell ringing through the small space could entice me from my hiding space and into the halls. I did wander into drama class just in time to get counted for attendance, but when it was clear Miss Francis was only going to run scenes for those students taking summer theater courses, I hid up in the back rows of the auditorium where no one could see me in the dark.

Lock joined me about ten minutes into class, flopping back into the seat next to mine with a sigh. I thought for sure he'd come to share all his insights into my case, but instead he just watched the movements of the class, saying nothing.

It wasn't as though we'd learned anything earth shattering, really. One of the magazines had come from that clinic, but it could just as easily have come from the trash in the building's alley, or from any of the hundreds of patients who came in and out of there on a weekly basis. It didn't have to be from Lady Constance of the Park. Or Mrs. Patel. Or even my

Sally Alexander, who we now knew was actually called Mrs. Greeves. That name fit her nicely. It also sounded familiar to me, in that way that random names sometimes do.

"What are you thinking?" I asked, after we watched a snubbed John Watson wander over to sit with a few of the set decorators, who were sitting in a circle onstage batting a Hacky Sack around using only the backs of their hands.

Lock shrugged at first, but he leaned forward to rest his arms on the seat back in front of him. "I was wondering how much Lily Patel hates you."

"Why do you ask about Lily?"

"Have you spoken to her at school?"

"Not much." I realized I hadn't told him about my accidental bonding time with Lily at her father's memorial spot in the park. But I wasn't sure anything said there was particularly relevant. It was obvious that her mother working at the clinic meant she had access to the magazines by proxy, but I couldn't imagine her hunching over them with scissors clutched in one hand and model glue in the other—not when she could just unleash her hyenas to rip me to shreds at school on a daily basis. "Why are you thinking about people who hate me?"

"In looking at the magazines left out in the clinic, it would appear they subscribe to six publications and change out the magazines every three months."

"And?"

"Even if we assume that one or two get taken home with a patient, or our sticky-fingered Lady Constance perhaps, that would still leave twelve magazines for Nurse Patel to hand off to Constance."

"Maybe. Maybe not. You can't know how many were stolen or damaged or didn't arrive in the post."

"True. But we do know how many were used to make your letter. Five. The letters used came from five distinct magazines."

He was being slow on purpose, which he knew I hated.

"And?" I said again.

"And Mrs. Patel only handed seven to the bag lady. The five used to make your letter were missing."

I frowned and let my mind drift a bit. "What is the point, though? What possible reason would someone have to send me a drawing and a threatening letter? What do they want?"

"They want you to confess."

"To what end?"

He shrugged. "Two possibilities. They think you're a conspirator with your father and want you to go to prison with him."

"Or?"

"Or they think you're the culprit."

"And want my father to go free?"

He was quiet, but my mind reeled. Suddenly, Mrs. Greeves's picket signs and screaming all felt more sinister. "You recognized our protester?"

Sherlock nodded and sat back in his chair again, steepling his fingers and resting them at his chin. "She has access to the magazines."

"And wants my dad free, though I've no idea why."

"She's older though. Too old to have a son who builds models. And I don't think she's our witness or artist either."

"Why?"

"You said she wants your father freed. Does she strike you as the kind to wait for your confession? I say she'd just go directly to the police if she had witnessed the act herself."

I pushed my fingers into my hair and rocked back in my theater seat. We'd gone from no suspects to too many in the space of an afternoon, and there were too many variables and not enough real data to find an answer that meant anything. It was all just randomness. No pattern.

"Have you heard of Ulam's spiral?" I asked.

"No."

"It has to do with prime numbers. There's not supposed to be a pattern to primes. They're distributed through the integer string seemingly at random. But when this mathematician named Ulam doodled numbers into a spiral, the primes started to line up diagonally."

"Line up?" He smiled at me like I was about to tell him the most fascinating of stories.

"It doesn't matter which number you start with at the center of your spiral or how many numbers you use. It doesn't even matter what shape your spiral is. If you write integers in a spiral pattern and circle the primes, you will have a diagonal line of circles. A pattern from randomness."

"A pattern from randomness? Is that what you see here?"

I shook my head. "Not yet. But it has to be there, doesn't it? If we just manage to circle our primes."

Lock stared at me and waited for me to speak again. When I did not, he asked, "Tell me what you're thinking?"

I focused on Lily, who sat down on the spot-lit stage, alone for once. Then I followed a taped-off line that came from under her uniform skirt and crossed the stage diagonally until it was interrupted by a knee—a knee that belonged to her Watson. I wondered then if he knew he'd done it. If Watson had connected them on the stage on purpose or subconsciously, or perhaps it had been a mere coincidence. Just two people sitting on a large plane with an accidental line drawn between them. A pattern from randomness.

"I wonder who will be at the end of my diagonal line," I said. I leaned on the armrest between us and tried my best to lighten my tone to hide the darker turn of my thoughts. "When the random reveals its pattern, who will emerge?"

Sherlock turned in his seat until we were face-to-face, suddenly closer than we'd been even the day before. "Don't turn away," he said quietly.

I still felt the need to put more space between us, but I resisted. Had the turning away just become habit? Was I thinking too much?

He started to speak a few times, taking small breaths, then huffing them out. Finally, he said, "No matter who is facing you at the end of your line, I will be next to you. Do you believe that?"

I wanted to believe, wanted to dismiss the way my brain screamed it wasn't true, couldn't possibly be true, that he'd only ever stand on the side of what he thought was right regardless of where I'd be standing. My thoughts fell into a blaring turmoil as I held Lock's gaze. And I was so tired of the noise of it. Of the unending mental noise whenever what I knew of the world warred with what I wanted. What I needed.

Lock reached up, and I almost flinched. He must have felt it somehow too, because he slowed the movement of his hand. And the very moment he rested his palm against my cheek, the noise stopped. My mind fell blank. Or maybe it was just that I suddenly became hyperaware of the rush of blood to my heart.

He traced my cheekbone with his thumb. "Can you believe that?"

I shook my head slightly, but covered his hand with my own so he wouldn't pull away. I wasn't sure I could take it if he stopped touching me just then. "Make me," I said. "Make me believe you."

He moved closer so slowly, I thought my heart would stop altogether. We shared one breath and then another, before finally his lips found mine. He kissed me softly but long, holding me close with his fingers twined in my hair. He stopped only to study my eyes, as if he couldn't believe I was still there. The next time he kissed me, I smiled against his lips and kissed him back.

We traded kisses and awkward glances until a giant crash onstage broke our spell. But Sherlock held my hand for the rest of class and all the way home. The very minute he let go and I closed our front door behind me, a hundred protests crashed through my mind, the word "temporary" flashing in red to mark each one. But I didn't care anymore. Maybe I was being selfish or stupid or whatever else. But I wanted him, my Lock. And for now he wanted me back.

Alice handed me another envelope after dinner that night—one without a postmark that faintly smelled of model glue. I should have opened it right away but instead placed it on my bed and stepped back to think a moment. Then I called Lock.

Before he could say hello, I said, "I got another envelope."

"I'll be right over."

"No. Don't come. I just . . ." I didn't know why I'd called him exactly, but I could hear him moving around, as if he was coming over anyway. So I opened the envelope and was surprised to find THANK YOU embossed in silver across the card inside. The glue smell had made me sure it would be another threat. "I think it's a drawing."

I didn't really know what I was waiting for, and it was uncharacteristic of me to pause at all. But I felt like maybe I didn't want to see what would be drawn there. Not this time.

I heard Mycroft call, "Sherlock!" and then the sound on Lock's end muffled, as if he was pressing his mobile against his shirt. I used the pause in our conversation to study the way the pencil lead smudged around the edges of the card, and then Lock said, "Call you right back?"

"Yeah."

And I was left alone with the card once more.

I opened it finally, to keep my self-derision at bay, and immediately wished I hadn't. Similar to the first drawing, this one had a main story in the background with an ornate, framed foreground and a male figure peeking in—no whispering princess, however. It had the same level of detail and it filled the entire white space of the card. In fact, the only style difference was that the main characters of the background story weren't wearing medieval gowns. Perhaps, if they were, I might have answered when Lock called back.

My phone blasted out that bloody barcarolle, and instead of answering, I stared at an almost perfect rendering of Sadie Mae in her school uniform. She was being pushed up against a willow tree by a large white man. Her perfect spiral curls, the look of abject terror on her face, his white fingers clamped around her throat. She was even missing a shoe, my Sadie Mae.

The card started to shake, and I realized I was gripping the card stock too tightly when I heard it start to crinkle in my fist. I dropped the thing, and still I couldn't look away. Which is also when I saw the hidden message in the leaves that formed the frame of the image. I thought maybe I was seeing things at first, but looking at it from far away and at the angle it had fallen, the words were definitely there: SECOND SIN.

"'Second sin,'" I said aloud. In the next second I was shuffling through my schoolwork and the other useless papers and books on my desk. And when I'd knocked near half of them to the floor in my rush, I found it. The first drawing. I could see that there were words as plain as anything, now that I knew what to look for. I dropped it next to its sibling on the floor and adjusted it until it was at the same angle. "'First sin.' Oh God."

I grabbed the lamp from my desk and pulled it to where the drawings rested, straining the electric cord to the farthest it would reach. Then I got down on my knees, studying every inch of the drawings. I found two anomalies. First, someone had doctored the drawings. While the original lines were drawn using a true black-colored pencil, the shading that created the "sins" messages looked slightly lighter, as if whoever had doctored them had used a normal lead pencil instead of an art pencil.

The second was more disturbing. That same lead pencil had been used again on the second drawing. The right hand of the man peeking around the frame had been messily erased, and, over the top, the person doctoring the drawing had replaced the hand with a stump and had drawn blood dripping down his upper arm in dark gray rivulets.

I wanted to obsess over the fact that someone was cataloging my sins, and not just my stupid mistake of throwing my father's sword into the lake. They knew I was responsible for Sadie's death as well. Somehow, whoever doctored the drawings knew enough to know what I'd never said aloud—that I'd invited my best friend into the house of a serial killer, when I wouldn't be there to protect her.

I shielded myself from the pain of that by focusing back on what my discoveries might mean. First, the smell of glue on what was clearly a drawing meant that Sherlock had been wrong that the drawings and threats were coming from two different people. Clearly, the card picked up the scent on a shared surface or by being handled by the same person who glued the letters on the threat. It possibly also meant that another threat would be coming to me in the mail.

Second, the fact that the drawings were doctored meant that the person sending me the drawings was not the artist. Third, whoever doctored the drawings had taken the time to sever the hand from the man character, which had to be a message. The hand found in our rubbish—it belonged to the man in the drawing. It was possible the man in the drawing was the artist.

So, I knew a few facts and several possibilities, and still I couldn't answer the larger question: WHY? Why would someone send these to me at all? What was her end game? Did the sender think she could scare me into some kind of confession? Did she really hate me that much? And how many more of my sins had been documented in this way?

When Sherlock's ringtone filled the room again, I was still sitting on the floor, glancing back and forth at the word "sin" written on each card. I didn't even know how long I'd been there. Without looking away from the drawings, I reached for my phone and answered, "Don't come over. I'll show you the second drawing tomorrow."

Lock paused just long enough for me to wonder if the change in costuming in the drawings was a message too, and then he said, "I need you."

The tone of his voice caught my attention. I looked up at my window. "Where are you?"

"Hospital. Charing Cross."

He hung up before I could tell him I'd be there, leaving me with a name I hadn't heard in almost a year, a place I never even allowed myself to think about. The place I'd left my mother. I had sworn that I would rather die on the street outside the front doors than walk the halls even one more time, but one phone call with three words from Lock and within minutes I was walking to the Baker Street Tube station, leaving the drawings and everything they represented on the floor of my room.

Chapter 13

My mobile rang again as I approached the bright blue awning of the Baker Street Tube station. I didn't recognize the number, but on the off chance it was Sherlock calling from a hospital phone, I picked up on the final ring.

"It's Lily."

"I have somewhere to be. How did you get my number?"

"I'm at your house. Where are you?"

I sighed. "Baker Street Tube station. What's this about?"

"Baker Street? Stay there. I'll come to you."

She ended the call, and I looked between the awning and my phone, trying to decide what to do. I scowled, but I stayed aboveground, watching the minutes creep past on my mobile. Just as I was about to give up on her, Lily appeared, her cheeks pink from running and a bouquet of flowers clutched in her hand.

"You hid the weapon." I could tell she was trying not to sound accusatory, but it didn't work. Her anger and confusion shimmered off her.

I wasn't sure how she'd found out, but I could guess. I

doubted Mallory would give that kind of information to the victim's family, but he was hardly the only member of the police that Lily could get her information from. She could have heard the accusations about me and the sword from anyone, really.

Maybe I should have lied to her, or kept quiet like I did when Mallory was the one interrogating me on the issue. But Lily deserved better from me than that. "I did."

Lily clutched the bouquet with both hands like a shield. "You said you wanted him to pay for what he's done."

"I do."

She thrust the bouquet at me so roughly that a few petals fluttered to the ground at my feet. "You said you wanted him to pay for what he's done! How could you? . . ."

I started toward the stairs, but Lily rushed to block my way.

"You knew where it was all this time, and you said nothing!"

She was yelling on the open street, oblivious to the stares we were already attracting. It was only a matter of time before someone recognized one or the both of us. I stepped toward her until our shoulders almost touched. She flinched when she thought I'd push past her, so I grabbed her forearm just hard enough to keep her beside me and spoke just loud enough for her to hear me over the street noise.

"I thought if I got rid of his weapon, maybe he'd stop— even if it was just for one day."

"But why?—"

"It didn't work." I closed my eyes against a wave of emotion, which was a mistake. All I could see in my self-imposed darkness was the look of terror Sadie wore in the drawing. Would I always remember her that way now? My "second sin," it had said. My greatest sin. "I've already lost something precious to me because of that decision. I don't need—" Lily started to move in front of me again, and I yanked her back to my side. "I don't need you to make accusations as though you could ever understand what it meant for me to find my friend . . . like that."

"Sadie Mae," Lily said. "She was your friend?"

I let go of her arm. "I have somewhere to be, and you've already made me late. Believe me or don't, but don't call me again."

She didn't try to stop me from going downstairs this time, but she followed me, saying nothing all the way to the Hammersmith & City–line platform. She sat next to me, but I didn't look at her. And when the train stopped at Paddington, she said, "I didn't know she was your friend."

I crossed my arms a little tighter around my chest. Then I looked the opposite way from where she sat and tried to think of anything but Sadie's muddy shoe. Of the way her body refused to move, even to take a breath. Of the bruising around her neck. And when I finally looked back, Lily was gone, leaving her tattered bouquet behind to rest on the seat next to me.

I texted Lock when I reached the bottom of the concrete steps that led up to the hospital's main entrance. It was already starting to get dark and I was exhausted, but I was there.

Where are you?

I stared at the screen for a few seconds, and when he didn't reply, I figured he was either angry or on a ward that didn't allow mobile phones. Either way, I'd have to find him on my own, which turned out to be much easier than I thought it would be. When I reached the top of the steps, I saw Lock sitting on a bench near the automatic glass doors. He was a rumpled mess of himself, his coat sliding off his shoulders, his mobile clutched to his chest, and his expression completely blank and staring across to the wall beyond.

When I got closer, I saw the cigarette in his fingers, slowly burning down so that half of it was already a tower of ash. I carefully sat beside him, but the slight shift of the bench didn't attract his attention. I was starting to wonder if he even knew I was there at all.

"I'm late," I said.

He waited a long time to speak. "Thank you," he said, at last. Then nothing again for a long time, before he added, "Never mind being late."

He still stared straight forward, and I knew this was where I should say something or do something comforting or helpful. I wanted to ask why we were there or what had happened to his mother—I assumed it was his mother. But I had hated that question when it was my mother in the hospital. "Is it worse?" they would ask, like they didn't know what the word "terminal" meant. Like we'd be spending our days at a hospital if she were even the slightest bit improved.

I thought about reaching for his hand, but it still held a

burning cigarette. I thought about just staying quiet, or even standing to leave, but he'd said he needed me. And for some reason I couldn't read him that night. Maybe my confrontation with Lily had thrown me off.

"You should go in," I said at last. When he didn't reply or make any movement toward leaving, I asked, "What if there's news of your mother's condition?"

"Mycroft will call me with news."

"What if she wants to see you?" I listened to the quiet sizzle of his next drag and his slow exhale, then watched as all the built-up ash was flicked to the ground. He never answered me. "You should go in."

"Will you go home if I do?"

"I don't have to go."

He didn't move or speak, even after he'd finished his cigarette and put it out on the ground.

I tried again. "You should—"

"I need you. I can't go in, because I need you."

I sat with that for a few seconds before I asked, "Tell me what to do?"

Sherlock lit another cigarette, but this time he took it from his mouth with the hand that held his mobile, so I quickly reached across the space between us to wrap my fingers around to his palm. He flinched a bit, but his expression softened when he glanced down at our hands. Then he looked back to the wall, and I thought maybe we'd just sit in silence, but he said, "Like this. Today, this is exactly how I need you."

We sat on that bench until it was dark and Lock was out of

cigarettes. When it started to get cold, I reached around him to pull his coat over his shoulders. As I straightened the collar, his arms came up around me, holding me close. He never met my eyes. He just brushed tentative fingers through my hair, smoothing it down and pushing strands behind my ear.

When he was done, I said, "I'm sorry." And I meant it in ways he'd never understand. It was a ridiculous time for a revelation, but right then, held in his arms, I felt all my anger and resentment wash away. The weeks I'd spent refusing to forgive him felt selfish and wasted as I wrapped an arm around his back. I rested my palm in the center of his chest and felt the faint thrum of his heart as his eyes finally tilted down to find mine, and I realized how stupid I'd been.

"I'm so sorry," I said. "For everything."

I still couldn't read his expression, but when he leaned forward to rest his forehead on my shoulder, he seemed lighter somehow. Unburdened, perhaps. I rested a hand on the back of his neck, and he said, "Just like this."

Chapter 14

I went back to the hospital the next day, without a summons. I half expected to find Sherlock sitting on the bench where he'd sat the night before, waiting for me. When he wasn't, I sat and sent him a text. *I'm outside.*

While I waited for his response, I caught myself tapping my coat pocket. Or, more accurately, I was tapping on the envelope that held both drawings in it. I'd told myself I was bringing them along as a just-in-case measure, if Lock needed a distraction from everything. But in truth, it had been a giant relief when I got home the night before to find the cards and my lamp still exactly where I'd left them. It occurred to me that anyone in the house could have wandered in and seen the drawings—my sins scribbled onto card stock in detail. I decided then not to ever leave them behind again. I wanted them with me.

I checked my phone to see if he'd texted me back, then sent him a new text. *I'm out front. Which is your mother's ward?*

Nothing again, so I watched the people file in and out of the hospital lobby as if it were a grocery store or an apartment complex. People laughed and sipped coffee as though the building weren't full of people fighting for their lives.

I tapped at my coat pocket again and started to wonder for the thousandth time who could possibly be sending me the drawings. "Have I really gained a nemesis?" I whispered. I hadn't expected a reply.

"Come now," he said. "I know we're not close, but I'm not sure I'd go so far as 'nemesis' to describe our burgeoning relationship."

I sighed. "Mycroft."

Lock's brother leaned lazily against the brick wall behind my bench and smiled at me, but the true state of him showed on his face. His eyelids drooped more than normal and seemed swollen, like he'd just woken. His clothes were rumpled and one side of his coat's collar was still tucked in by his neck.

"I'm still planning to get you a bell," I said, standing. "Your sneaking days are numbered, Elder Holmes. Cherish them."

"Noted. Sherlock told me you were here last night. He seemed in better spirits when he returned to the ward. Well done, that."

I couldn't decide which was more unbelievable, that Mycroft was praising me or that me sitting on a bench had any impact at all on Sherlock's mood. "All he did was smoke. I'm not sure you should be so approving."

Mycroft shrugged. "There are worse vices. Like naming your boyfriend's brother as a nemesis." He stood up from the wall and held a melodramatic hand to his chest. "That hurts."

I reached over to straighten his collar. "He's not my boy-friend."

I wasn't sure why I'd said that. No, I knew exactly why. I just didn't want to think about it there in front of his brother. Regardless, Mycroft seemed taken aback, though he shrugged it away in the end and started walking toward the entrance. "As you say."

"Is he inside?"

Mycroft raised a brow. "He didn't come here with you?"

We stared at each other for a few seconds.

"When did you last see him?" I asked.

"He left before midnight last night. I assumed he went home or to your house."

I shook my head, and then raised a hand to stop Mycroft from rushing past me. "You stay with your mother. I'll go find him."

I held his gaze until I was sure he would do as I said, and then I nodded once and walked toward the line of taxis.

I tried calling Lock most of the ride to his house, but he never answered. I did get a text, however, the very minute I started to walk up the steps to his front door.

I'm on my way.

I wasn't sure what that meant, but I headed home. I supposed whether he came to me or to Mycroft at the hospital, at least we'd know where he was.

My front stoop was uncharacteristically barren. No reporters. No protesters. No police. There weren't even any of Alice's men posted that day. I could almost have tricked myself into believing we'd found a bit of normalcy. I should've known better.

"Who are you?" a gruff voice called out from behind me.

An older man in a threatening posture was holding a sleepy Sherlock by the arm. The man shook Lock once, perhaps just to prove he could, and then he demanded again, "Who are you? And what were you doing lurking in the bushes there?"

That's when I recognized him as the man from the grocery. Alice's savior prince. Only, instead of the gentle concern that had wafted off the man when he dealt with Alice, now his eyes were boring into Lock like he wanted to burn him from the earth. Lock, in contrast, didn't seem overly concerned about any of it. He gazed off into the distance as if his mind was taken up with too many other things to care.

"Let him go right now," I said.

The prince stood firm. "I won't. Not until I know who he is and what he's doing here."

"What he's doing here is none of your business." When he still didn't let go of Lock, I ground out, "He is here because I want him to be here."

The prince let go of Sherlock and said, "Sorry, then, lad."

Sherlock shrugged and wandered up the front stairs and into the house, leaving me to deal with our resident guard all on my own.

"Who the hell are you?"

He cleared his throat and assumed a soldier's at-ease stance before answering. "Stuart Tucker, miss. And I came because your aunt—"

"I know. Just . . ." I tried my best to calm down. "That one who just went inside? He comes and goes as he pleases. Got it?"

"Yes, miss."

"My name is Mori." My voice was softer this time, but I didn't wait for his reply. Instead, I texted Mycroft quickly and then followed Sherlock inside.

By the time I got to my room, a Sherlock-shaped heap of boy was sprawled on the floor right on the spot where he used to sleep when my dad was still about the house.

"Where have you been?" I tossed my coat over my desk chair and kicked at his shoe twice. "Mycroft wants to know as well."

He rolled over to stare at the ceiling. "Working a case."

"The phone theft again?"

He didn't answer in word or gesture, and I let it be, leaving him to muse into the rafters. I wasn't sure why he was in my room instead of with his brother at the ward, but I didn't have the energy to form the words into a question, so I grabbed a book and sank down onto my bed to read. Almost the minute I lay back on my pillow, however, I couldn't seem to focus on the words. My mind was a tornado of half-answered questions, potential dangers, and endless unknowns. I put the book aside and let my mind spiral through the storm a bit. Then I watched Sherlock for a while, and when I shifted my gaze from him to the corner of envelope sticking out of my coat pocket, I caught him watching me. I draped my arm over the side of my bed so that my fingers could trace over the pattern of the rug and tried not to think about anything.

"Was it your second sin?" Sherlock asked, bringing me fully back to my senses in a way no other question would have. "The new drawing was your second sin?"

He'd seen the hidden text in the first illustration. Of course he had. And he hadn't mentioned it yet, because ...?

"Why didn't you say anything?"

"I knew you'd find it yourself. This new one is of you lying to the constable in the park about your dad being with you. Right?"

"No. It isn't." Apparently, Lock had decided my "sins" were merely my mistakes.

He tilted his head to look directly at me. I looked across the room at my coat.

"Sadie." I answered before he could ask, then watched him scowl and stare up at the ceiling again. I thought he might press me about it, so I asked, "Why didn't you go to the hospital today?"

His expression was blank as he seemed to ponder that question. "She stopped breathing last night. Mycroft had to give her CPR." His voice sounded a little more distant when he said, "She's had heart troubles since she was my age. I never knew that about my own mother."

"Mothers keep secrets."

"They do." Lock kicked one foot up and rested his heel on the toe of his other shoe. "She was supposed to be going in for regular treatments. She was supposed to be taking medications. But she stopped."

"Why didn't you go to the hospital today?"

"Sons are supposed to take care of their mothers, and she has two. She should've been doubly cared for."

"She is." It was a stupid thing to say, because I knew he wouldn't believe it.

Lock shook his head. "She isn't, though. Because it's too late now for us to take care of her. So much of her heart is damaged, she can't breathe right. The doctor said her next heart event will . . ." Lock took a quick breath and seemed startled by his own inability to finish the sentence.

"But you ask why I didn't go there," he continued. "It's because of Mycroft. He's intolerable on a good day, but do you know what he said to me after the doctor left? He said, 'Then we'll have to make sure she doesn't have another.' As if we can control her heart just by sitting at her bedside."

Lock rubbed his eyes angrily, but it didn't keep me from noticing how wet they were.

"Would you like me to hit him with a stick, or shall I hold him while you do it?"

It was a small smile, but Lock did indulge for a brief moment. Then he frowned at me. "Bartitsu weapons are called staffs or canes. They are not sticks."

"Yes, of course," I said. "Never a mere stick."

I closed my eyes then, but before I gave in to sleep, Sherlock's hand found mine and held tight.

Chapter 15

I'm not sure why I decided to descend into the bowels of the theater instead of going to chemistry. Was it perhaps that going to class seemed a waste of time now that I'd already taken our final exams? Or that, if I had to sit next to that moron Marcus Gregson for even one more hour, I would probably explode with all the insults I'd managed to keep at bay the entire school year?

I was surprised to find Sherlock there, directing his beakers and pipettes as though his mother wasn't presently dying in a hospital bed.

"What is it?" he asked without looking up. "Busy."

"Are you?"

He spun in place to find me with eyes as wide as if I'd rattled ghostly chains. But then he smiled and said, "You."

I'd never seen that side of Sherlock Holmes and found I missed it as soon as he recovered, which was much more quickly than I liked. "Me."

"How did you know to find me here?"

"I wasn't looking for you. And what on earth are you doing

in this basement that is more important than being with your mother?"

Lock scowled and hunched back over his experiment, which seemed to have something to do with how far different volumes of the same liquid spread across different kinds of flooring. He had various sizes of carpet samples and a table full of pipettes and beakers that were all filled with the same red liquid. "Mycroft kicked me out."

"For no reason at all, I assume."

"We might have had words about his habit of saying useless things."

I frowned in solidarity with Lock. "He's a bossy thing."

Sherlock barely responded to that with a grunt. He was already absorbed in his experiment once again. I watched him for a while, but there're only so many times you can watch pools of liquid expand through cut sections of carpet fiber before you find you would rather carve the periodic table into your skin than continue on. And still I sat and watched. There was something comfortable in this dank basement lab of his.

"This liquid has the same viscosity as blood," Lock said, as if I had asked him what he was doing. "If we imagine a wound dribbling blood in a steady stream onto a floor—"

"Because who doesn't?" I interjected.

"—and we know how the blood will react with the surface, we can estimate the victim's blood loss based on how far the pool of blood has expanded."

"And the point of knowing that is?"

Lock watched the last of his liquid bleed out onto a tightly woven carpet, like the kind one might find in an office building. "For when a bloodstain is all you have."

"You mean at a crime scene. If the victim is no longer in the room, you want to know if you're looking for a corpse or a living victim."

He shot me an impressed look and then set his beaker aside. "I can tell you that the man who left this stain most likely survived long enough to get to the hospital, but this man . . ." He pointed to a carpet sample in the corner that had a much wider stain across the square. "I don't need to see the body to know that the man who made that stain is dead. They use a similar method to train nurses in a hospital setting—"

A call from Alice stopped Sherlock's mini lecture short. She sounded like she'd just run down the stairs when she asked, "Mori, where are you?"

"With Sherlock. Why?"

"Stay out for a while. Mallory's here. Apparently it's not just anonymous calls coming in anymore. There's a real witness."

"To what?" I stood and moved to the far side of the room.

Alice paused and I could hear her thudding steps on the kitchen floor. "Some woman came forward to make a statement about seeing you with the sword in the park. I think I can keep Mallory away from your school, but we're going to have to go to the station. Probably right after your last class."

"Okay."

Alice paused again. "What are you going to tell Mallory?"

I lowered my voice, though I wasn't sure there was enough

noise in the room to mask what I said completely. "I need you to do something for me."

"What is it?"

"I need to know who it is. See if you can make him tell you."

I could hear the smile in Alice's voice when she said, "God, you're like her. You're just like her."

I did my best to control my expression as I ended the call and turned back toward Lock, just in time to witness another pool of liquid expand until it was threatening to overtake the edges of the carpet sample. Lock didn't ask about the call, which meant we were back to him playing mad forensic tech and me playing fascinated observer. But the longer I watched him moving around the room, the more I wondered whether or not I should tell him about the witness, about my impending trip into custody for questioning. Would it be a welcome distraction or just another stress on top of all that he was already dealing with? Wasn't his need for distraction the whole purpose of his experimenting when he should have been in class?

I watched as Lock flicked the cap from his pen to write an observation on a glass board standing behind him and then popped it back into place before moving on to a new pipette and the next beaker. He was so fully immersed in his task, I felt like I had somehow merged into the background of the room. I wasn't sure he was even aware I was there anymore. Or perhaps he was. I thought he would pour out the liquid onto the shaggy rug sample that was up next, but instead Lock looked up from his experiment and right into my eyes. He immediately set the pipette down, straddled a rolling office chair, and propelled himself across the floor to me, stopping only when he was close enough that I could smell vinegar on his hands.

"What is it?"

I ignored the question at first, instead focusing on his proximity and the complete lack of emotion in his expression. While he wasn't impeccably dressed, he wasn't rumpled like Mycroft had been. He was normal rumpled. Everything about him was normal—or might have been, if I hadn't known better.

He seemed to find my silence entirely amusing. "Or remain unfathomable. Either way."

I wanted that playful quirk to stay on his lips, so instead of telling him about me, I said, "I've decided to be mad at you for ignoring me, like a proper needy girlfriend." It felt weird to use the title, but Sherlock seemed pleased to hear me say it.

"Very well." He stood and swiveled the chair around before plopping back onto it and draping one long leg over the other. "I'm sure you've a long list of grievances. Have at me."

I stared at him blankly, then looked over his shoulder to stare at the blue flame coming out of a lit burner that had no reason to be lit, at the half of a rag draping out of his autoclave, like he'd only just started to sanitize it before moving on. There were pipettes lined up, each with a little white pill sitting in the bottom, but only half had been filled with liquids. Everything half done. Useless. He was desperate for distraction and nothing was working. Some kind of pain flared in my chest, and I had the sudden urge to throw my arms around his neck and hold him until it faded.

"Come on, then," he challenged.

"I've no intention of 'having at' you."

"So, is it to be silent seething then? You are so lovely when you seethe."

"I really am." I reached across the space between us to smooth his hair down. "But it's neither today, I'm afraid. I've somewhere I need to be."

I got up to leave, but he kicked his foot out to block my way to the door.

"Don't go. It's no fun if you go."

"You'll have plenty of fun staining carpets without me."

He stared at me for a few seconds before a thoughtful expression replaced his playful arrogance and he stood suddenly, blocking me with his whole body and forcing me to look up. "Tell me?"

I shook my head quickly and made sure my grin didn't drop. "Last week of school. I can't miss all my classes."

He nodded, but he didn't move out of my way. "I have somewhere to take you after school."

"Not today. I promised Alice I'd be home. I probably won't be able to come to the hospital tonight either."

Sherlock's expression went blank for a few moments, and I almost told him about Mallory right then and there. I wondered if learning about this new evidence against me would make him worry for me or if he'd just be fascinated to see another piece of the puzzle. But then he smiled again, and I decided it wasn't worth the risk.

"I'll take you tomorrow," he said. "You'll like it, I think. I may finally have an answer to our great mobile phone heist."

"Jealous girl secretly in love with your client and hoping to steal him from his first love?"

Lock's smile widened. "You'll have to wait until tomorrow."

"Is this your ploy to get me to come with you this afternoon? Did you think I'd be too curious to stay away?"

"Is it working?"

"Sadly, no. But we'll go tomorrow for sure. Our lover boy deserves a proper ending to his torment."

"And me? Is there no end to mine?"

I grabbed the front of his shirt and pulled him down until we were eye to eye. "Your torment will also have to wait until tomorrow." I kissed him quickly and spun around him to walk freely toward the door. But at the last minute I ran back to him and handed him the envelope with the drawings in them. "More evidence for my case."

He nodded, his expression sobering a bit. "Yes. I'll hold on to these for you. See if I can find all the things you missed."

I pulled him down toward me again, which seemed to brighten his mood back up. "Shall I give you a hint?"

"Are we playing a game?"

I nodded. "The artist is not the one sending me the cards." I released the front of his shirt and called out, "Tell me when you see it!" as I left his lab.

"I'll know before tomorrow!" he called after me. And the smile in his voice meant he hadn't seen the fear in my eyes.

"I might be in jail tomorrow," I told the staircase as I made my way back upstairs. One last class until I had to face Mallory, and I had no idea what to do. One last class.

Chapter 16

Lily sat next to me in drama, to the open shock and dismay of her friends. She didn't say a word to me, however, ensuring they didn't completely implode. It was an odd development, but I tried not to take it too seriously, tried to be the same as I always was.

Once Miss Francis had properly addressed her teacher duties, she left us to study for other exams while she finished up grading the last few final performances. Lily, as usual, reached for her music scores, but her bag tipped over, spilling paper and folders out onto the floor. I scooped up the pages that fell at my feet and as I handed the stack to Lily, her necklace fell from under her shirt.

It was the first time I'd seen Lily's bronze cross up close, a Celtic cross with vines wrapping around it. The image was instantly familiar, though it took me longer than usual to put together just where I'd seen it before.

"The attic," I said to myself minutes later, when everyone else had gone back to minding their own business. Thankfully, only the two people closest to me heard what I'd said, and one was Lily, who didn't even bother to look up from her cello scores.

But the symbol was on a box in my attic—a box housing cash and a lock pick with a really heavy lid. And, really, I should've put it together much sooner than I did. Even without seeing Lily's cross, the box was obviously what had been buried at Patel's murder site. The money must have been Patel's getaway cache, which meant the empty wrappers once contained money my father had spent.

It was suddenly intolerable to spend even one second more in the theater that afternoon. So I feigned sick to a distracted Miss Francis, and as I stood to leave, I dropped a note in Lily's lap that said, "Right after class. Park. Important." Then I left to sneak home somehow and fetch Lily's money.

I got to the tree first and realized that the last time I'd been to the place in daylight, Sadie had been with me and I'd been looking for the clover symbol and proof of Lock's and my theories of the crime. Had that really been only a few weeks ago? I lined myself up with the clover symbol, just like I had before, and paced toward where Sadie had stepped into the box's previous burial site. When I reached it, I could see another carving just ahead in a tree not six feet from where I stood. The etching was rudimentary and dirty, but a recognizable Celtic cross. The box had been buried exactly in the middle of the two.

I placed the container right above where her dad had hidden it and then sat next to it to wait. Lily was there before school ended, carrying flowers and beer, which meant she hadn't managed to stay through all of the drama herself. I thought for sure she'd recognize the symbol on top of the box, but she didn't even look at it.

"Why are we here?" she asked.

I nodded toward where a bundle of wilted flowers had been kicked behind the clover-marked tree. "You first."

She followed her ritual, though she seemed more aware of my presence this time. Once the beer was poured, she came over to sit next to me in the dirt and watched the foam settle. I probably should have shown some kind of respect for her thoughts, but my patience didn't extend for more than a minute or two. I pushed the box wordlessly in front of her crossed legs and watched for her response.

She clutched the pendant to her chest and traced the cross on top of the box for a few long seconds. "Where did you find this? How do you have it?"

"Was it your father's?"

Lily started to shake her head, then stopped and said, "I don't know. I've never seen it before. But it must be, right?"

"I think so. Look inside."

She used her thumbs to push open the lid and slide it back slowly, almost like she was afraid of what the box might contain. I'd cleaned out all the empty tissues, leaving only the three bundles of cash and the lock-pick multitool. I watched quietly as she went through them, letting her have whatever kind of moment would suit her best.

She tore open only one bundle before pushing them aside

to seize the lock pick. One by one, she opened the tools. She nodded at most, but a few of them seemed to be new to her, and she didn't close any of them until they were all out of their hiding places looking like a tiny metal arm topped with a dozen frightening claws.

When they were all put away again, she flipped the tool over in her hand a few times before pulling the cash free from its tissue.

"Do you ever wonder what it was like?" Lily fanned the money so that only her eyes could be seen above the edges of the bills. Still, I could tell she was smiling.

"Does the money make you that happy?"

She shook her head. "It's not the money."

"What then?"

She dropped the notes into her lap, reached into her purse to pull out her father's lucky clover coin, and then met my eyes. "We should start again. Sorte Juntos. We should do it again."

It was a ludicrous idea, but my heart still began to race. "So it *is* the money?"

"No. Not money. Legacy. We could revive our parents' greatest years. We could immortalize them by continuing their work."

I stared out at the gathering shadows. It was impossible. I didn't have the time. My priorities were protecting the boys and finding a way to keep my father from torturing us from his prison cell. All of that, while trying to keep out of prison myself, was far more important than some pipe dream from my mother's wild years. But still, a spark of something had ignited in my mind at Lily's suggestion. I didn't care about legacy or immortality. I didn't much care for amassing great sums of money, either. But the idea of re-creating a network, of the power and freedom that could bring. Something about that felt right.

"You're thinking about it," Lily teased.

"It's ridiculous." Only it wasn't.

"But you want to. I can tell."

If I'd sent someone else to the lake that day with the sword, I'd be untouchable just now. If I'd sent a team of somebodies to take care of my father problem, he'd probably be dead. If I could sit back as the mastermind and send others out to do the work of it, never knowing why or how, just that they'd be paid.

"We don't have the skills," I made myself say, though I wondered if that was really true.

"I know how to use this." Lily held up the lock pick and flicked open one of the tools with her thumb. "I also have access to copies of keys to every important building my dad's ever serviced."

Mr. Patel, the locksmith. Yes. That could be useful.

"And you can be our leader, just like your mom."

I didn't bother to hide my surprise that she'd worked out which of the women in the picture was my mother, but it couldn't have been too hard of a deduction. "The pictures."

"You look just like her. Not necessarily in feature, but your expressions are identical to your mother's."

I nodded and looked back out at the shadows.

"She was beautiful," Lily said.

I should have said something. My silence was giving away too much about how I felt right then. I wanted so much to see those pictures. I just didn't know how to ask, and I didn't trust Lily not to ask for something in return. I didn't want to owe her.

"My dad told me that she was the cleverest person he'd ever met. The way her mind worked, yours is like that too, isn't it? I know it is. You were the one who figured out the truth about your dad, not Sherlock like they said. I'm right? It was you?"

I looked up and Lily's expression had darkened. She was suddenly greedy, maybe. But for what, I couldn't say. I was almost sure it wasn't about the money, however.

"I had more information than he did."

She wouldn't look away from me, and her expression was unnerving, but when she pulled her dad's coin out of her handbag and held it in her palm, she seemed suddenly very pleased with herself. Like she'd been proven right about something. We stared at each other quietly for a few beats, before I realized that her greed was for me. She wanted something from me—or, rather, she'd just figured out a way for me to be useful to her.

"We should start it again," she said, confirming my guess.

She flipped her coin and it landed on the damp earth between us, clover-side down, which is when I realized that all the coins were different. Instead of the Tree of Life I'd expected to see, Lily's coin had her dad's cross emblem. All the members had their own symbol on their coins, and I was willing to bet that all their hidden cache spots were marked with both the clover and their specific symbol. I wondered then, just how much money was hidden around London and in the outer boroughs now that everyone was dead—hidden fortunes marked with symbols no one else would understand.

"Sorte Juntos had an entire team of people to rob those places. We have just the two of us. It's not enough."

Lily frowned at that. "Then we'll find others. We'll find who we need."

"To do what?"

"Anything we want."

The way she looked at me then brought to mind what Lock had said before—the statement I'd dismissed so easily. *I was wondering how much Lily Patel hates you.* The answer was in her eyes just then. She hated me. But she also wanted something from me, and the war those emotions created inside her was fascinating to watch.

"And what do *you* want, Lily?"

She looked down at the contents of her dad's box again, smiling to cover whatever else it was that she was thinking. And then she stood and grabbed all her things. "Think about it," she said.

She left me there, sitting between the now-meaningless symbols of her father's coin.

Chapter 17

I should've gone straight home, but that only meant being bustled off to Mallory and his inane questions, and facing down some unknown witness bent on destroying me and releasing the monster. And I was tired. Tired of fighting things and people I couldn't see, of not being able to move on with my life.

In the end I couldn't seem to make it past the bandstand. Past the willow tree at the edge of the lake. That was where I'd found my best friend dead, where I'd known for sure my father needed to die. Would it also be the place I made the one mistake that could free him? Would that one lame attempt to disarm a killer become my greatest regret?

My mobile rang before I could find an answer, and I ignored it at first. Texts came next, but I knew I couldn't neglect Alice forever. So I called her back.

"Where are you?"

I kicked my heels up and let them thud back against the cement base of the bandstand. "I'm in the park."

"He says if we don't show up by seven, he'll come arrest you at school tomorrow."

"Then I won't go to school."

Alice grunted out a laugh. "You want to run? Over some witness who might not be any threat at all?"

I loved Alice for posturing just then. Her false confidence was probably the one thing I needed to bolster mine.

I sighed. "I'll be home in a few minutes."

"I'll call a taxi."

I was approaching the end of hour two of being stuck alone in the flickering fluorescent-lit nightmare that was Interview Room 2A. I sat in an orange chair that once was cushioned but had probably been in active duty for at least a decade. It was a mirrored room, rather than one with a camera, which meant there was at least one officer silently watching me through the glass like a creeper in the night. Worst of all, the vent just above my head had a rattling part that was starting to tear at my reason and sanity.

"Police interview rooms are inhumane," I declared for whoever was behind the mirror to hear. "If you're going to waste so much of our taxes on chasing after innocent school-girls, you should at least spend a little to fix your ventilation system."

I'd given up on my original plan to affect a stony silence until I was allowed to leave. I justified my talking into the void by deciding that as long as I cut off all speech the moment they came in the room to question me, my protest of silence would still stand. But perhaps I was just drunk on boredom.

"Could you at least give me something to read?"

A sudden scuffle in the hall distracted me from my request. The door burst open, but instead of Mallory, the Lady Constance of Regent's Park barged in with a constable struggling to restrain her.

"You!" she said, thrusting a finger at me so that the bag wrapped around her wrist swung out and knocked the interview table sideways a few inches.

Mallory rushed in, red faced and angry like I'd never seen him. "Get her out of here!" he bellowed. I honestly didn't think he had it in him.

Try as the poor constable might, however, Lady Constance would not be moved. "Vivian can never win!" she cried, smacking the constable with her clutch. "You can't keep him locked away forever!"

More King Arthur references? She was calling me "Vivian" this time, which was just another name for the Lady of the Lake from the Arthurian romances. But I had to wonder if the "him" I was keeping "locked away" referred to my father or to Merlin—or if they were both the same in her mind.

That's when everything fell into place. As Mallory and his constable tried their best to guide and then push Constance out of the room, I realized that this was their witness. Or, rather, the Lady Constance had witnessed Nimue returning Arthur's sword to the lake in Regent's Park, and she'd come to the police to name me as Nimue. That meant she was also the figure whispering about what she'd seen to the artist in the drawing. And now that I knew who she was, finding the artist couldn't be all that hard. The relief I felt was matched only by the slapstick humor of the Lady Constance and her constable punch doll.

Alice rushed in when they were gone and looked relieved herself to see that I was okay. "What happened in here?"

"A miracle," I said with a grin.

She raised a brow and sat next to me. "Who was that woman?"

"I believe she is the witness against me."

Alice opened her mouth to ask something else, but then Mallory came in, looking more harried than I'd ever seen him. That didn't seem to strip any of the all-knowing condescension out of him, however. He took his time sitting down across from Alice and me, and even spent a few vital seconds looking through the papers of his manila folder.

"Do you have any enemies, Miss Moriarty?"

I had not been expecting that as his first question. "Just the one you've got locked up in your jail."

Mallory didn't scold me for bringing up my dad like I'd expected. Instead, he pulled a glossy picture from his folder and pushed it toward me. "Do you know this man?"

The face looked familiar in a face-in-the-crowd kind of way—like maybe I'd seen him around our neighborhood enough times. But I shook my head.

"Do you know the name Charles Ross?"

"No. What is this about?"

Mallory took the picture and straightened all the papers in his folder, then he leaned back in his chair and stared at me expectantly. Though I had no idea what he was presuming I'd do.

"Why am I here?"

"That may be something only you can tell me."

"Is she free to go then?" Alice asked.

After nearly a minute of more silent staring, Mallory seemed to come to some kind of decision, but instead of sharing it with us, he opened his folder and started to arrange the papers inside of it for us to see. Once they were all laid out, he pointed at the photo of the familiar-faced man, which was farthest to my left.

"This is Charles Ross. His hand was in your bin."

I looked more closely at him, wondering if I might have recognized him better from his back—if he was the man in my drawings. It was possible, of course.

"Are you sure you don't know him?"

I shook my head. "Never met. Should I know him for some reason?"

"A reason other than his severed hand in your bin? He's dead, by the way. The coroner believes he was dead when the hand was removed, though we have yet to recover a body."

My heart sank a little. That was a detail I'd forgotten. If the man in the drawings was the artist, then he was the one missing a hand. That also apparently meant that he was dead. I didn't figure the artist was the one sending them to me, but now we'd never know whom he'd given them to either.

Mallory pushed a statement forward next, which was typed out but lengthy. "This is a statement given by Constance Ross."

I looked up. "Ross?"

Mallory nodded. "The wife of Charles. Constance was in the Master of Letters program at Oxford twenty years ago when Charles was completing his Doctorate in Fine Art."

Which meant he was the artist. He had to be.

"Charles Ross secured a teaching position for a time, but they both mysteriously left the school and the city of Oxford two years ago. Neither has a current permanent address that we could find, but it appears Constance spends most of her days in Regent's Park, which is where she claimed to see you returning Excalibur to the lake."

"Me?" I wasn't even slightly nervous, but I did try to act surprised.

Mallory narrowed his eyes. "Here is where I wonder about your enemies." He pushed a single sheet of paper forward that said "Call Log" at the top. "A female witness called in to tell us you'd put the sword in the lake, three days ago. That woman was not Constance Ross."

But it was Constance who had seen me and relayed the story to our artist, which is why I was drawn in Arthurian clothing on the card. If the foreground of the illustrations meant anything, Lady Constance was the princess whispering what she'd seen into our artist's ear, and my second sin he'd seen for himself. And if the man with the severed hand in the drawing was our artist, then Charles Ross was our artist.

And now he was dead, and no longer able to confirm or deny what he'd seen or who he was. I hardly expected we'd get a straight answer from his widow. Which meant we really would never know who was dropping the cards into our postbox or if that person had also made the phone call three days ago.

"Someone out there is doing a fair job of pointing fingers

at you, Miss Moriarty. Are you sure you want to leave here without telling us who that might be?"

"She's a sixteen-year-old child," Alice interjected. "What kind of enemies could she possibly have made?"

"No threats have come to your house? No one following you around?"

I stared down at the picture of Charles Ross and said, "Does this mean I can go?"

Mallory gathered all the papers up but one, straightened them, and placed them in the perfect center of the file folder. I glanced over at the remaining paper long enough to see that it was a custody form with my father's name at the top. He was evidently fighting Alice's guardianship. "I expect we'll find a body soon for Mr. Charles Ross. I also expect we'll find some kind of evidence of you on or around that body."

"What are you trying to say?" Alice asked.

Mallory pushed the custody form toward Alice, but she didn't bother to look down. Instead, she kept her hands folded neatly in her lap and her gaze zeroed in on the inspector. He was focused completely on me. "I'm saying, Mori, that you should be very careful whom you trust. We found evidence of a murder in your rubbish and have a witness statement that you hid evidence of five more murders."

"Four," I corrected him. "He killed Sadie with his bare hands. He didn't use the sword on her."

I thought perhaps I saw a glint of pain in Mallory's eyes, but he quickly covered. "Someone is orchestrating this campaign against you."

That's when Mallory finally looked at Alice. He suspected her. But then, he would. Regardless of whether or not he was still in my father's camp, I was sure he'd heard a mountain of stories about Alice's evil ways.

Alice, unfazed, said, "Exactly. And I hope that the police catch whomever it is and bring him to justice."

Mallory's smile was tight lipped and short lived, and still he didn't take his eyes off her for a long moment. But when he spoke, he addressed only me. "Leave this to the police. This is no place for that little detective boyfriend of yours to stick his nose in. Let us handle it."

"The way you've always handled my problems?" I asked.

He tried not to react, but I could see his anger in the clenching of his jaw.

"If we're done here." I stood, and Alice followed suit, but Mallory reached across the table to grab my upper arm.

"If you keep secrets from us, we can't help you."

I pulled free of his hand. "If I need your kind of help, all is lost anyway. But I'll make sure to keep that in mind."

Chapter 18

In the middle of the night, my phone blared the barcarolle through my dreams until I finally found it with one fumbling hand and answered. "Sleeping."

"I can't find him." It was Mycroft's voice, only barely recognizable. And as the silence opened up between us, I started to realize why. He coughed to clear his throat, but he sounded like he was about to weep. "I can't find him, and it probably wouldn't matter if I could. He needs you."

"What's happened?"

He didn't respond, and suddenly I remembered standing in the hall of my mother's ward, facing the patient, expectant faces of three nurses who wanted me to answer a similar question. And I couldn't seem to say the word "dead."

"Where would he go?" I asked.

Mycroft barely answered, "I don't know," then ended the call.

I didn't know what to do at first. The ringtone was Lock's, which meant Mycroft had his phone. And Sherlock could have been a thousand places or even on his way to my house.

Still, I got myself together and went out with no real plan.

I doubted heavily that he'd be at his house, but I decided to check there first. The door was locked, so I used the key hidden in the rocks to let myself in. I could tell no one was home the moment I stepped into the entry. The house had that empty feel to it, like no one had been there for a long while. But I ran up the stairs just in case, deciding to start at the very top floor of the house and work my way down.

His mother's room was spotless but not sterile. It was welcoming, actually. Her bed was turned down and a side table lamp was on, spotlighting a novel that she'd never finish, despite the silver marker holding her place. Next to it, an ornate frame housed a picture of the brothers from when they were young. A floral robe was draped across the foot of the bed, slippers lined up perfectly beneath. It was a room waiting for someone to come home.

It was also the only tidy room in the house. The rest were in more of a crumpled state, where perhaps the boys had rushed home to change clothes or grab belongings before heading off to school, work, or the hospital. Regardless, Sherlock wasn't there, so I pocketed the key and went back downstairs.

I checked my phone for the time. Four in the morning meant there were more places he couldn't be than could. The school was locked up. Technically, the park was closed too, though that didn't mean he wasn't there, or one of any number of places that were important to him and I wouldn't know about. There was also the very real possibility that he was going nowhere. Wandering around London like I would, taking trains or buses just to be moving, but with no real destination in mind.

Out of desperation, I thought to go back home, hoping to find him at our kitchen table with a cup of tea and a hovering Alice. But as I stepped out onto the landing of Sherlock's stoop, the headlights of an oncoming car revealed a silhouette moving toward me, a recognizable shadow man, made ever more defined by the orange glow of his cigarette.

It hit me, then, the level of his despair. It wafted off him with every step. Or perhaps I was transferring onto him how I'd felt on a similar night, pressing my swollen face to the cool wrought iron fencing of his stoop.

Lock didn't see me until he was standing on the bottom step, and when he did, he immediately looked away.

"Didn't bring my keys and the spare is missing." He took one last, long drag and then ground out the embers and tossed the dark brown butt down into the rocks. "Seems I left my bag at the . . ." He paused and then never finished what he was going to say. "I can't get into my own house."

I moved down a couple of steps and held out the key as an offering, but he only stared at it for a moment before fixating on my shoes.

"You rushed out tonight," he said. "Your laces are undone." His gaze slowly drifted up to my face, and then away as he stepped up until he was on the stair below mine. He grasped my wrist, as though he thought I might get away if he didn't hang on to me, and he turned to face me, eye to eye, pulling me to the left until I was leaning against the wrought iron.

I didn't realize why until his fingers came up to my cheek, never quite touching my skin. "Are those tears for me?"

The street lamp. He needed light to be able to see my face. I wanted to wipe at my cheeks, bat his hand away, but I couldn't move for the pain in his eyes. I could feel it, like it was happening again to me, only the ache was different, compounded somehow.

A few of his own tears fell just as his thumb came up to brush mine away. "I don't like to see you cry."

I composed myself as best I could and wiped the rest of the moisture from my cheeks with my shirtsleeve. "Then I will not."

He took my face in his hands and shook his head, staring into my eyes. "No. Don't hide from me. Will you . . . ?" His eyes pleaded with mine, and his voice sounded almost as broken as we both felt. "Will you tell me something true?"

I nodded, and then couldn't think of a thing to say. Was my life so much a lie that I no longer knew truth? Or was it that I didn't trust anything I knew to be the truth?

He waited with expectation, and I could only gaze blankly back, my mind a scattered mess. "I don't know."

"Tell me your last thought."

"Your pain hurts me more than my own." His eyes widened in a way I could only see because of our closeness. "And it scares me."

"Why does it frighten you?"

"I don't know."

"Why?"

"Because I can't stop the pain." I blinked away a few more tears, which he smeared with his thumbs. "I can't make her come back and I know what that means. I can't make it better."

He was still for a long time. Another tear dripped from his eye to his cheek, and before I could lift a hand to dry it, he pulled me into him, wrapped his arms around me as tightly as they would go. I stood frozen in his embrace for a few seconds before I lifted my hands to hold him, tracing them up his back to his shoulders.

"You do," he gasped in my ear when he could find his voice again. "You do make it better. Even when you shadow yourself. Just knowing you are there in the world makes it better."

I felt something tear inside me, a gaping, open thing that left me out of breath and out of restraint, out of everything that held me together. More concerning, I wasn't sure I'd ever be able to fix it.

Sherlock slept fitfully and ate hardly anything that day and the next. I didn't press. I still didn't remember more than bits and pieces of the days directly after my mother died. My strongest memory was thinking that everything was just too much of itself. It was too quiet. The boys were too loud. My bed was too soft. The shower too harsh on my skin. My tea was too hot and then too cold and definitely too bitter. The world felt like it was sensory overload, but hiding from it meant facing silence and my thoughts, and that was worse.

So I sat by his bed and brought him food, just in case. I

waited and watched. I'd gotten so used to his fitful tossing and turning, I didn't recognize when he was dreaming. When his huffs and grunts turned to cries and then Lock shouting my name, I didn't know what to make of it at first. I sat frozen as he yelled for me twice, then came to myself enough to wake him up and hold his hand while he recovered.

"It's okay," I whispered. "Whatever you saw was just a dream."

He scrubbed his eyes with his palms and cursed. It took him a few moments to go still, and then he sat up and stared at me, like perhaps I was just a dream as well.

I reached a hand up to smooth his hair. "Are you hungry yet?"

He shook his head and I dropped my hand to his forehead, which was still dewy from his nightmare.

"Do you want anything?"

"I want you to stay."

"I won't leave."

He scooted closer, so he could grasp my hands. "I want you to stay with me."

I stroked my thumbs across his knuckles and met his teary eyes. "I promise. I won't leave."

That didn't seem to reassure him, but he didn't ask again. Instead, he pulled me down onto his bed, facing him so he could keep watching me. I forced myself to be still and to watch him back, even when it was so painful, I thought maybe I wouldn't be able to breathe soon.

Still holding both my hands in one of his, he reached up

with the other to trace the way my hair framed my face. "I sometimes think I'm losing you."

I said nothing. The word "temporary" was flashing through my mind again, and as much as I wanted to shoo those thoughts away, I wasn't sure I could say the words he needed me to say right then—not confidently, anyway.

"But then, I suppose you can't truly lose something that never belonged to you. Can you?"

I cleared my throat a little before answering. "No. You can't."

"And if I were to tell you that you could lose me?" he asked.

I wanted to answer that I knew I would. That as much as I wanted him to stay, I was sure he'd most likely hate me in the end. But instead I asked, "Could I?"

He attempted a smile but failed. "You ask the question, but you don't think you could."

I didn't answer, even after his smile dropped and his hand came up to cup my cheek.

"Don't go," he said.

I looked up at the ceiling, traced a tiny crack that curved around one of the light fixtures and then out the door. "It was just a dream, Sherlock. I'm still here."

"For how long?"

"For as long as you need."

He attempted another smile and then leaned in to kiss my forehead. "I wish that were true," he whispered against my skin.

I held my tears until he fell asleep, and when he did finally drift off, I couldn't seem to cry anymore. I got up and went to the window. When I rested my forehead against the glass, I could just see my house from where I stood. It looked peaceful without me there. So did Sherlock, resting in his bed alone, finally at peace. All of this peace in the spaces without me. As if I was the reason for the chaos. As if maybe, if I just removed myself from everything . . .

I really was the worst kind of person. All of Lock's pleading for me to stay, and I suddenly could only entertain thoughts of running away, of the endless relief it would be to just escape and start over. I could use Detective Mallory's theory as my excuse, that all the recent happenings were because of some enemy I'd made without knowing. I could leave behind a note that said my leaving would end the chaos.

I could almost believe that, too, if it weren't for one thing—my father's obsession with my brothers. He'd never leave them alone, regardless of how far away I ran. I was nothing more than an obstacle to his prize when it came to those boys. And I could never leave them to him. Not while I still lived.

I supposed that meant I hadn't lied to Sherlock. I'd stay. But it also meant he was wrong. I knew I could lose him. And I knew my father would probably be the reason why. Just then, watching Lock from the window seat, I wished so much that I were a different Mori, from a different family—that I could be Lock's Mori, the girl he wanted me to be. I wished I had the freedom to stay only for him.

Chapter 19

I woke up sitting in the chair by Lock's bed, my neck sore and my body feeling anything but rested. Lock was up and dressed already and waiting for me in his window seat. He met my eyes briefly, then looked back out the window and took a long drag of his cigarette.

I ran fingers through my hair and watched him for a bit before I asked, "Are you going somewhere?"

"*We* are going to resolve my most pressing detective case."

There was a split second when I thought about telling him to go back to bed, to "let himself grieve" or one of the other hundred platitudes people had told me when I went back to school before it was deemed proper by whoever keeps track of those sorts of things. But I had gone back to school for the same reason Lock wanted to go finish his case. He needed something else to think about. Giving him that felt like the very least I could do.

"And I get to watch the great Detective Holmes in action?" I stood up and stretched my arms to the ceiling.

"I'm finished with the case of the stolen mobile phone."

"Sifted through the data already?"

"The day you couldn't go with me, I learned two facts I didn't know before." He twisted out the dark brown cigarette butt on the windowsill, then stood and reached for my hand without looking at me. I let him take it. "So, I'll tell you those two truths, and you have until we reach the client's house to come up with the answer."

"Very well. What are your facts?"

"I found the missing SIM card in an odd place."

"Is that so?"

"And I discovered that I'd been given inaccurate information about the state of the phone. Once those two facts came to me, it was all very simple, really. Had I known, I could have solved it in minutes."

I waited for the details, but he didn't give them. Instead, he tightened his grip on my hand slightly and tried to pull me toward his bedroom door. I didn't budge.

"I have some new data for you as well, perhaps we could trade."

"About the mobile phone case?"

I shook my head. "About my case. Or, to be more specific, about where I went with Alice the day that I couldn't go with you."

Lock frowned and looked down at his watch, then back up to me. "Okay, we'll trade. But you first, and you have to tell me on the way."

"Deal."

I told him about my little trip to the police station, the

Lady Constance's accusations, and Mallory's sudden change of mind about my role in the murder case as we walked over to my house and while I got washed up.

Lock's eyes brightened when I got to the last part. "He *showed* you the evidence?"

"Kind of. He showed me a photo, a statement, and a call log."

"Do you think he'd show you again? Or give us a copy?"

My rueful stare did nothing to quell the hope in his eyes, and so I said, "He literally told me to leave this to the police and make sure you stay out of it."

Lock nodded. "Still, it's good to know what we're looking for."

"Looking for?"

Lock only grinned and turned his back to stare out my window onto Baker Street.

After a quick shower, I spent most of the time while drying my hair trying to figure out what evidence we'd be looking for and what facts he was still holding back on the mobile phone case. I didn't actually ask, however, until we were walking toward the Tube station, but he only shrugged and said, "I'll tell you on the train."

We didn't say more than a few words to each other as we wound our way through the crowd to our train platform, but I was watching Lock, waiting for that break in his shield that would reveal the grieving I was sure hid just beneath the surface. But even as we stood on the platform silently, hand in hand, he acted like it was any other day. He seemed to be thinking something through but showed not even a trace of the emotions I'd expect to see from anyone else in his situation.

I envied that—his ability to put things out of his mind for good and focus on the present. I couldn't even seem to focus on Lock for long. The minute I looked away from him, my mind filled with the story of Lady Constance and her caretaker husband, imagining the life they must have had at Oxford when they were young, and the pain he must have felt every time he watched her Arthurian fantasy world torment her away from his reality.

I looked down at the ground because no thoughts of my artist tormentor could pass through my mind without bringing Sadie Mae's face from the drawing to the forefront. I couldn't seem to scrub it from my mind no matter how hard I tried. I'd thought that seeing her dead was the worst kind of torment, but seeing the scene re-created on paper and not being able to reach in and get my father away from her was far worse.

My expression must have given me away. When Lock leaned closer to meet my eyes, he seemed confused for a moment, then concerned. I thought I was in the clear when he wrapped his arms around my shoulders and held me. I should have known better.

"I want to know what is hurting you like this."

"Did you look at the second drawing?"

He paused and then said, "Her death isn't your sin. It's his."

I had used my question in an attempt to deflect, and I couldn't decide if I was angry at him or myself for letting him see right through me. "You promised once. Do you remember? We were just like this on a similar task, on a similar platform." I pressed my cheek to his chest and continued, "You promised you wouldn't try to solve me like one of your little games. Do you mean to keep that promise even now?"

He didn't answer. He didn't say anything else, not until we were seated on the train. "The SIM card was in the phone owner's desk, tucked into the back corner. And while the phone had been wiped clean of data, her home phone number and a note were added after."

I'd almost forgotten about the stolen phone. "What did the note say?"

"Does it matter?"

I smiled. "Of course it matters. It matters to everyone but you."

"But we know who did it without that information."

"Did you honestly not read it?"

Sherlock shrugged and stared past me out the window as the train started to move.

"She did it, of course," I said. "The phone's owner. Some bizarrely complex romantic gesture to make him call her. But the note would tell us why she felt the need to go to this length."

"Her motives are immaterial."

"But why would she say it was stolen in the first place?"

"She didn't. She asked to borrow a friend's phone and then was too embarrassed to correct the assumption that her phone was stolen. She tried to explain it was just lost, but by then no one would listen to her. And when they found the phone in his bag, she couldn't exactly say that she'd put it there."

"Her embarrassment was more important than his academic career. He'll be pissed about that."

"Overjoyed, actually."

I stared at Lock and he shrugged.

"Happiest I've ever seen him."

"But if you've already told him the happy news, why are we going to his house?"

Lock grinned. "My most pressing case has always been yours. We still need to figure out who's threatening you, and my client now says he owes me."

The client's name was Jason Kim, not-yet-convicted computer hacker. His room was almost a flashing neon advertisement for his unscrupulous hobby. No fourteen-year-old in London needed a setup like he had for anything casual. But instead of being rightfully suspicious of what his son was up to, Mr. Kim, the client's father, spent the entire walk to Jason's room bragging about his genius son.

"Just brought him a few of the retired computer bits and bobs from work. He knew exactly what they were for, my boy. That's my way of apologizing for the state of his room. Really can't be helped, though. Genius is never tidy."

I smirked a bit, thinking of the state of both Sherlock's lab and room and my brothers' rooms as well. Perhaps it was truer to say that boys were never tidy.

I was officially introduced to the back of Jason's head first, silhouetted in front of a sea of white-blue monitor glow. Two of the monitors shifted from white-blue to black with green type dumping onto the screen much faster than any human finger movement could produce.

"You've got visitors, son."

Jason nodded, and kept on with his typing, waving off his dad, who left quietly with a bright smile on his face.

Once the door closed, Jason spoke without turning around. "Two minutes and I should at least have his login to the MPS website. As promised."

Lock seemed impressed. "Your text said it would take at least an hour only half an hour ago."

"What can I say?" Jason finally turned to face us, with his father's same bright smile. "I'm just that good."

From the front, Jason was one of the more beautiful boys I'd ever seen. Creamy skin, dark, wide-set eyes, and perfect teeth surrounded by full lips. His thick-rimmed glasses tried to hide all that, to no avail, and when he swept them from his face, I couldn't keep from staring. This boy had to be surrounded by girls everywhere he went, and he'd had his heart set on only one from his childhood?

I was suddenly pretty sure of our mobile phone culprit's motive. This was exactly the kind of boy that elicited bizarrely complex romantic gestures.

My thoughts must have shown on my face, because when I glanced over at Lock, he looked thoroughly unhappy, which he quickly tried to cover by widening his eyes in a challenge. I shrugged at him.

"You're Mori, then? Sherlock tells me you're more clever than he is." Jason gave me a little wave, then crossed his arms.

I didn't wave back. "That's entirely true."

Sherlock's expression warmed a bit. "She asked me the same question you did."

"I guess I should just be happy that Kay wanted me to know her number." Jason's smile didn't falter, but he did settle his gaze on me. "I'm told any further motive is immaterial."

"Oh, I can guess what the note said." I glanced over at Sherlock's unhappy face and gave him my best smug grin. "Regardless, I hope you call her directly."

"Shall I?" There was a bit of panic in Jason's tone, and then he shook his head and stared down at the floor. "I'm not sure I could. Every time I try to talk anywhere near her, I end up sounding like a complete ass."

I stifled a laugh. "Do what you will. But why exactly are we here? And what is all this?" I gestured at the monitors.

That question seemed to brighten Jason's mood. He copied my gesture toward his monitors, but his seemed more flippant than mine. "This is all for show. Makes my dad think I'm a superhero and keeps me flush in equipment and upgrades. This, however"—he slid a small laptop forward from the mountain—"is where the magic happens. Gotta be light and portable. Just in case."

He threw me another bright smile that distracted me from my original question, though I was sure he hadn't answered it. Thankfully, Lock came to my rescue.

"He's trying to get Mallory's log-in so we can look at your case file," he said, sliding his hand in mine.

"Wait. MPS stands for Metropolitan Police Service?

You've asked this poor boy to hack the police?"

Jason answered. "Don't need to. We just need to figure out how he logs in to the website, which is run by a third-party service." Jason spun back around and started up his rapid-fire typing again. "That gives us an IP address for both his work and personal PCs and . . ."

Watching the windows open and close on his laptop screen was both useless and a little bit dizzying. I had no idea what he was doing or how, but then he laughed and said, "It's always so nice of them to leave their remote desktop software running for me." And less than a minute later, he opened a window that looked like someone else's desktop, complete with a rather arty-looking picture of Big Ben on the left side of the screen. Jason did a search for my name in the directory and copied the first few files that came up, then closed out of everything as quickly as he could.

"Okay," Jason said. "What are we looking for?"

Sherlock leaned over the desk as Jason opened the files. "There should be something about a call log in there, with numbers from the anonymous tips."

"Okay, we have the phone numbers right here," Jason said. "And . . ." He stood and reached behind his laptop to switch out a couple of cables and flick a switch of some kind. "We've got this to tell us who they belong to." He patted a small black box next to him. "Dad works for Vodafone. He hand-delivered one of their old servers over the weekend. With a little restoration and a backdoor to reconnect . . ." He typed for a few seconds and opened and closed a couple of screens, then seemed to find what he was looking for. "There. I'm in."

I leaned forward as well. "Who is it?"

"One call was made from a high-end boutique on Church Street. And the other from what looks like a burner phone, though . . . yes! It's still active!" He spun around and his eyes shone with his excitement. It reminded me a little of how Lock looked when he was closing in on something fascinating. "Hand me your mobile?"

I nodded and pulled it out of my pocket.

Jason snatched it from me and started thumbing through my screens with the same speed he'd used on his laptop. "As long as the phone is still on, you can track it." He tapped the screen a few dozen times. "And whoever it belongs to happens to be at the boutique right now."

"Meaning both calls probably came from the same person." Lock pressed his fingertips together and started to wander out of the room without even a good-bye to Jason.

I wanted to apologize on his behalf, but Jason seemed more amused than offended. I reached out a hand for my phone.

"Just a minute," he said. "I'm setting up an app that will allow you to track the burner, in case the caller leaves the boutique before you get there."

"Thanks for doing all this."

"Anytime," he said, handing back my phone. "I mean it too. You ever need anything, let me know."

I nodded and was about to leave, but at the last minute I said, "The note."

"You really think you know what it said?" He looked

down as he blushed, then peered up at me through his bangs. "Would you tell me?"

For the briefest of moments I thought I should meet this Kay girl, find out what made Jason adore her so. "It takes a good while to think of an elaborate and ridiculously flawed scheme like hers. A girl has to like her boy quite a lot to take those kinds of steps just to get him to notice her."

Jason hid behind his glasses again and ran a hand through his thick black hair.

"You should call her." I back-stepped to the doorway of his room. "And when she fumbles over her words and acts like a complete ass, try to be nice about it."

He lifted his hand to wave at me again as I backed out of his room, and I was pretty sure I'd just unwittingly added matchmaker to my list of accomplishments.

Chapter 20

The train ride to Church Street was only eventful in that we spent most of it arguing about who we thought would be holding the mysterious burner phone when we found it. Sherlock was obviously refusing to see reason.

"It's not about reason. It's about objectivity!" Sherlock punctuated his point with a finger in the air that I kind of wanted to rip off his hand.

"So you're saying I'm incapable of being objective."

"I'm saying your guilt is keeping you from looking at the most likely suspect."

The man in the seat across from mine pretended to be reading something on his mobile, but his shifty eyes made me lower my voice. "Why in the world would I feel guilty toward—"

"Lily Patel."

"*You* are fixated on Lily Patel."

"I'm fixated on the evidence."

"If Lily hated me, she could torture me at school. If she had any evidence against me or my father, she'd go directly to the prosecutor. She obviously has someone there updating her about the case, because she knew about the police finding the sword and that I'd been accused of throwing it in the lake. She doesn't need to make anonymous calls and resort to magazine-collage threats."

"Maybe." Lock grabbed my hand. "We'll find out soon enough."

I was trying to decide whether to let him continue to hold my hand or whether to use it as a counterbalance to toss him into the aisle when my mobile rang. I used it as an excuse to pull free.

"Mori, where are you?" It was Alice. "Tell me where you are." She was crying. "It's Michael. He's been hurt."

"Hurt how?"

"It's bad, Mori. We're at Charing Cross."

I'd thought I'd never have another reason to enter Charing Cross, but after Alice's call, I couldn't seem to get through the doors fast enough. I followed the signs toward the emergency room and found Alice, Freddie, and Sean sitting vigil in front of two giant doors covered in warnings that only hospital staff were allowed beyond.

I turned to Alice. "Is he in there?"

Alice reached for the hand I'd used to gesture at the doors and held it like she was afraid I'd run through them if she didn't. "He's in surgery. His arm is broken and there's pressure on his brain."

Something inside me cracked in half, but instead of pain

or fear or anger, I just felt numb. "His brain?" I sank down
onto the bench next to my brothers. A broken arm would
heal, of course, but my mind spun with all the ways a head
injury could change Michael's life forever.

Alice sank down next to me, but Lock kept standing, still
holding my hand. "They said he should be fine, but they
won't know—"

"Until they relieve the pressure on his brain," I finished for her.

She nodded, though I wished she had argued with me,
told me there was no chance that my sweetest, most gentle
little brother might have brain damage. I closed my eyes and
an image of his scared face streamed through my thoughts. All
of the numb turned to heat in my chest, so that by the time I
spoke again, my words came out shaky and low.

"Who?"

Alice's free hand came up to hold my arm. "Calm down
and I'll tell you what happened."

"Who? Who did this?" I was feigning calm, or attempting to. But I imagined even a complete stranger would have
noticed the way every muscle in my arms and shoulders was
tensed. I was a cat ready to pounce.

Alice glanced between Lock and the boys, then stood up
suddenly, pulling me to my feet as well. "Come with me."

We left Sherlock behind with an ashen-faced Freddie and
a glaring, angry Sean. Alice pulled me past the elevators that
led to the wards and into the dimly lit staircase. The light
was flickering above us as she sat on a step and I leaned back
against the cold concrete wall.

Alice started to speak, but I cut her off. "If you don't tell me everything, I'll leave right now to find out for myself."

"We need you here. Those boys out there have done nothing but ask for you since we got here."

"WHO DID THIS TO HIM?" My shout echoed through the stairwell so that everything seemed especially quiet just after. I took a breath that did nothing to calm me down. "Tell me what happened!"

Alice paused, and then in her most quiet voice, she said, "Someone tried to take Sean when we were walking back from the market."

"What do you mean, 'take' him?"

"A black van pulled up just in front of us, and when we walked by it, some big guy jumped out and grabbed Sean. Freddie and I managed to fight him off, but when the driver jumped out too, Michael panicked and ran out into the street."

Big guy, black van. It was just what Michael had described before, and back then Officer Parsons was sitting behind the wheel. Of course he panicked.

"I was so focused on keeping Sean and Fred away from the van, I didn't even realize Michael was gone until someone screamed." Alice closed her eyes and hung her head. "Another bystander shouted to call for the police and the guys in the van ran for it, which is when I saw Michael lying out in the street."

The image of that only fueled my anger. "Did you recognize either of the men from the van?"

"No. They were wearing masks."

"Did Michael recognize them?"

"I don't know," Alice said, but then she paused. "He did say something when the van first pulled up." She stopped to think again, then shook her head in frustration. "No, I don't remember. I was so focused on keeping the other boys from being taken."

I slammed my fists against the wall and Alice stood.

"I have something else to tell you," she said. "But first, promise me you won't run out of here."

I didn't say a word, just stared at her, and after a while she sighed. She put her hands on my arms. "Okay, so that petition your dad put in to question my guardianship rights? He was denied first thing this morning."

"He lost," I said, staring up at the underside of the stairs that led to the floor above us. "And then he sent Parsons to steal the boys from us."

"You don't know it was him."

I jerked my arms free of her and slammed my fists back again. "Michael saw Parsons last time. Michael ran because it was happening *again!*" I yelled the last word and Alice jumped. I took the opportunity to step toward her, but her eyes seemed more fascinated than frightened. "Get out of my way."

She shook her head. "Mori, stop. What can you accomplish by going to the police station?"

"Get out of my way!"

"No." Alice grabbed my arm with both of her hands and pulled me in close to her.

I reached up with my free hand and grabbed her around

the neck, pushing her up against the wall. Her eyes only challenged me, but her fingers were like vices on my arm. She was afraid of me.

I immediately let go and stepped back, running my hands through my hair as if I couldn't trust them to have nothing to do. I wasn't really mad at Alice; I was mad at myself. This was my fault, in the end. I'd let the threats against me distract me from protecting my brothers. I'd forgotten all about my father—trusted his cage to hold him, when I'd already had proof that it wouldn't. And now Michael was injured and it was my fault for failing to see the greater threat.

My voice shook when I spoke again. "Do you think he's done, my father? Because I don't. He just lost guardianship of the only people he cares about in the world to a woman he blames for the death of his sainted wife. He will not give up until he has those boys hidden away from us and is out of prison to be their dad again."

"I won't give up on the boys either. Or you." Alice spoke with the conviction I'd seen when she'd come to free me from Mallory's interrogation. And I believed she cared. Despite how little time she'd spent as our surrogate guardian, she seemed to care about my brothers. She would protect them as well as she could. But even if I were to include Sherlock, we were two high school students and a con woman against police officers hiding behind masks and the law.

"Do you really still think you can protect us from him with a handful of lovesick middle-aged men?"

"Not without you here."

We were weak together. We were useless alone. I knew that. But I had to find a way to keep my brothers safe without me, because my father wasn't my only enemy. I knew for sure that whoever was clutching a burner phone in a shop on Church Street wasn't going to stop just because I was stuck in a hospital waiting area. I wasn't the safety Alice assumed I was. And I couldn't figure out who was trying to get me thrown in jail from the hospital. If my new threatening enemy was successful, if they really could somehow blame my father's crimes on me, I'd be locked away. Helpless. And worse, my father would be free.

But the moment I opened my mouth to explain all that to Alice, her mobile rang. She held a finger up in front of me as she answered. "Yes? Mallory, this is hardly the time."

I grabbed the phone from her and tapped the screen to put it on speaker.

"... isn't something to put off. Can you locate her?"

"Mori is here with me. We're at the hospital. Her brother was hit by a car."

The pause on the other end was perhaps one or two seconds, and then Mallory sighed heavily into the phone. "Which one?"

"What do you need from Mori?" Alice asked.

"Constance Ross is coming to the station first thing in the morning to make a statement."

"I'm sure it'll be just as coherent as the last one."

"I'm told the woman has been medicated and is still claiming to have witnessed Mori disposing of the murder weapon."

Alice and I exchanged panicked stares, but she recovered more quickly than I did. "She's probably just mixing fantasy and reality in her memory. Surely—"

"That might have been the case if we hadn't found the sword right where she'd said it would be. There's no way around it. Mori's going to have to come in for more questioning."

I started to shake my head, and Alice placed a hand on my shoulder to calm me.

"Can't it wait until we know her brother came out of surgery okay?"

Mallory paused again, then said, "Twenty-four hours. It's all I can give her. Then she has to come to the station."

"Twenty-four hours," Alice echoed, then ended the call.

Our eyes met and then I said, "I can't stay."

"I know. Take your boy with you."

I shook my head. "No, he can be here to help you."

Alice suddenly grinned. "I'll make do. If I can't turn a couple of hospital security guards into my soldiers, what good am I?"

This is exactly why my mother loved you, I thought. But aloud I said, "Thank you."

I practically ran into Sherlock on my way back to where we'd left him with my brothers. Mrs. Hudson was there, pulling Seanie and Freddie into a hug.

"Oh, my special boys! How I've missed you."

"*We* used to be her special boys," Mycroft said, from somewhere behind me. "I might need to spend a little more time with the old girl to win her back."

I spun in place to face him. "I've an opportunity for you, then."

Mycroft immediately caught on to my scheme. "Leaving us so soon?"

I ignored his question to ask one of my own. "Did Sherlock call you?"

"No," Lock said, stepping up beside me. "I didn't."

And yet there was Mycroft, with Mrs. Hudson. With the distance he had to travel to leave his work and collect her, he would have had to have found out about the accident before I did.

Mycroft's expression fell and his voice was gentle when he asked, "How is Michael?"

"We don't know yet. How did you know he was injured?"

He glanced at Lock and then back to me. "I heard about the accident through . . . channels, and—"

"And you dropped everything to come here?" Lock asked. "I don't think so."

Mycroft pulled at the cuffs of his shirt and looked past me to where the boys were sitting with Mrs. Hudson. "There was nothing pressing."

Lock made a noise somewhere between a laugh and a cough. "What do you know?"

"I know that Mori needs answers to much more important questions than yours."

He was right. I squeezed Lock's hand to keep him from voicing the protest I clearly saw in his expression, and then asked Mycroft, "How long can you stay here and look after things for me?"

Mycroft checked his mobile. "Four p.m. tomorrow." He seemed amused at my surprise and said, "I came prepared to stay." His eyes drifted down the hall to where two men in black suits sat, one reading and the other playing a game on his mobile. But their eyes followed every passerby until each was clear of the bench where my brothers sat. "I came prepared for a lot of eventualities."

"Why?" I asked. It wasn't as though he hadn't helped numerous times before. But this time was different. This time he came without my request and brought backup. Not only that, Mycroft was grieving himself, and here I was asking him to spend the night in the place where he'd just lost his mother.

"I've grown rather fond of your brothers," he said. "You promised me that man would never get his hands on them again. I plan to hold you to that."

I stood there dumbly, because I didn't know what to say. I suddenly didn't even know if I could leave, now that I was faced with it. Could I just walk away, not knowing how Michael was or if he'd even survive? Could I live with myself if he woke up for a short time and found I'd abandoned him?

Alice must have seen my inner fight somehow. "Go. I'll call with news."

I glanced between Mycroft and Alice and then made myself leave. Sherlock followed along like a good soldier for a few strides, but we'd barely made it halfway across the lobby when he resisted enough to stop me.

"Where are we going?"

"I'll explain on the way."

He pulled me back toward him. "Maybe you should stay here as well. What if your father sends someone after you?"

"Then I should be as far away from this place and my brothers as possible."

"You're more vulnerable out there. What if someone hurts *you* this time?"

"Better me than them." I looked directly into Lock's eyes when I spoke again, and somehow, despite the boiling heat I'd felt rise in me at the mere mention of my father, I managed to keep my voice steady. "Let him. Let him hurt me. Let him kill me in their place if it will make him stop."

Lock paused then said, "It won't."

He stepped closer to me again, and I didn't move away this time. He wouldn't keep me from leaving, but I needed him to focus on what was important, not on what could possibly happen.

"You're right that he won't stop. While he breathes, wherever he is, he will come for those boys. This will happen over and over again, and if I am in his way, he will cut me down to get to them." I met Lock's gaze, moving closer still so that all he could see was my sincerity. "Maybe you don't understand the level of my priorities when it comes to those three boys, because I'm not good at being their sister most days. Perhaps if they had better . . ."

Lock adjusted his hand to lace his fingers through mine, but he didn't say anything.

"Do you understand what I would give up for them?"

He didn't answer again. I didn't need him to. All I needed

was for him to come with me. To focus with that beautiful brain of his and see what I couldn't see. It took him a few beats, but his expression finally shifted from worry to determination. "To find the black van, then?"

"No." I held up my mobile, which was already running the app Jason Kim had loaded onto my phone. "We're going to follow this." I took Sherlock's hand in mine. "And whoever's at the other end of this burner phone is going to wish they'd never heard my name."

Chapter 21

Sherlock and I got off the bus at Regent's Park and wandered through the closest entrance. We followed paths I'd never seen before, trying to get my little red dot closer to the blue dot that was supposed to be the burner phone. But the blue dot didn't stay still, and the app didn't work well on the unmapped expanse of park. Sometimes the dot would disappear altogether only to reappear in a place far from where it had been. I was so turned around by the time the dots were almost on top of each other that I didn't realize where we were until I heard overly boisterous laughter followed by a voice I recognized. "Cheers to that as well! Cheers to that bloody woman you married!"

It was Lily Patel, kneeling in the mud and facing the tree where her father's body had been found. Behind her, the clearing was cluttered with the scattered remains of a mixed-flower bouquet and four crumpled, empty beer cans. She poured a bit of liquid onto the ground from the can she held, then drank deeply, not coming up for air until foam was escaping from the corners of her mouth.

"Cheers!" she cried again, crashing her beer can against the tree trunk so hard, it sprayed up a bit onto her head. She took turns laughing and coughing.

"Looks like I was right," Lock said quietly.

I looked down at my phone, which showed the blue dot moving in weird stuttered circles around my dot despite the fact that we were both being relatively still. But it didn't matter what the app said anyway, because if it was Lily, there was one way to find out for sure. I shoved my phone into my pocket and pushed through the brush toward Lily right as she lost balance and started to tip over in slow motion.

I caught her before she fell completely and righted her. "Okay, let's be done with this, yes?" I pulled the beer from her hand, which was practically empty, but she grabbed it back with both hands and scowled at me.

"No! This is mine."

Sherlock released a soft laugh, and I glared at him through the growing shadows of dusk. "A little help maybe?"

He managed to hold her up so I could focus on keeping the girl from drinking any more. "Can we share more of this with your dad?"

Lily smiled and let me tip her hand enough to pour what little remained onto the ground at her knees. She instantly smashed the can in her hand and tossed it over her head to join its brothers. Before I could stop her, she had the last unopened beer in her hands. Luckily, her depth perception was gone, and she couldn't get her hand on the pull tab. She winked one eye shut and still couldn't make her fingers land on the top of the can. Nor was she a patient drunk, it seemed. After three misses, she held the can out in front of her and whined. When I didn't immediately take the can from her hand, she whined more loudly and bounced her whole body against Sherlock until I relented.

"Open," she commanded.

"I'm pretty sure your dad's had plenty. Maybe save this one for next time?"

Her face crumpled a bit. "There is no next time. Give it." She lifted her arms and made grabby hands in the air. She even crawled toward me on her knees a couple of steps.

I knelt down next to her and tried not to wince away from the smell of alcohol on her breath when she whined pitifully. "Enough," I said.

She shook her head for a good ten seconds before she said, "No, no. You don't understand what she did. She took it, but it was mine." Lily grabbed for the can, and when I held it too high for her to reach, she yelled, "I hate you! Just like her!"

At least the alcohol was making her honest for once. I shifted my body a little and slid the can behind my back out of her sight line. It felt familiar, this game, playing hide the booze from the angry drunk. "What did *she* do?" I asked, to distract her as I patted down her coat pockets. I shook my head at Lock. No phone.

"She took it all." Lily's expression dropped from anger to despondence in the time it took me to blink. "That was for me and Dad, but she took it and threw it away."

"What did she throw away?" The phone wasn't in the pockets of her trousers either.

Lily started to tip forward, and Lock caught her before she scraped her face on the bark of the tree. "Dad's beer. She found where I'd stashed most of it." Lily waved her hands around her head at the cans behind her. "Those are all that's left."

"And now those are gone too."

Lily immediately started to cry. "You shouldn't take it. Not the last one. It's mine."

"I'll just hold it for you, then. Just so you still have it tomorrow."

Lily wiped muddy hands across her cheeks, her tears all but forgotten. I spotted Lily's handbag, slung across a wilted bouquet of flowers on the far side of the tree. I upended the bag and scattered the contents across a patch of grass. No burner phone. Not even her regular mobile. And as I shoved all Lily's things back into her bag, I realized what that meant.

"It's not her," I said to Lock.

Still, according to the app, the phone was right next to us, which meant the person who was after me was somewhere close. Somewhere close enough to be watching. Lock stood up and while Lily whimpered in the mud, we both looked around, but all I could see were bushes and trees falling deeper into shadow by the second.

"Anything?" I asked under my breath.

Lock shook his head. "I've a question. Why was the burner hanging around near Lily before we got here?" He leaned closer to speak into my ear, so that Lily couldn't hear what he said next. "And what might have happened if we hadn't shown up when we did?"

I hadn't thought of that, but the minute he said it, all I could imagine were headlines of Lily being slaughtered at the same place where her father had died.

"Help me get her up." I slung her bag over my shoulder and we helped Lily to her feet. But then Lock let go and started backing away from us toward the trees.

"What are you doing?"

"We're so close," Lock said. "We need to know who it is."

I pulled out my mobile and watched the little blue dot stuttering away from my red dot slowly. Then I shoved the mobile at Lock. "Take this and find whoever it is. I'll take Lily back to my house."

There was almost no light left in the sky, but I could see Sherlock's expression in the glow from my mobile, and his eyes were already bright with the adventure of chasing off into the night. "Be careful."

"Maybe I'll look for a stick on my way."

"A cane or staff," I called after him. "Never a mere stick."

And then he was gone, and I was left in the dark with a groaning, drunken Lily Patel.

"You're bad," she said once we'd made it up onto the path. "You're a bad one."

I gritted my teeth to guide her around the corner when she threw her full body weight the other way. "That's the rumor."

She swung her body around so that we were eye to eye, her face so close to mine, all I could smell was stale beer. "Bad stock."

I took a quick look behind us, but it didn't seem like we were being followed.

"Not feeling well," Lily mumbled into my hair. It was suddenly very tempting to leave her there in the park, sprawled out on a bench for one of the park staff to discover at closing. But I didn't. She and I weren't friends, but I didn't want her to die. Not by some creeper with a burner phone, anyway. So I hoisted her, step by step, out of the park and up Baker Street to my empty house.

What would the paparazzi have made of us? I wondered when I got to our stoop. Apparently, Alice's marks had gotten the memo that the family was at the hospital. All but me, the wayward child who couldn't even sit vigil beside the brother for whom she claimed to care so much. And the press? Who knew. Maybe Alice's men had run them off for good.

"Bad stock," Lily slurred again. I leaned her back against the door to dig out my keys. "Daughter of a thief and a killer."

"Shows what you know." I unlocked our door and repocketed my key. "They were both killers."

Lily smiled. "I've only just the one killer. Got you beat."

She lifted a finger and tried desperately to make it touch my face somewhere. Was she saying something real? Or just hyperbolizing over her angst with her mother? "Do you have secrets too?" I asked quietly.

Lily's fingertip finally connected with my cheek just above my jaw and she burst out in a fit of giggles. I indulged in a deep breath, which I huffed away. More likely, she was extremely drunk and had no idea at all what she was saying.

I managed to haul her inside the house and lock us both in, but I knew I'd never be able to repeat the feat all the way up our stairs, so I dragged her into Alice's room and fell back onto the bed with her to catch my breath. A knock at the door brought me right back to my feet. Lock pushed his way inside, out of breath, covered in dust, twigs, and leaves, and practically glowing with excitement.

"Did you see who it was?"

He shook his head. "The signal went dead just outside the park, and when I reached the spot, a bus was driving off. No luck."

I nodded and took back my mobile when he held it out.

"I'll get Jason to put that app on my phone as well so we can surround whoever it is next time. How's the drunkard?"

"Whimpering into Alice's pillows."

"Ah. Alice. She called."

Michael. I started to dial her back on my mobile, but Lock covered my hand with his.

"It's no good. She's turned hers off for now. Michael came out of surgery and is in intensive recovery."

"And she can't have her phone on in there."

"He hadn't woken up yet, but she said the surgery went well and she'll call in the morning."

I nodded, and scowled at the floor. A few twigs had fallen, and it was difficult to keep from picking them up. I needed something to do just then, to keep my mind off of Michael.

"So, what's next?" Lock asked.

"For you? A change of clothes and sleep."

Lock waved off both suggestions with one sweep of his arm. "Not tired."

"You might as well go home and change. I've got a school-mate to babysit, at least until she sobers up enough to tell me her address so I can call her a cab."

"Leave her here and we can go out searching again."

"Not a chance. The very last thing I need is to have the daughter of one of my father's victims die of alcohol poison-ing in my house while I'm out." On cue, Lily groaned and I pushed a still-reluctant Sherlock to my front door.

"Call me the minute you get rid of her? No matter the time. I'm not going to sleep."

I managed to push him out the door, but by the time I went back in the room, Lily had fallen into some kind of fitful sleep. "Hey, wake up. Give me your address, yeah?"

Lily winced away from my voice and curled up into a ball, this time with her back to me.

I pushed at her shoulder again. "Give me your address. You need to go home and do this. I'm not your nursemaid."

When she wouldn't budge, I gave up and lay down next to her on the bed, staring up at the ceiling. I really didn't have time to waste like this, but I also couldn't think of what to do next. The app wouldn't do us any good until the burner phone was turned back on, and our only other lead was the posh boutique that was definitely not going to be open until the morning. I was stuck, and in just a few hours, Constance Ross would be giving a mostly coherent statement to police that she saw me throw my mother's aikido sword into the Regent's

Park lake. And there was nothing I could do about it.

But there was one thing I could do. I could go back to the hospital to see if Michael was out of surgery. To sit with my family like a caring sister should and wait to see if he would still be himself when he woke up.

"Is this your room?"

I started to shake my head, but decided she wouldn't want to know that she was sleeping in Dad's old room, so I nodded instead.

"It's big."

I sat up and leaned back against the excessive number of throw pillows Alice had staged against the headboard.

"Are you sober enough to call for a taxi?"

Lily shook her head for a little too long, then held the sides of it, like she couldn't stop the back and forth without her hands. "Don't want to go home."

"You can't stay here. I have to go to the hospital."

"For what?"

I ignored her question. "You can't stay here."

Lily waved me off. "Yeah."

She was quiet for a while—a lulling quiet that made me think maybe she'd gone back to sleep. But then she said, "He can't go free. He can't get away with it." She paused. "What if he gets out?"

"I will kill him." I shouldn't have said it, of course, but there was something satisfying about saying it aloud. "If he gets out, I'll finish what I started."

Lily managed to roll over and face me.

I kept my eyes trained up, but I could feel the intensity of her stare.

"I'll help you," she said.

I met her gaze, nodded, and then looked back up at the ceiling.

We lay on Alice's bed just like that until morning, me staring up at the ceiling and Lily staring at me. When the sun was just starting to lighten the sky, Lily called for a cab. A few minutes later she stumbled out of the room, fought with our dead bolt, and left the house.

The next time I opened my eyes, the sky was a bit lighter and Alice's clock said it was almost six a.m. I knew I needed to wake up, but my mind was warring for more sleep, right up until I felt a cool breeze blow into Alice's room.

I sat up and leaned forward to peer into our entry way. The door was open, but only a bit. I moved slowly off the bed, trying not to make a sound, then crept out into the entry until I could just make out a shadowed lump of something pushing through the opening of the door. I was almost on top of it when I realized what it was.

An elbow.

The Lady Constance wasn't going to make her meeting with DI Mallory after all.

Chapter 22

Her body was draped across our stoop, her right foot hanging over the top step. And she was definitely dead, the Lady Constance of Regent's Park. The killer had apparently propped her up against the door—a door that must not have been shut all the way when Lily left. And now my accuser had fallen across our threshold, her vacant eyes staring down at the dusty tiles of our entry.

My accuser.

I couldn't seem to move from where I stood, but I could see the future so clearly. Someone would call the police, if they hadn't already. And then the press. And there I'd be, the nasty daughter of a killer, who'd slaughtered the only witness to her own crimes. Maybe, just maybe, Mallory would believe that I wasn't stupid enough to kill a person at my doorstep. But he couldn't be counted on to rescue me from this. He never could.

This story would be a whisper of doubt about my father's guilt that could only grow into a scream of accusation against me. In the press? I could become the real Regent's Park Killer by the end of the week. No mere detective inspector could keep me out of jail when there was a body lying at my feet. And my father? There was no world in which he wouldn't jump on the opportunity to point all fingers at me—to claim it'd been me all along and he was merely protecting me as best he could. And with the help of his few remaining lackeys, I was willing to bet they'd find key pieces of evidence against me within hours. And then it would take only a judge's signature to free him.

They couldn't possibly pin it on me forever, of course. It was an obvious setup—one more piece of paper to add to Mallory's file of proof that I had an enemy. But it wouldn't take more than a day of my father's freedom and my imprisonment for him to steal away my brothers to somewhere I could never find them again.

I didn't know how long I'd been standing in the doorway, staring down at a dead woman, but that thought—the thought of me in prison and the monster free to torment my brothers—that thought was what finally made me move.

I grabbed a bag, Alice's scarf, and one of Freddie's baseball caps from the hooks near the door. Mallory would have to take me in on suspicion of murder, and I'd have to endure it. But first I needed to talk to Alice. She needed to get my brothers out of town, and it needed to be now.

I tried to call her, but her mobile was turned off, as was Freddie's. "Because they're in the hospital," I said aloud. And every extra second I spent in this house made it more likely I'd be taken into police custody before I could even find out if Michael had woken up, if his surgery had been a success. So I pulled the cap down low on my brow, wrapped the scarf around my neck to cover some of my face, and ran from the house.

"Who is that woman?" An older woman, whom I recognized as a neighbor from two houses down, stood at the bottom of our stairs, a look of pure terror on her face. "The police will be here any minute."

My escape route was cut off by this neighbor—a woman who never seemed to notice the banged-up kids coming out of our house or hear the drunken rantings of our father but managed to see a dead woman sprawled across our stoop. Of course she did.

As if on cue, I saw a couple of cars with flashing blue lights coming down the street, which meant I was out of time.

"Free our sergeant! Free Moriarty!" Mrs. Greeves came stomping down the street from the other direction.

"God," I whispered, for the first time hating that woman with every fiber. I no longer cared about her agency or attitude. I just wanted Mrs. Greeves to see reason. More important, I wanted to know how she knew to come to my house at all.

A small crowd of people gathered around me as I stood there. My senses became overwhelmed as they shouted, flashed their mobile phone cameras at me, and pushed in closer. I tried to break away from them, but it was as though the crowd moved with me and reformed no matter which way I went. And then I saw some news vans zoom around the corner.

A hand reached out from the throng, grabbing my wrist with a grip made of iron. I couldn't shake it off or break free. All I could do was duck and weave around bodies as the hand pulled me through. Soon, I was pulled up alongside a body that smelled of clove cigarettes and felt like my Lock. He pulled my hood over my cap and smashed my head against his chest so that I was walking in awkward sideways steps and trusting him to help me maneuver.

He guided me into the backseat of a town car and shoved people out of the way to close the door behind us. One last flash went off before he could, and I heard words that echoed through the silence long after we'd pulled away.

"Aren't you Sherlock Holmes? Where are you taking her?"

Sherlock Holmes. The crowd had named him, which meant it was only a matter of time before he was named to police and to the press. And because he came to my rescue, he'd now be tainted as that kid who lied for the real killer.

"Are you okay?" the question came from the driver's seat, which was occupied by Mycroft.

Lock's question came next. "Did they hurt you?"

I tried to catch his eyes with mine, but he was too busy looking around my arms and legs for nonexistent injury. Would he be labeled the coconspirator, I wondered, or the idiot who believed the girl he liked? Either way, he was stained. No more cases from school friends. No more avenues in with the police. This one act might strip him of the future he wanted and I'd so easily dismissed.

"She's bleeding," Lock reported. And while he leaned over the front passenger seat to retrieve a small white box from the glove compartment, I looked down and found that he was right. Someone must have scratched my arm. They left trails of claw marks, two of which were a line of blood drops getting ready to drip down.

"Does she need the hospital?" Mycroft asked.

"Just a scratch," I reassured his reflection in the rearview mirror, though I caught myself shivering. My thoughts still weren't coming together well. "But I do need to go to the hospital. Alice isn't answering her phone."

"Sorry it took us so long to come get you," Lock said. "I thought Mycroft's car would be better than a cab."

"How did you know to come over at all?"

Lock held gauze across my scratches, which instantly started to sting. "I couldn't sleep, so I kept checking out the window to see if your house lights came on. I first saw the body at 5:45. It wasn't there at 5:15. It was Constance Ross, yes? The woman who'd given a statement against you?"

I nodded. I must have been shivering again, because he held my hand still without taping the gauze down for a few seconds. I looked up at his eyes, which were bloodshot and glassy. "You didn't sleep."

"I told you I wouldn't." He tilted his head a bit and lifted a brow—his way of asking if I was okay. I didn't answer.

"I need to go to Alice. I don't think her mobile's on, and she needs to know what's happened."

"Alice knows," Mycroft said. "I told her as soon as Sherlock called me."

"And you can't go to the hospital. The police will be waiting there for you."

Really, it didn't matter if they were there or not. All that mattered was getting Alice and my brothers out of town as soon as possible. I thought to plead my case with Mycroft, but he looked pensive as he turned down a side street to avoid the traffic ahead. And when he caught me watching him, he shook his head, as if he somehow already knew what I was about to say and had already decided against it. So, when he rolled to a stop at a light, I made my own decision.

"I'm out of here, then." I grabbed for the door handle, but the locks engaged before I could open it.

"Just a minute," Lock said, his eyes moving back and forth as he calculated something. "If I can just find the reason . . ."

"Unlock it," I said to Mycroft, trying my best to be commanding. "Neither of you should be seen with me. It'll only mean questions and rumors." I pushed to unlock the door manually, but it locked again immediately.

Mycroft sounded playful when he ignored me and said, "Sherlock will put it together eventually."

"Seriously. Let me out."

"She knew something!" Lock cried. "Constance Ross knew something important."

"Yes. She knew that I'd tossed the murder weapon."

Sherlock waved his hand through the air, like he could bat away my words. "No. It had to be something more important than that. Something bigger. Her statement about you doesn't matter, because the police already have the sword. They've already heard the accusation. There has to be something else she might say if she's medicated. Something about the killer."

"There he is," Mycroft said. "And that means . . ."

"I've been an idiot!"

Mycroft smiled widely. "That's true on more days than not, but I'll listen."

Lock's eyes were calculating again, but they were brighter from his discovery. "You were right. This isn't Lily Patel."

The minute he said her name, some pieces started to come together for me. Pieces like a high-end boutique that sells costume jewelry and handbags—the kind of bags that Lily collected. Like magazines culled from the doctor's office where her mother worked. Like a little red dot sitting in Regent's Park while my blue dot danced around it, all while I'd been standing near Lily.

She hadn't had the burner phone. And I'd seen myself the way the little blue dot moved off while Lily stood right next to me. But the phone could have been passed off to someone else right before we got there. "It can't be her," I said with less vigor.

I'll help you, she'd said. But we weren't friends. We'd never been friends. And what was that she'd said about a killer and a thief? Did her family have a killer too?

"What is it?" Lock asked. "You're frowning."

"Tell me why you know it's not her," I said, which made Lock study my expression.

Still, he answered me. "The motive of this doesn't match her. She'd never do anything that might make your father look innocent of the Regent's Park crimes. If she's coming for you, it's because she wants both of you in prison, not you at the expense of your father going free."

I nodded. It couldn't be Lily who killed Constance anyway. She was with me all night.

Until she left in the wee hours of the morning. Before the killer had struck.

"It is possible that whoever is behind this wants me to think that Lily is involved?" I asked.

Lock asked, "How so?"

"She collects handbags, like the ones at the boutique at Church Street. The message was built from magazines at her mother's work. The burner phone led us right to her last night, and a body turns up on my front porch the morning after Lily spends her first ever night in my house. Too many pieces there for them all to be coincidence."

"Could it be her?" Mycroft asked.

"No. Lock is right. She wants my father to rot forever in prison. She would never do anything that might give anyone even the tiniest doubt of his guilt."

"And we saw the burner phone moving away from her," Lock added. "We know that the person holding that mobile is the one who called in accusations about Mori."

We all fell into a thoughtful silence for a while. I thought about bringing up my theory about her passing off the phone, but his thinking on the motive was right. Not that it helped me to know she didn't do it. Deciding who *wasn't* our culprit did nothing at all to solve the actual problem at hand. I could come up with a hundred people who *didn't* kill Constance Ross, but that wouldn't stop me from being arrested for a crime I didn't commit. And, at the moment, I had no other suspect to offer them in my stead. I was just the girl who had stepped over a dead body to flee from the scene in front of witnesses. Just like everyone would expect of me.

I sat up straighter in my seat. All my enemies would expect me to shout my innocence until the end. Even my father would expect me to evade police and lie about what had happened and when. The very last thing anyone would expect was for me to come clean, which was why telling Mallory everything was the exact right thing to do. And I needed to do it as soon as possible.

This time I didn't give Mycroft any warning.

I pushed to unlock my door and jumped out. I ran down the street, though I didn't know where I was going. I only knew it felt good to be out in the city, to feel the drizzle on my face, to be anonymous on an anonymous street. But then the buildings got nicer, all red brick with perfect white windows and white brick trims, and I knew I was in Mayfair. I walked to a crossing and saw the Italian flag on one side of the street up ahead and the low shrubbery wall of Grosvenor Square on the other. Which meant I was only a ten-minute walk from where I needed to be—West End Central Police Station.

I stood at that corner for a few minutes as all the other pedestrians picked a direction to cross, and I couldn't find it in me to take the crosswalk to my right. I stared down the path I would take, tracing it as far as I could see, which is when I noticed Sherlock, leaning back against the red postbox to my left, hands in pockets, like he was just waiting to see what I'd choose.

I was sure Lock had been following me since I jumped

from the town car, but he hadn't yet approached. I should've been grateful for that, really, but instead it made me a little sad. Perhaps he'd heard what I'd said in the car after all, that he shouldn't be seen with me. That was still true, but I didn't believe he cared all that much about things like appearances and associations. Still, when he did approach, I'd only have to send him off again. I couldn't let him get involved with this any more—not when someone was killing people to get my attention.

But the very thought of sending him off made a question pop into my mind.

Was this the place where our "temporary" became "finished"?

Pain lanced through my chest. I closed my eyes against it and crossed my arms, then another set of arms held me too. Did my pain draw him to me? He managed to always be there when I was falling apart. He pressed his cheek against my hair and pulled me back against him.

"Tell me what to do," Lock said.

Was this where I was supposed to become a noble girl? Because a girl more noble than me would pick a fight and tell lies until her boy ran off, hurt but safer for being apart from her. I, on the other hand, leaned back in Lock's arms, closed my eyes as he tightened them around me. I'd never been very good at being selfless. But I couldn't let him be ruined either.

"Call your brother. Have him take you to the hospital."

"And you?"

"I'll be at the West End station, waiting for Alice."

Lock turned me around to face him, and even though we

were still standing close, even though his hands were still on my arms, I suddenly felt cold. Another slash of pain shot through me. Could I do it? Could I become that noble girl?

"You're giving up? You're just going to walk into a police station and turn yourself in? For what? You didn't do anything."

"Better to walk in by myself then let those smug bastards catch me and feel accomplished for it, right?" I wondered what Mallory's expression would be when I finally told him the truth about everything. I found I couldn't even guess.

"Then I'm going with you."

I shook my head. "Not this time." I reached up to rest my hand against his cheek. "I need you to help Alice get the boys ready to leave town."

"Leave?" His hands dropped from my arms, and the cold seeped through my skin to my veins. It was all I could do to keep from shivering.

"She'll need help with Michael. He'll still need medical care, and they won't want to let her take him from the hospital."

Sherlock stared at the sidewalk. "Will you leave too?"

"I don't know," I lied. I knew I couldn't leave. They probably wouldn't let me, even if I wanted to. "But if they let my father out, my brothers aren't safe here. I need them to be safe."

"Mycroft can help them. I'm going with you."

I looked up then, waited until he did as well before I spoke again. "What can *you* do?" I hadn't meant to sound so cruel, but my tone affected Lock enough that I knew pressing a few more buttons would possibly send him away from me after all.

"What is it you think you can do for me there? Do you think they'll let you sit in the interview room and hold my hand? Do you think they'll listen to your theories? Can you logic away the death of a witness against me?"

"I'll clear your name."

"How?"

He didn't have an answer, and I knew he wouldn't, but still he persisted. "I'll find a way."

"How will you do that from inside a police station, Sherlock?" I watched a pack of students cross the street to the square, sack lunches in their hands. "Nothing you say holds any weight with the police. Especially not now that you've been stained by me." I looked back at Lock, and he was scowling in that way that meant he was about to argue with me. "You said you wanted to do this work in future? Then do it properly. You can't let your emotions get in the way, and you can't do a proper job if you're with me."

His expression fell blank and I crossed my arms and closed my eyes to make it through another flare of pain.

"Go and help Alice. Tell her what's happened. Then—"

"Then I find the real killer."

I nodded and offered up the best smile I could in the circumstances. And then I backed up a step. And another.

"I'll find out who it was," he said.

I nodded again, knowing I should have reassured him a little more. But it was all I could do to keep myself walking away from him, when every step I took made me feel colder and more alone.

Chapter 23

It was strangely freeing to walk into the police station on my own. No one recognized me at first, or cared why I was there. So I found a row of chairs across from the front desk and sat in the one farthest from the door. It took exactly seven minutes before I got a panicked phone call from Alice.

"Where are you?" she demanded, like she seemed to always do these days.

The constable behind the desk glared at me as I answered. "I need you to come meet me. I'm at the police station in the waiting area."

"Huh." She laughed a little. "You're a constant surprise. I thought for sure you'd lied to your boy." Alice lowered her voice and I could almost see her con mask settling in over her features. "Get out of there. We'll find another way." She definitely no longer sounded panicked.

I shook my head and met the eyes of the constable, who seemed suddenly much more interested in me. "This is the way. Come down and we'll listen to their accusations."

Alice paused a few seconds just as the constable made a phone call, his gaze never leaving mine.

"Do you have an alibi?" Alice asked. "Do I need to create one?"

"I don't have one that will help. But you'd better get here soon. I think they've finally discovered me."

I heard Mallory's voice in the background of Alice's call. "She is *where*?!"

A sudden amusement overtook Alice's voice when she said, "Seems you're right. Should I just hitch a ride with the inspector? It would save on petrol."

I smiled, despite everything. I was starting to wonder if Alice wasn't the best gift my mother ever gave me. "You are nothing if not conscientious."

The constable must have been given orders to stay put, but another uniformed officer came out from the back to stand near the door, which meant I wasn't to leave either. I toyed with the idea of going to the ladies' just to mess with them, but in the end I stayed put myself. Even after Mallory came rushing into the station like he was there to save a life, I stayed in my same chair, tinkering around on my mobile.

"Did you know the prime minister just got a new cat?"

Mallory didn't reply, but he did walk over to stand in front of me imposingly with four officers at his back, not including the one guarding the door and the one behind the desk.

"One more, and I believe he'll qualify to become a member of the Cat Ladies' Society. I wonder if they have a gentlemen's branch in London?" I glanced up at the giant crowd of police in front of me, then bowed my head a bit to greet Mallory. "Detective Inspector."

He was trying very hard to keep up his cool, disinterested persona just then, though his eyes were almost manic with anger. "Bring her," is all he said, before he pushed through the double doors and into the back offices. I stood and two of the officers lunged toward me and grabbed my arms, holding them up while a third officer ripped my phone from my hands.

Right as he did it, however, the door to the station opened again, and Alice stepped inside, in full fire mode. A man in a suit also entered, holding a briefcase behind him and keeping one or two steps behind Alice, who walked straight at the officer and grabbed my mobile from him before he could drop it into an evidence bag.

"What are you doing, miss?"

"This phone is in my name," she said. "Do you have a warrant?"

"It's evidence. We're allowed to seize mobiles without a warrant."

The man who'd come in with Alice raised a finger in the air. "Excuse me, but that's only technically true if you are arresting the girl. Do you, in fact, have a warrant for her arrest?"

The officer scowled as the uniformed constable behind him leaned in to secure a zip tie around my wrists. Once he heard the sound, the officer pointed at Alice. "You stay here until we invite you back."

Alice's man still had his finger in the air when he cleared

his throat. "Once again, I'll point you to the law on this matter—"

"Who the hell are you?!" Officer Scowls bellowed.

I grinned. "Just guessing, but I believe that's my barrister."

Alice nodded, and her man held up his briefcase, as though that proved his credentials. "Evan Golding, solicitor advocate, actually. But I have a barrister standing by should we require her services."

Officer Scowls turned and smacked open the double doors, following Mallory's path. We all followed him, including Alice and the solicitor, who stood on either side of me.

"Legally, you are allowed both a guardian and an attorney in this instance, you see."

I glanced over my shoulder at the man, who cowered back a bit and glanced at Alice for approval.

"Yes, Evan. You're doing a fine job."

The expression on Evan's face over such a tiny encouragement told me that he could only be another one of Alice's men. And despite my previous issues with Alice's manipulative ways, there was something comforting about that. He was so eager to please. Though he was also exceedingly awkward as we waited in the interview room for Mallory. The DI entered the room soon enough, however.

Mallory walked in with one other officer, who placed a laptop and two file folders on the interview table before taking his place by the door. Mallory sat and stared down at his papers, which I knew was all a part of his theater. Not even Evan fell for it.

"The twenty-four hours you are allowed to hold my client here started the moment you took her into custody, which means you have only twenty-three and a half hours left. Use them wisely."

Mallory didn't speak. He opened a file folder and slid a form across the table toward Evan, who immediately frowned.

"I see," Evan said. "You have thirty-five hours, then. Not a minute more."

"We have submitted to the court for a ninety-six hour hold," Mallory countered. "Based on the seriousness of the crimes."

"I'll look into that," Evan told Alice.

Mallory seemed to find Alice's authority over Evan amusing. "Where were you between the hours of four and six this morning, Miss Moriarty?"

Evan rested a hand on my arm to stop me from answering. "Miss Moriarty will not answer any questions until you present us with a reason for holding her."

Mallory opened the laptop and turned it toward us. With the press of the space bar, a video started, which was obviously from a CCTV camera somewhere near the Regent's Park York Bridge. It showed a few scattered pedestrians walking along the sidewalk in front of the bridge. But because there was no foot traffic coming in and out of the park that early in the morning, the appearance of a woman being dragged by a dark figure instantly drew my attention. The two figures moved closer to the camera as they left, close enough to see that the dark figure was female, her hair tucked into a hat that hid her face. Not that her face would have been distinguishable without the hat. The footage was so blurry, I knew the other figure was Constance only because of the bags.

"That's not—," I started, but Evan rested his hand on my arm once more.

"That could be anyone," he said.

Mallory looked right at me. "I asked you before if you had any enemies. Are you ready to tell me what's going on?"

I started to speak, only to be cut off by Evan again.

"Still waiting for the evidence that would allow you to hold her here."

"The body was found sprawled halfway into her house."

Alice spoke up then. "Which actually proves she didn't do it. Why in the world would she kill someone and put the body where it would most implicate her?"

"Because she's arrogant," Mallory said. He was still staring at me, but it was obvious he didn't think I'd done it. "Because she doesn't think the police are smart enough to beat her. Because she's been playing us all this time."

Evan was unfazed by the inspector's little speech. "That's all your conjecture and contains not a shred of evidence."

"Yes, and it's exactly the conjecture that will appear in newscasts and across the Internet before the next hour has passed. Let her tell us where she was. What does she have to hide?"

"Nothing," Evan said. "She's neither hiding nor revealing anything, because you have the burden to prove why you are holding her."

Mallory opened the final file folder. "We have a witness who saw her going into the park last night." He flipped a page. "We have a statement from the victim that she saw Miss Moriarty tossing a murder weapon into the lake." He flipped a page. "We then found that weapon and have confirmed that it is the weapon used to kill at least two other victims in Regent's Park—crimes Miss Moriarty has accused her father of committing. And finally," he said, flipping yet another page, "we have confirmed that the victim of this morning's crime was killed with a weapon similar to that used in the previous crimes."

I shook my head and sat back. I'd come there to tell the truth, but I was starting to second-guess that decision. I was pretty sure Mallory would listen. It was even possible he'd believe me. But I was also sure the "similar weapon" bit was a lie meant to trap me somehow. I hadn't taken the time to inspect the body, but if it had been slashed, I'm sure I would have noticed a giant pool of blood dripping down our stoop.

Evan leaned forward. "That is all circumstantial."

"Perhaps," Mallory said. "But it is enough to hold her. And if she didn't do it, then there is someone out there doing their best to make it look like she did. If for no other reason, we'll hold her for her own safety."

"Or until your thirty-five hours elapse."

Mallory gathered his papers and walked from the room, leaving us to fall into an awkward silence.

That was until Alice asked, "What now?"

"Now we wait and see what they find," Evan said. He turned toward me. "Tell me, what is it they are going to find?"

Chapter 24

Evan and Alice left me after I'd told them where I'd been the night before, Alice to see to the boys and Evan to check that the police were following all the rules correctly and to file a response to the request for the longer hold.

"Once again, it's you and me," I said, to whichever officer was behind the mirror to babysit me. He, of course, didn't respond, leaving me with my thoughts, which for once was exactly what I needed.

I'd let everything that happened to me exist in a swirling chaos for far too long. I needed order. I needed to pin everything I knew, like mapping equations on a graph, then draw the lines between the pins to reveal the pattern. I needed to solve for X.

No, I needed a time line. I needed to start from the beginning and order the steps of the crimes against me. I needed to see them all in sequence and find my connections.

I touched my finger to the table on the very left edge.

First pin: Constance Ross saw me throw my father's sword in the lake.

I moved my finger an inch to the right and touched it down again.

Second pin: She told her husband, Charles Ross, who drew the scene like one of her fantasies.

And again.

Third pin: Charles Ross saw my father kill Sadie Mae and drew that scene as well.

Fourth pin: Someone killed Charles, cut off his hand, and took his drawings.

Fifth pin: Someone put the hand in my rubbish bin.

Sixth pin: Someone altered the drawings and sent them to me.

Seventh pin: Someone sent me threatening collage letters.

Eighth pin: Someone talked Constance into telling the police.

Ninth pin: When that didn't work, someone medicated Constance to make her statement more believable.

Tenth pin: Someone killed Constance before she could make her more-believable statement.

I spent minutes walking through the pins in my mind, trying to make sense of them. But there were too many unknowns. Too many someones, and not all of them could be the same person. Would the person who killed the artist put his hand in my rubbish? Wouldn't it be better for the killer if no one ever found any of him? Why had the artist been killed? Why use it to implicate me? What was the point of it? I could buy that the person who called in tips about me and brought Constance in to make a statement would make her take medicine to clarify her thoughts. But why would this person then kill her?

No. It was like two equations in one.

I sat up straighter.

I needed to group the sets.

Someone had put the hand in my rubbish, sent me threats, and found Constance to give a statement.

Someone else had killed Charles, altered his drawings, and killed Constance to keep her from giving her statement.

There were two. It was the answer to everything. There had been two people all along. The problem wasn't solving for X. It was solving for X and Y, two forces working opposed to each other. X was trying to blame me for my father's crimes. Y was trying to stop X. And Y was killing people in the process.

Which meant X was in trouble.

I stood up and walked over to the mirror. "Hey! I need Mallory. Tell him I'm ready to talk." No response, so I knocked on the glass and got louder. "Go get Mallory! I need to talk to him. It's important!"

Nothing.

I paced the room, sat for a while, then got up to tap on the glass again, but still there was no reply. I was starting to wonder if I had a babysitter after all. I tried counting down the minutes, to track time, tried to use all these wasted minutes and hours to think of what to do next, but there were almost too many contingencies and not all that much that was in my control.

Were I to be released, my first priority had to be getting Alice to take my brothers out of town. And then I needed to find X and . . . do what? Protect whomever it was from the threat of the equally mysterious Y? Would I really protect someone from a killer who was trying to protect me?

If I didn't get out of this bloody station, I still had to find a way to convince Alice to leave me here and get my brothers out of town. And if Mallory wouldn't listen or see reason? If I ended up being incarcerated for good?

I sighed and felt the drag of that hopeless thought on my mind. But it wasn't only hopelessness that dragged me down. It had been days since I'd had a proper sleep in an actual bed. As much as I tried to keep my focus, my eyelids kept drifting shut, and closing them felt so good.

I didn't know how long they let me sleep, or what time it was when Mallory next came in the room, but he was breaking the rules—I knew that for sure.

"Where were you between the hours of four and six yesterday morning?" he asked. He had slammed down his files as my wake-up call, which was bad enough. But he'd almost immediately shoved a microphone in my face and compressed some buttons on an ancient-looking machine I assumed would record our conversation.

I barely lifted my head in acknowledgment of his question, and, when I didn't answer him right away, he leaned toward the mic and said, "Suspect refuses to answer the question."

I grunted and Mallory asked, "What did you say to the victim to lure her from the park?"

I met his gaze and sat quietly.

"Suspect refuses to answer the question."

I again said nothing.

"Where is the weapon you used?"

Nothing.

"Suspect refuses to answer the question." He flipped open his file folder security blanket then, and I decided to take the opportunity to ask a question of my own.

I leaned as close as I could toward the microphone and asked, "Where are my attorney and guardian?"

Mallory flipped a page from his file and opened his mouth to say something else, but I cut him off.

"Inspector refuses to answer the question."

He slammed down the page in his hand and said, "Interview ended at seven thirty-nine," then compressed another button to stop the recording. He sat back in his chair and stared at me. "I've done my due diligence."

"A.m.?" I asked.

Mallory looked confused.

"Is it morning?"

He didn't say, of course, but I guessed it must have been morning already, because Mallory was wearing a different-colored shirt from yesterday's blue.

I asked, "Who brought Constance Ross to the station to give her statement?"

I didn't expect Mallory would answer, and he didn't. Though he did look at me oddly.

"Who was giving her medicine to bring her back? You know, right?"

"Why do you want to know?"

I studied Mallory's eyes for a few moments. "I think that person may be in trouble."

Mallory looked like he was about to answer when the door swung open and a rather triumphant-looking Evan Golding practically jogged inside the room.

"Let's go," Evan said, gesturing toward the still-open door.

I didn't get up at first, half expecting Mallory to argue.

Evan smiled. "She's free to go, isn't she, Inspector?"

"How exactly am I free to go?"

"New evidence," Mallory said, trying his hardest to seem nonchalant to the words, I was sure.

"And what exactly is this new evidence?" I asked.

Evan's grin was back. "You've got an alibi."

Evan led me out into the main office and right up to where Sherlock was standing. "It's all down to him, I'm afraid."

"As promised," Lock said, gesturing to the desk next to us.

"Lily?" I hadn't even noticed she was there. Lily Patel was sitting next to a DS at one of the many desks in the room, studying a white piece of paper carefully. She looked up at me and nodded slightly before going back to her reading. "What is she doing here?"

Sherlock smiled as Evan filled in the details. "She's giving a statement about spending the night at your house. This lad talked her into it, of course."

"But she left in the early morning."

"She did," Lock said, and his eyes brightened. "At four oh-nine a.m., exactly."

"You have the exact time?"

"I have video," he said, holding up his tablet. He tapped the screen and turned it toward me, and I watched a time-coded video play that looked as if it came from the cab's black-box camera. It pulled up to the road where Lily was standing, looking like she'd spent the night vomiting in my house. She got into the cab, and it pulled away before Lock stopped the video. "That's how I knew she didn't do it."

"Yes, yes. We already knew that."

But Sherlock wasn't done.

"It's also how I got the idea to look for this." The next tap on his screen started up another black-box video, though this one didn't look to be from a taxi. The car didn't move at all, just sat there, with the camera pointing down Baker Street. I could just make out our front stoop at the very edge of the frame, and only knew it was ours, really, because I watched Lily coming out of the house, waiting for the taxi, then watched the taxi pull away.

After about twenty seconds of nothing else happening on screen, I looked up at Lock. "The point of all this nothing?"

"Nothing is exactly the point." He tapped to fast-forward and other than a couple of cars, a bus, and a few pedestrians, nothing happened on the street for at least ninety minutes.

"No doors opened," I said, suddenly breaking through the mind-numbing effects of twenty-four hours in a police inter-view room. Then I smiled. It was rather brilliant, actually. Not that I'd ever feed Sherlock's ego with that kind of compliment.

"Bloody brilliant," Evan said. "I never would've thought

to look for a parked car with a black box to prove you *didn't* leave. That's—"

"Actually rather obvious," Lock said.

"You really need to stop telling people that," I said.

Lock quirked a brow. "But there's more."

Just as the sky started to lighten a bit, a rather large shadow tromped up the street, stopping just outside our stoop. With slow, labored steps, the form moved up toward our front door, and then half of it was dumped on our top step.

"It's too far away to see who it is, but it proves it wasn't you," Evan said. "And that's all we care about, right?"

I exchanged a look with Lock, and then answered Evan's question with one of my own. "What does all this do to my father's murder case?"

He seemed surprised at the question. "I don't imagine it'll do much, really."

"They've found the sword and a witness that caught someone else trying to get rid of it. No one could use that to spring him?"

"Well, I suppose that depends on the level of the other evidence they have against him."

Not much, was the answer to that. Purely my supposition, of course, as I wasn't privy to the police files. But my father had acted like I was the key witness against him when we'd had our little breakfast visit, which meant they couldn't have had much other evidence. "Could you find out the status of his case for me?"

"I could ask around."

"Why?" Lock asked me, suddenly on alert.

"I need to know if they're going to release him. And if they are, I need to know when."

Evan swung his briefcase a bit. "Sure. I can find out."

I offered him the best smile I could, and said, "Thanks. Call as soon as you know anything." I patted at my pockets and remembered that Alice had my mobile. "If Alice answers, tell her. I have to go home right away."

Chapter 25

They took the longest time to release my belongings to me. I might have skipped the step altogether, but the constable at the evidence desk said that Mallory insisted he do everything precisely by the book when it came to me. Of course he did.

Then came an overlong taxi ride home through horrid traffic, with Lock sitting in complete silence and Alice calling him every five minutes to find out why we weren't home yet. We were just a minute or two from home when Lock finally did speak up.

"You won't go with them?"

I stared out the window at the graying sky. "Not yet. I have something to do."

He held my hand, bringing the back up to his lips, but he didn't say anything more until we were at the house and the driver had been paid. I tried to run up the steps, and Lock used our still-clasped hands to bring me back to him.

"What is it?"

He rubbed his thumb over the top of mine.

"Sherlock."

He looked up, holding his blank expression like a mask.

"I'm too tired to guess. Give me the slightest hint."

His brow drew in again and he glanced at the door to our house, which was perhaps as far away from me as he could look. "For as long as I need. That's what you said."

For how long? he'd asked. His mother had just died. I told so many lies that day, and among them, I'd said I'd stay. *For as long as you need.* What he didn't—couldn't—know was how much more I needed him, and how selfish it was for me to need him at all. He was the only one I had left, really. Or would be, once I walked into my house and sent my brothers away. But I had to somehow convince myself that I was better off alone—or maybe that he was. And then I had to send him away.

That pain lanced through me again, the kind that came with the word "temporary." And with him staring at my door, and people walking past us on both sides, I moved closer to him, and rested my head against his shoulder.

I wanted to say all those things that the lovers in Sadie's books said to each other and hear Lock say them back to me. But I couldn't speak for the pain. It pulsed along with the thought that something had just ended for us. And I couldn't explain that. He was still with me and probably would be for the balance of the day, but when he slid his fingers into my hair and pulled me in closer, he still felt so far.

My eyes were hot and wet when I pulled away from him, so I glanced up and away, blinking them dry as I pulled him toward the front door. We walked in to a complete chaos that I was thankful for. Freddie and Sean were practically running circles around a pile of every suitcase and bag we had in the house, along with a few boxes. As Lock closed the door behind us, Seanie ran up the stairs to grab some completely unnecessary set of books from Michael's shelves, which he tossed downstairs one at a time to Freddie to be packed.

Alice walked through the bare inches of space between the bags and boxes, closing them and taping them shut in a perfect dance with the boys. She smiled at me and handed me my phone. "I've packed you as well," she said, pointing to the large blue bag by the staircase. "Check to make sure I got everything you want."

"Michael?" I asked.

Alice's smile fell a bit. "He's still not awake. I've arranged medical transport as far as Brighton. Then I have a nurse who's agreed to help the rest of the way. She owes me."

A horn honked outside, and Alice twirled past us to open the door. She waved at a large rented lorry on the street. "Okay! He's here. Start hauling everything down, boys."

Seanie ran right between Sherlock and me to greet the driver, ripping my hand from his. I smiled, but when Lock wandered over to help Alice carry a rather large box, I caught myself holding my freed hand up to my chest.

Like a nostalgic idiot, I chastised myself, but still I couldn't seem to shake this dark feeling. "The end," I said aloud.

Leaving the house was just as chaotic as entering, full of shouts of "one last thing" and juggling bags and boxes out to the street. But I used the mess to kick my bag behind the door of Alice's room, so it wouldn't get packed off with the others.

And I made sure I was the last one out the door, jumping into the front of the lorry just before it took off for the train station.

The driver was an old friend of Alice's, who had once been an airline pilot, which meant the boys' questions filled up the trip to Victoria Station. It also meant that we could leave the boxes behind with the driver's promise to post them on ahead. And then Alice shoved a roll of pound notes into Lock's hands and asked, "Could you take this one"—she shoved Seanie at Lock—"and buy us five tickets to Brighton? Two adult and three child?"

"With a connection to Lewes?" he asked.

She looked at me. "You'll have to explain how he knows that later."

I nodded and when she looked away, I met Lock's eyes and held up four fingers. He grinned a little and guided Seanie with a hand on top of his head toward the ticket counter. I helped Alice and Fred navigate a cart full of luggage, which miraculously was only one bag for each of the boys and two for Alice. She didn't notice mine was missing until everyone was packed onto the train but Sherlock and me.

Lock walked over to talk to the boys through the train windows the minute Alice exploded on me.

"What do you mean you're not coming?!"

"I can't. Not yet. It'll just look like I'm running from all this police mess."

She put her hands on her hips. "And?"

"What do you mean, 'And'? That's the reason."

She stared at me, her eyes full of fire, though some of her

exhaustion was seeping through. For all that I'd been forced to handle in the past week, Alice, too, had spent long hours at the hospital and police station, trying to keep us safe. Together. And there I was ruining all her work.

I glanced over at Lock, who was somehow managing to avoid having his hand slapped by Seanie's, even with his eyes closed.

"Is it because of that boy?"

Wouldn't it have been so much easier had that been my reason? Alice probably would've approved of that as my reason. But I shook my head.

"You've never cared about Mallory and his lot. I don't buy that you're starting now."

I glanced at my brothers then looked straight into her eyes. "Their safety is what matters now."

"So does yours. And what are you going to do all alone here? What great mission is making you stay?"

"I have to atone for my sins, apparently."

Alice's expression dropped. "What do you mean by that?"

I shook my head. "More important, I have to make sure Father atones for his."

"You don't need to do anything about your father."

I wished that were the case. Sadly, I knew better. "There is only one way to make us safe."

Alice grabbed my arms and stared into my eyes, as if she was trying to read my mind. "Just what do you think you're saying? The last time you tried something stupid, he almost throttled you. You're coming with us."

"I can't. They'll probably let him out now. You know there are some who've been searching for an excuse to proclaim his innocence. And then he'll scour the earth for those boys and we'll never be safe. And he's not my only problem."

A little of Alice's intensity fell away. She was starting to give up. "And if I make you come with me? I can't let you do this. You know that."

I pushed her hands from my arms and stepped back. "You can't stop me."

She started toward me, but the train signaled that it was ready to leave. Lock walked back toward us. She was stuck.

"You'll miss your train."

Alice growled out her frustration and took a step back toward the train, but she pointed a finger at me. "I'll come back for you. This isn't over."

In the end, she got on the train. I waved to my brothers from the platform and yelled out my good-byes. Only Freddie seemed concerned that I wasn't going with them, but my promise to follow them in a few days made him seem slightly less nervous about the whole thing. I waited on the platform until I couldn't see the train anymore. Maybe if Alice knew just how much I trusted her to let her take those boys with her, she wouldn't have been so angry. She had everything most precious to me in the world. She had to keep them safe.

Chapter 26

I told the cab driver to take us to 221 Baker Street, which I thought would be a hint to Sherlock of what was coming, but he seemed to take it as a good sign. Or maybe there was another reason for his sudden lift in mood. I turned away from him after a while. His subtle grins made my heart ache.

Once we reached his house, he said, "I'll pack a bag and meet you at your place." It was our second time standing out on the sidewalk that day, and I still didn't know what to do about him.

That was a lie. Because I knew very well what I could do to make him leave, I just wasn't sure I could do it. Not in the way I needed to get the job done. He looked at me with such a mix of expressions just then. Pride for saving me once again, for being the reason I was free to walk the streets. Relief? He'd gotten his way when I didn't leave with my brothers. But something on my face must have clued him in to my own internal struggle, because he fell silent, making no moves toward his house to pack.

I opened my mouth to speak, still unsure what I would say, and then my phone rang. It was Evan.

"Miss Moriarty?"

"Yes. Were you able to find out the status of my father's—"

"You were right. He's still under charges, but his lawyers are using the similarities between this latest case and the previous ones to apply for your father's release on police to court bail. If everything goes smoothly for them, he'll be out by the end of the week."

Three days. I had three days to make my plans. Three days to make myself ready. And that started with Sherlock.

"Thank you for the information. I'll be in touch."

As I ended the call, I noticed Lock starting to walk down the street toward my house.

"Lock, what are you doing?"

"Your door is open," he said. After he'd taken a few long strides down the sidewalk, he looked back at me. "Do you think one of your brothers forgot to lock up?"

"I was the last one out. I know I locked it."

We looked at each other, then ran down the street to the house. The door didn't seem to be damaged, which meant a key had been used. I pulled Sherlock back before he started up the steps of my stoop.

"That call was from Evan. My father's getting out at the end of the week. What if he sent one of his thugs ahead of him? He's the only other person who has a key. It would probably be with his personal affects."

Lock paused a moment. "Umbrella still by the door?"

I nodded. "In the stand, but probably just the old-fashioned long one."

"That's exactly the one I need."

We crept up the steps to the gaping front door. Without stepping inside, Lock reached around the doorjamb for the umbrella. Weapon in hand, he stood taller and surveyed the entry.

When he didn't move, I moved up next to him in the doorway and almost choked on the smell of fresh paint.

The place was trashed. All the bedding from Alice's bed had been torn and was strewn about, so that ripped fragments of her sheets peppered even the stairs. It appeared the bedding from upstairs fared no better. Sheets and duvets as well as cotton batting and stray feathers were everywhere, up and down the stairs, hanging over the banisters, in and out of the kitchen and out the gaping open French doors to the back patio.

But worse, someone had pulled the full-length mirror from my room and tossed it down the stairs to shatter across the front entry. Book covers had been torn from their pages and thrown everywhere. And the paint smell—messages were spray-painted all over the walls and even up the steps. Red paint that dripped down from the corners of the letters like blood.

CONFESS, the blood said.

MURDERESS . . .

I KNOW YOU DID IT. . . .

And across the door to Alice's room, the blood threatened, CONFESS OR DIE. I walked closer and touched a paint drop that stained my finger. Still fresh.

Lock moved me behind him, as if he was going to protect

me with an umbrella. So I decided to arm myself as well, and retrieved a golf club from the floor. Annoyingly, I held it between my hands as if I were at another of Lock's Bartitsu practices. Evidently, my body was going to instinctively wield any sticklike object in that fashion from now on.

We could plainly see that no one was in there, but still Lock made us walk around the center table and check behind the door. We walked the rest of the rooms in the house and found them similarly empty. Lock seemed almost disappointed when he slid the umbrella back into the stand, but he immediately steepled his fingers and stared at the ground, chasing his thoughts.

I caught myself watching him fondly. His eyes were the brightest blue just then, filled with clues and possibilities. He was in his element, and something about that broke my heart. But I didn't want him to continue on this case of mine. Or, more accurately, I couldn't allow it. My father's impending release was all that mattered from here forward, and Sherlock was sure to either distract me from what I had to do, or attempt to thwart it. Either way, I couldn't afford to have him near me for a while. And it had to start now. I'd run out of time.

I set the golf club up against the banister and turned toward Sherlock. "You can go."

Only his eyes shifted when he looked at me. "If you think you're staying here alone after this—"

"Whoever it was is gone. They didn't damage the door, just picked the lock, probably. I have a bolt lock no one can get through, even with the key." I paused too long and he started to argue, but I cut him off. "I need you to go."

He fought away an exasperation that seemed to take his words, but managed to ask, "Why?"

I ignored him and stepped gingerly toward the door, trying to avoid the glass of the mirror.

His anger was evident when his next question burst forth. "Why am I leaving you with this mess all alone in a house that's been broken into?"

"Because my father's getting out of prison at the end of the week." I gathered all my strength and looked up at him. My expression must have been adequately cold, because he dropped his hands and stood up taller.

"Don't do this." His face went completely blank, almost as if he were mimicking my coldness. But I knew better. I knew he was afraid.

So I pretended he hadn't said a word. "And I need time to prepare."

"Why are you doing this now?"

"I only have the three days, and I've no idea where he'll go first when he gets out, or if the person who broke into our house will have told him that the boys left town. There are a lot of contingencies."

Sherlock crossed his arms. "Why are you sending me away for that? I could be helpful."

I wanted to explain that he couldn't be involved in what I was about to do. That I needed him unstained and unbroken. I needed to know that he would still be Sherlock Holmes four days from now. But he'd never leave if I did that. Because he was still Sherlock Holmes, and I had a puzzle to solve. So, instead, I rested a hand on the doorjamb.

"I need you to go."

"I won't."

I didn't entertain his petulance with a response. I just stood at the door and watched him until his anger returned.

"Why? Why! WHY!"

"Because I don't trust you!" I shouted back. "I don't trust you to help me. How could I?"

The subtle shift in him from righteous anger to guilt— would anyone have been able to see that but me? "It won't be like last time. I'll—"

"Because even if by some miracle you don't betray me outright, you'll get in my way, and then I'll have to cut you down to get to him. And don't think I won't."

His expression was ice then. I'd seen it before; I'd caused it before. He was in pain again, and I'd done that. Did it matter why?

"So now I need you to leave."

Lock took three steps toward me, the glass crunching with his every footfall, but he didn't look at me, only out at the street. "I'll go get my bag."

"I won't open the door for you. And I'll call one of Alice's men if you try to sleep on my stoop."

He took another step so that we stood side by side, our shoulders almost touching, he looking out and I looking at him. I clenched my hand into a fist at my side to keep from reaching for him.

"Then I'll come back," he said. "I'll always come back."

I couldn't show him the pain I felt at hearing my own broken promise tossed in my face. I remained perfectly still, feeling the sharper edges of my pain lance through me until I was gutted. Without looking, Lock reached out a hand to surround my fist—my one tell of the turmoil inside. Of course he'd seen it. He was Sherlock Holmes.

He pressed his thumb into my clenched fingers to relax them away from my palm. He traced his thumb across the indents my fingernails had made and down along my fingers. And then, slowly, he released my hand entirely, and I had to press it up against my leg to keep from grasping at the air where his hand had just been. I couldn't look at him anymore, but I held him in my periphery.

"You'll . . . ," he started, but his voice broke, and he cleared his throat before speaking again. "You'll lock the door behind me?"

I nodded.

He mirrored the gesture. He cleared his throat again, and this time his voice was soft. "I'm going to call you at intervals throughout the night. If you don't pick up within two rings, I'll be back here. And I will break down the door if you don't let me in."

I should've protested, but I didn't trust my voice. I nodded instead, justifying myself with the thought that I didn't have to speak to him, just answer the phone and then end the call.

I thought he might linger there in my doorway. And maybe I would have broken down if he had, begged him back inside to stay with me. But he immediately stepped out onto our stoop and made his way down the stairs. I watched him until he crossed the street, and then I closed the door.

Which is when I found the picture.

At my eye level, on the back of the door, there was an old, stained picture of a young boy, no more than Seanie's age, wearing a white shirt with red sleeves and black shorts. Someone had affixed it to the door using one of the small carving knives from the kitchen. I knew the boy's face. I'd seen it before. Somewhere.

I studied the image then closed my eyes in an attempt to capture the memory. I was pretty sure I hadn't seen him on the street. It was more like I'd seen that photo before. I let my mind follow memories of family photo albums, pictures hanging on walls, television shows, and then finally newspapers. And because there was some law that what a person needed to find would inevitably be in the last place they searched for it, the thought of newspapers finally brought the memory back to me.

The scrapbook in the attic. The picture stabbed to my door was even the same picture of the boy, only the red sleeves were hidden in the black and white of newsprint. I closed my eyes trying to picture the article or the words of the headline for about thirty seconds before I realized I didn't need to. The scrapbook had the article, which meant I probably even had a name.

"In the attic," I whispered.

And then I heard two crunching steps behind me.

Chapter 27

Had I dodged left, I wouldn't have gotten cut, but I also wouldn't have had a weapon to deflect the next blow. I grabbed the umbrella from the stand, just in time to hold it up above my head as the knife came down again, high enough to see the look of hate contorting the woman's features into a mask I knew all too well, down to her curly hair and bright-red-painted lips.

Our Sally Alexander was trying to kill me.

My brain recklessly tried to piece everything together, when I should have been more focused on the shift of her arm as she stabbed at me, which meant I got cut again, this time on my hip. I didn't feel the cut, but a quick glance showed blood blooming through the slice in my jeans.

Nothing too serious, I told myself, holding the umbrella up again. At least she was attacking in patterns. In a moment of inspiration, I noticed she was left handed, and I released the left-hand side of my umbrella shield just as she sliced down, using her impact to spin my umbrella around and slam down on her hand with a satisfying crack. She dropped the knife. I stepped down on the blade and, like I'd practiced with Sherlock, kicked it away. But with all the rubble on the floor, it didn't go near far enough.

Sally lunged for it, but the crook of my umbrella was just coming around and connected cleanly with her face, which sent her staggering back. I pushed it against her neck before she could recover and pinned her to the banister.

She glared at me and hissed, "This is your fault. You should have just admitted what you'd done."

"Is that your son?" I asked, gesturing toward the picture affixed to our door.

"No one cared about my Mickey. Son of a whore. Lost while I was out with my tricks. No one cared but our sergeant."

"And then he found the killer."

"No. I found him and killed him. And Sergeant found me. Papers said there weren't justice, but I got my justice. I got to stand over the body of that animal and spit on it for my Mickey."

I huffed out a laugh. "Fine, then. So you think my father is innocent. Why in the world would you come after me?"

Her eyes narrowed to slits and her lip twitched. "You killed all those people in the park."

"I didn't."

"You killed them and blamed him!" She reached her hands for me, her nails extended like she wanted to tear me apart. But I pressed my weapon against her neck until she gave up.

I loosened my hold a little, to make sure she could breathe. "I didn't kill anyone. You have it all wrong."

Mrs. Greeves's voice was thin and tight when she said, "You were seen. Connie told me she saw you—"

"I was hiding the weapon from my father! *I* was trying to *stop* him."

"No! You threatened him too! I saw that with my own eyes."

"What are you talking about?" I loosened the crook from her neck just a little bit more, hoping she'd calm down now that we were talking. But I still held it against her skin in warning.

"I came here the night they took him away," she pointed toward the kitchen. "I saw you through the window, standing in that room there, holding a knife to Sergeant's throat."

"You don't know what you saw." I shook my head and looked around at the room. All that rage and damage over nothing. I'd wasted all that time trying to figure out who she was for nothing—for what amounted to the misinformed rantings of the neighborhood gossip and her misdirected loyalty. She'd killed the man who killed her son and this is what she'd turned into all these years later. Is this what Lock was afraid I'd become? "I was trying to make him stop killing people."

"Liar."

"I wanted him to leave London. I was going to pay him money to leave so I could protect my brothers."

"Liar!"

Mrs. Greeves knocked the umbrella aside, and in the next moment we were on the floor, shards of glass cutting through my shirt to embed in the skin of my back. She pushed up to face me only to punch me as hard as she could and fall on top of me again, pressing the glass still deeper into my back. "And then you killed Charlie!"

I grabbed her wrists to keep her from hitting me again, but there was already blood in my mouth when I said, "I didn't. I didn't kill anybody."

"You killed him and cut him up! But I found the piece you left. I found his hand and put it where the coppers would find it." She ripped an arm from my grip and hit me over and over as she screamed, "Why didn't they lock you up!"

I managed to deflect only half the blows, and the one that smacked against my temple made me dizzy. She suddenly stopped hitting me, staring at me through her hateful mask, her cheeks wet with tears.

"Do you know how lost Connie was without her Lord Charles? You didn't have to kill him. He was on your side— said Sergeant killed your friend. But I knew better. Then I found his hand."

Mrs. Greeves connected another blow to my temple before I could grab her hand again. "Then you killed Connie!"

She was practically sobbing at that point but was still stronger than I would ever have guessed. And even though my back screamed in protest, I shifted my body under her as I was taught, turning all the simple punctures into slices along my skin. Then, when she pushed up her body to free her hand again, I brought my knees up to my chest and kicked her stomach as hard as I could so that she launched into the rubble.

I spun over and, quickly as I could, crawled toward the

knife. My fingers brushed against the hilt just as she jumped onto my back to stop me. I inched forward and she grabbed my hair, pulling back to limit my reach. But it didn't work. My hand closed around the hilt and I swung my arm back, stabbing the knife behind me with as much strength as I could at that awkward angle.

I didn't even know where I'd hit her until she rolled off me and I was able to sit up on my knees. She seemed a lot more delicate with blood pouring out her side. I must have punctured a lung, because she was gargling when she coughed, and her chest was moving in an uneven way when she breathed.

"I didn't kill your friend," I said while trying to catch my breath. "I don't know who did, but I know one thing for sure. My father is a serial killer. What you saw through the window that night was me trying to stop him."

She swallowed a few times and managed to growl out a "No!"

"You and I are just two more of his victims now." I looked down at her tiny frame, which had still managed to toss me around, and I knew she'd probably survive this. She'd probably survived worse.

"You killed her and if—" Mrs. Greeves coughed into her fist and I saw blood on her skin and lips when she glared back up at me. "If they don't get you on that, you'll go to jail for trying to kill me."

Maybe I would. She was obviously the X I'd spoken to Mallory about just hours ago at the station. *I think that person may be in trouble.* Even the inspector would have to see a threat in my words. Or maybe Mallory would see her for the home invader that she was and let me off. But in the meantime, I'd most likely be held in custody. Alice was no longer here to come to my rescue. And every hour I was in that station would be another hour closer to my father's release. I couldn't afford to let him run off somewhere out of my reach. I had to be prepared.

I gripped the knife hilt that was still in my hand and slowly brought the blade up to her neck. Just a nick and I could ensure she wasn't around to accuse me of anything. But I could barely keep the blade held to her skin. She really was just another victim of my father, and just like me, she had become like him to get her revenge.

Mrs. Greeves coughed and made another gargling sound in the back of her throat, and then she gasped out, "Bitch."

"Yeah, I am. But I'll let you in on a little secret. He'll be out at the end of the week, your sergeant. All of your coming after me worked."

I'd maybe expected surprise or relief to filter somewhere into her expression, but instead she clenched her teeth and tried to hiss out another response that I couldn't fathom.

But I nodded anyway. "You've freed a murderer. And now, because of you, I have to become a murderer too, to protect the world from him."

In my imagination, I saw hands covered in blood, only this time, instead of my father's body beyond, I saw Alice dead, and Freddie. I saw Michael and Seanie cowering as our father moved toward them. All of that and more would happen if I went to prison now. And all it would take was a slice to stop her from ruining everything.

You would not be you anymore.

I heard Lock's voice so clearly in my mind right then, I half expected to hear his crunching steps behind me. I gritted my teeth against the sound of it and blinked away the hot, wet feeling in my eyes. I screamed in my mind that he was wrong, that I was already changed, that I had to do this!

But a tremor in my hand moved the knife and nicked her skin, and the blood drop that formed over the wound made me toss the knife aside. I crawled off her and away, until I was sitting in a pile of feathers that used to be Alice's duvet. I thought Mrs. Greeves might get up and run off when I did, but she just lay there, coughing more than she had when I'd been on top of her. She didn't even move her hands. She coughed twice more and her eyes were closed. Maybe she was sleeping, I told myself. Maybe she'd fall into unconsciousness and stay there. Maybe I'd already killed her in the end.

I covered my tremoring hand with the other and stood slowly. I stepped gingerly toward Alice's room. Once there, I turned on the faucet in the powder room and washed my hands and face before the water could turn warm. Then, and only then, did I decide to face my own reflection. It wasn't as bad as I'd thought it would be. There was a scratch along my cheekbone under one eye, and a bruise was forming at my temple. But for the most part, my wounds were all in places that could be hidden under my clothes and by my hair. I'd had worse. Much worse.

My phone buzzed in my pocket, but I ignored it.

"You have to go," I told my reflection. "Quickly now."

I reached under the bathroom vanity for the first-aid kit I knew was kept there. I hugged it to my chest, walked out into the room, and saw my bag behind the door, miraculously untouched in Mrs. Greeves' destruction. I shoved the kit into it.

It wasn't until I was looking in Alice's closet for an unshredded sweater that I heard another cough from out in the entry. My reminder that a woman was dying out there. I took a moment to close my eyes and squeeze my hands together again, and when I opened them, I found a wrap that would work perfectly. It was thick and long enough to hide the blood on my body.

When I reached for my bag again, I winced at the pain in my shoulder, where a piece of glass still felt wedged into my skin. My hip wound ached from all the walking around and standing. I needed to get to a hotel as soon as possible, a thought that made me remember that I needed money. And I'd hidden the cash that Alice had given me in Piddinghoe. I hoisted up my bag, grabbed the wrap, and headed for the kitchen. I knocked along the wood panels of wainscoting in the kitchen until I heard the empty one, then kicked it free to grab the bag of cash.

I shoved the cash bag into my bigger bag, then swung the wrap around my shoulders, making sure I could still use my hands without revealing the wounds at my shoulder and hip. A flare of pain went off in my injured shoulder, and I gritted my teeth against it. The ache in my shoulder set off a kind of ripple effect, bringing to life all the little pains in my back and making my hip pain worse. I needed to get to a hotel to clean up. I needed to lie down.

I slung my bag up on my uninjured shoulder and made for the door. The picture of the little boy stopped me for a few seconds. I reached a hand up like I would touch it, but I never did.

"I'll call for help," I whispered.

Chapter 28

I was halfway down Baker Street when I decided to call Alice.
She answered before the connection could even ring on my
side.

"Where are you?" I asked.

"Safe. Near Battersea Park."

"You should be closer to Brighton by now."

"Yeah, we had to take a little detour. I thought I saw someone who was too interested in us, so we jumped off the train
to make sure we weren't being followed. I've booked tickets to
take a more circuitous route for later tonight. And before you
ask, Michael is safe as well. My friend will meet the transport."

For the slightest moment I thought about not telling Alice
what had happened. She had enough drama on her plate just
getting my brothers to her farm. But she had to know how
toxic London would be from now on. What if she'd brought
them back here tonight?

"I was attacked when I got home. And the house is trashed."
The quiet on the other end of the line made me peek to see
if the call had dropped. When I found it had not, I said, "I'm

fine. But it was that protester woman who has been around the house. She's the one who put the hand in the rubbish bin, and she's been coming after me for weeks."

"And she's been sending you threats." There was something off about Alice's tone, but I couldn't say what it was. I suddenly wished I could see her face to figure out what she was thinking.

"You knew about those?"

"I saw one in your room when I was cleaning up."

"Well, she got pretty badly injured when I fought her off. Do you think you could find a phone to call someone to help her? Anonymously, of course."

"Where is she?" Again, her tone made me wary. It was like her words were clipped. Was she angry? Angry with me?

"She's in the house, bleeding pretty badly. I just know if I call it in, it'll be worse for me in the end. But she's really hurt."

"I'll take care of it. Where are you right now?"

"I'm going to find somewhere to lay low for a bit. Figure out what comes next."

"Text me where you end up."

She was definitely angry. Not that I could blame her. I'd tricked her into leaving town without me and then made a huge mess of things. And now I was involving her. Like she wasn't already doing enough for us. Still, I wasn't going to text her. I knew that.

"I'd better go."

"Yeah. Go find a nice place. Text me and I'll take care of the bill."

I paused just a second before ending the call. "Thanks, Alice."

I thought I heard an amused grunt before she hung up. And for some reason her insistence that I text her made me think of the way Alice snatched my phone from the officer's hand in the police station lobby the day before.

This phone is in my name, she'd said.

Which meant she could probably find it using my GPS if she was really determined. I tapped into my settings and turned off the GPS. Just to be safe. Then I took one last look back at our house, sure that I'd never see it again, and I forced myself to turn the corner away from Baker Street.

By the time I got to Gloucester Place, my whole body ached so badly I was ready to stay at the first hotel I could find. I tripped up a set of stairs into an inn with a white and gold entryway. It looked posh enough for the staff to mind its own business, but was still a retrofitted town house, so not a place that would have too many expectations of me. I managed a smile as I paid for three nights in cash and somehow made it to my room without faltering on the steps.

All I wanted was to fall face-first onto the white and silver linens of the bed, but I knew I would regret not taking care of my wounds. I undressed completely, bagging up my ruined, bloody clothes, then started a bath. While I waited for the tub to fill, I got the tweezers from the first-aid kit and reached back to pull out one off the embedded glass shards I could feel at my neck. The pain was so intense, I couldn't help but whimper, and my plastic tweezers kept slipping on the blood.

I was out of breath by the time I pulled it free and wondered how in the world I'd manage the rest when a knock at the door made me freeze in place. I turned off the bath faucet and waited silently, thinking whoever it was would move along when they realized they had the wrong door. Then they knocked again.

I pulled a towel around me and crept toward the door.

"Mori. Let me in!"

I slid the chain lock into place and opened the door just far enough to see Sherlock out in the hall. "How in the world are you here?" I asked in a loudish whisper.

"Let me in and I'll tell you." He looked over both shoulders, scanning the hall.

"Tell me and I'll let you in," I countered.

Lock made a face and crossed his arms. "The longer I am out in the hall, the more likely someone will recognize me."

I clenched my jaw as I closed the door to undo the chain for him. The minute I opened the door, his arms were around my neck. Thankfully, he was gentle in his embrace.

"I told you what would happen if you didn't answer your phone."

I maybe should have pushed him off me and out the door, but it felt so good to be held by someone, I didn't want to move. Not until I remembered that he shouldn't have known where I was. I pushed against his chest to face him, despite the aching protest of my entire body. "How did you find me?"

He smiled in that way that meant he was about to describe how clever he'd been. "I called Jason Kim to track your phone."

"But I turned off the GPS."

Lock nodded. "Yes, but Jason's app meant he was able to turn it back on remotely."

I cursed, and rushed over to where I'd set my phone on the bedside table. I disabled the GPS again and then deleted Jason's bloody app off my phone for good. I stared down at the bedside table and sighed. "You're not the only one who'll think to use that, Sherlock—"

Before I could finish his name, his arm slid around my middle, to hold me still. His other hand brushed gently over the still-bleeding wound at my neck.

I tried to wave him off me and break free of his hold. "I'll be fine."

Sherlock held me tighter to him, pressing his hand over my hip, so that my legs gave way and I winced at the pain of it. He quickly adjusted his grip, and held his now bloodstained fingers out in front of me.

"Don't speak." He paused, as though he was trying to compose himself, then said, "I'm not asking for the story of how you got this way. I'm not asking why you are here instead of at your home or at the hospital. And I'm not asking if I can stay or not."

"Lock . . ." I turned to face him, but even the barest glance at his expression and all my protests withered away. I'd seen Sherlock full of passion and determination, facing down adventure and even a bit of danger, but I'd never seen him as resolute as he was right then.

"I'm staying," he said. And all I could do was nod and

keep very still, as he painted me with his gaze, taking in every injury he could see. His hand brushed over my hip, where blood was staining through the towel. "Let's get you cleaned up."

I let him lead me over to sit on the edge of the bathtub while he prepared all the supplies. I didn't make any noise when he started plucking glass shards from my back, not even when it hurt so bad I thought I might bite through my lip.

"This one may scar," he muttered, when he reached the last of them, this one right above my left hip.

The relief I felt having the object removed overshadowed any talk of scars. But I reached back all the same. Sherlock stopped my fingers before I could touch the spot.

"I just cleaned that."

A scar. And I'd be able to reach it once it healed over. "What's its shape?"

Sherlock didn't answer at first. He covered the area with a square of gauze and taped it in place. He rested his hand just below the bandage. His fingers curled around my side. "I'm telling you your wound might permanently scar, and you want to know the shape?"

He brushed his thumb lightly over the top of the bandage and I shivered.

"It'll be my memento of this night." I turned slowly until I was facing him, and suddenly I felt shy. Maybe it was the affection I saw in Lock that his concentration couldn't mask. Or possibly the affection I felt for him, compounded by our closeness. He glanced down at my lips briefly.

"You want to remember tonight?" He moved so close that my vision blurred trying to take in his whole face.

"I want to remember every night I've spent with you." *And tonight will be our last.* I wanted to say the words aloud, but I didn't need to. His eyes were so sad. He knew the truth already. When he retreated from me, I felt the pain of it so acutely, I brought a hand up to my chest.

He cleared his throat and said, "One last thing and I'm done. It may hurt."

I nodded, thinking it couldn't possibly hurt more than the twisting and tugging I'd already endured. But when he cascaded antiseptic down my back, I couldn't keep from crying out. After the initial sting, everything started to throb, but by the time he'd closed all the larger wounds with butterfly bandages and covered the lot in gauze and plasters, the stinging had mostly subsided.

When I stood, my entire body ached. I had to rely on Sherlock to help me to the bed, and then I didn't even have the strength to put my clothes back on. I pulled my towel tight around me and got under the covers. He didn't turn off the light or say anything else. He just crawled onto the bed next to me.

After a bit, he reached up to push some hair back from my forehead and said, "I'm ready to hear who did this to you now."

I shook my head. "I can't tell you."

"I didn't expect you would."

"Thank you," I said, and I could hear a trembling in my voice. "I'm sorry."

He traced the scratch on my cheek with his thumb. "No need." He leaned forward to kiss my forehead, then held me close to him. And being able to hide my face against his shoulder let me say all the things that were tripping around my mind just then.

"You can't help me anymore after this," I said. "I need you to stop trying. I can't keep fighting you off. I don't have the will."

"Shhhh. Just rest right now. We'll talk about all that later."

It couldn't have been much past three or four in the afternoon, but sleep sounded like the very best idea, so I let myself fall into it. "Later," he'd said. Yes. Everything I needed to say could wait until then.

Chapter 29

I woke up to sunlight streaming onto my face and my mobile buzzing. I still had my eyes closed when I answered.

"Where are you?" It was, of course, Alice.

I cleared my throat. "I'm safe," I lied. I probably wouldn't ever be safe again.

"Where? I need to know."

"I'm at Sherlock's."

"Don't lie to me."

My heart sank. I looked around the room, but there wasn't any sign of Sherlock. There was a note on the little desk by the door, however.

"I'm at a hotel. It's not like I could go back home."

Alice sighed. "You can. I had the place cleaned out."

"What do you mean?"

"I mean the woman and the vandalism. It's all been taken care of, so go home."

"What does that mean, 'taken care of'?"

Alice was quiet for a long time, but I wasn't going to give

her an out, so I waited. "Please go home. I can't protect you when I don't know where you are."

"I don't need you to protect me," I said. "You just focus on protecting the boys."

"Do you remember last time, when you asked what I would do if your father came for us and we needed real muscle to keep us safe?"

I paused, then said, "Yes."

"I made that call. But it's all for nothing if I don't know where you are. So tell me or go home where I can find you."

I thought about it. Alice had managed to protect me all this time with her contacts. She was just doing it again. I should've been grateful. But something about her voice made me think that this time it would come with a cost. "I'll think about it."

Alice cursed and then lowered her voice. "Think fast. Your dad's getting out day after tomorrow, and—"

"I know he is. That's why I'm here and not there. That's why I don't want you to know where I am. That's also why I don't need your protection."

"Mori, you're being a stupid little girl right now."

I'd thought Alice had been angry the night before, but that was nothing to the anger I could hear in her voice just then. There wasn't even a hint of the playful, sarcastic Alice that I knew.

"You think your mother never wanted him dead? You think she never tried? If someone like Emily couldn't take him down, you never will. Go home. Someone will be waiting there to bring you to the country house. We'll find another way."

"I can't do that."

"And I can't let you throw your life away over that piece of human trash."

We both went quiet, so that I could hear my own breathing echoed through the mic of my phone.

"Okay, kid. If this is what you want, I'll find you on my own. And you'll come with me, whether you want to or not. I'm not leaving you behind again." She ended the call, and I stared out the little window in my strange room—a window that had been covered with a curtain when I went to sleep last night.

I sat up and immediately regretted it. My body felt like it had been pummeled thoroughly as I slept, and all my wounds were aching and throbbing. I wondered how many days I'd have to rest to be fit to face my father. Too many probably. And I wouldn't have the luxury.

I somehow managed to stand and wobble over to the desk where the note waited for me, but I fell back to sit on the bed as soon as it was in hand. I recognized Sherlock's handwriting right away, but instead of a short note telling me he'd gone out for coffee or an errand, the writing filled most of the page.

You didn't wake up for our late-night fight over whether or not you still needed my help, so I'm forced to write it all out here. Lucky for me, you can't argue with a letter. I suppose this means I'll win no matter what. Well done, me.

I could easily imagine the expression on his face as he congratulated himself in writing, and the image lightened my mood instantly.

. . .

*You'll notice I'm not there right now. It was difficult to
leave you in such a vulnerable state, but I knew I had to do
the right thing for once. I'm not wrong in wanting to protect
you when you're vulnerable; still, I knew you needed to
think about things without me there to muddy the waters.*

But I'm not the wrong one right now. You are.

I laughed and said, "Of course I am."

*I've been thinking about what you said to me yesterday,
that you didn't trust me to help you. I don't think you
were being honest about that. I'll not betray you. No
matter what you think, I never have. I've maybe been
stupid in my decisions in the past, but you have the
singular ability to reduce a great mind like my own to that
of a Neanderthal. You know that.*

*You also know you can trust me, so that's not why you
keep pushing me away. I know you think you're attempting
to protect me, but you forget sometimes how well I can take
care of myself. How my choices are mine to make. How I can
sometimes see things in a way you can't. How you see things
in a way I can't. How well we see when we look together.*

*What I'm trying to say is that I want to be with you.
I don't care about any of the rest of it. I just want to be at
your side. I won't stop you. I won't get in your way. I just
want, if you'll allow me, to occupy that space next to you.*

And your allowance is the key, isn't it? I can't force

myself into that space, can't keep following you around like
some kind of resentful mutt who's been domesticated despite
myself. I can't do any of that and still be of any use to you.
And you need me at my best just now.

So it comes to this. You take a think, and I'll be
waiting for you at the bandstand when you've decided.
Don't make me wait too long?

He signed off the letter with a giant *S*. I traced the curve
of it with my finger and then set the page back on the table.

It was perfect, his letter. Arrogant and reckless and lovely
and full of him. And it shattered me in a way I didn't expect.
I'd built this wall made up of all the excuses I'd given myself
and him for why I should push him away, why I should separate myself from the one person I wanted with me. But Lock
had managed to shatter my weeks and weeks of wall building
in just eight paragraphs. He'd done it with hope.

I wondered if he knew how much I needed his hope. I'd
spent so much of these past weeks resigned to my fate—to
my need to stop my father for good and the sacrifices I'd
have to make to do it. I'd hoped the police would keep my
father in jail. I'd hoped his police brothers would stop letting
him use them as his weapons. I'd hoped my brothers could
stay safe and that we'd somehow manage to wring a successful life out of the ruins of our family. But the idea that I
wouldn't eventually be alone? I hadn't dared to hope for that.

And as if that weren't enough, he'd left the decision in my
hands. He'd trusted me in a way I hadn't expected he ever

would. Eight paragraphs all culminating in his willingness to wait for my decision meant that he trusted me with something precious to him. He trusted me with our future, and then asked me to trust him as well.

And for the first time, I could see it, *our* future. I could believe in a future of us together. No more thoughts of temporary. No more thoughts of false nobility. No more thoughts of anything but my Lock waiting for me in the park.

I left the hotel a few minutes later, my bag slung across my body in the least painful way possible. Getting dressed, packing up, and checking out had all felt like separate eternities now that I had somewhere to be. I willed my body to be less broken so that I could get there faster.

But something about being out on the streets and among the people of London made me start to second-guess everything. In that hotel room, all alone, Lock's letter had seemed the starkest truth in the sea of my empty concerns over what could be. And with strangers all around me, laughing and arguing and rushing this way and that, the dim, clean comfort of the hotel room felt more like a total fantasy. My hope, an exercise in wishful thinking.

Still, I forced myself on. Lock was waiting, and I could see it, our future—even if it was only a year from now, I could see it.

It wasn't until I reached the very center of York Bridge that I stopped walking. I wanted to move forward, but my thoughts buzzed with "what if" scenarios, the most prominent being, *What if keeping him with you gets him killed?*

I closed my eyes in an attempt to bury the thought. Needless worry over something that wasn't even a remote reality. Within four minutes I could be walking into Sherlock's embrace. I could have a partner, an ally. Maybe I could even protect him from being corrupted by me. Maybe if I held him close enough . . .

I took another step to cross the bridge, but I was stopped again.

What if loving you ruins him?

Because I couldn't afford to engage in wishful thinking. Lock saying he wouldn't get in my way didn't mean he could stand by and watch me end my father's life. Or that he should have to. And that was what I'd be asking of him, if I met him at the bandstand.

But he'd said that his choices were his to make, and I had to respect that if I wanted him to let me make my own choices as well. I couldn't get angry at his incessant need to tell me what was for my own good, only to turn around and tell him the same. I wouldn't do that to him. Not anymore.

So I took a few more steps, and thought I'd make it all the way to the end of the bridge, only to be stopped again, this time by my father's voice.

What if he can't love who you really are?

That one hurt more than the others, because I believed it. Perhaps he wouldn't. Perhaps, as I'd told Mycroft all those weeks ago, I'd be the one who was broken in the end. But that wouldn't change my decision that day.

Because I loved Sherlock Holmes. Was that a good enough

reason to war with myself in the middle of a bridge?

I stood there, on the edge of the bloody bridge, because he was mine. Sherlock was mine and I wanted him. I loved him, and maybe it was wrong, or twisted, but I couldn't be swayed. Not again.

I paced off York Bridge toward Regent's Park lake. I went to Sherlock because he was my hope, and I needed him. Because he was right. We always did see things better together. I knew my crimes would taint him the way they'd taint me. I knew he'd feel the pain of my destruction, but still I walked the path, past the rubbish bin where the wallet man used to search for recyclables, past the bench where the Lady Constance used to rest with her bags. I was almost to the bandstand. I could see the silhouette of my shadowed man, waiting there with nerves that made him stand stock-still.

I smiled, but before I could move more than a step farther, I was stopped again, this time by hands that came out of nowhere, pinning my arms to my sides and stuffing something over my mouth and nose. As my world turned gray and then black, I could still see Sherlock just up ahead, but I couldn't make a noise. Couldn't move. And then I couldn't see him anymore at all. Right before everything went black, I saw someone hurl my mobile down at the ground and heard feet stomp it to bits.

Chapter 30

The pain woke me up. My head felt like someone had beaten on it with a bat. Everything smelled weird. The minute I tried to move, my shoulder screamed at me to stop. I groaned aloud but made myself sit up, which made my hip join in on the pain party.

"You're awake."

I recognized the voice, but I couldn't figure out where I was or what had happened.

"Alice. I think my dad tried to attack me."

"It wasn't your dad," she said.

I forced my eyes to open, despite the pain, and thought I was seeing things at first. I was sitting on a bed, but the floor was covered in straw. And I could see Alice sitting in an old leather recliner across the way, but there were silver bars between us. I tried to look around, but moving my head made me feel like I would vomit.

"Just keep your eyes closed, Mori. You'll recover faster if you keep them closed."

"Where am I? What is this?"

"You're safe," she said. "You're at the farm."

I sighed and squinted my eyes open again to gain some sense of where I was. The room I was in looked like it had been converted from a horse stall. And there was a door to my right that was open just enough for me to see a small bathroom beyond. But instead of a door to get out of the stall, there was an opening with silver bars.

"You have a jail cell on your farm?"

I closed my eyes again, but I couldn't ignore the pain in my shoulder and brought a hand up to hold it.

"I have someone on the way to treat those. Was that caused by that woman in the house?"

I nodded. "What is this?"

I heard rustling, and when I opened my eyes, Alice was standing at the bars holding a white card between them. "This should explain things."

"Not really in the mood for show-and-tell." It took me a while, but I lay back down gingerly, shifting until my back stopped stinging. "Just tell me what I have to do to get out of here."

I heard the card flop onto the straw somewhere close to my cot. "You'll want to see this. It's your third sin."

That got my attention, but sitting up took me much longer than it should have.

"What drug did you give me?"

Alice smiled. "Several. You had a long trip to take."

I grabbed the card and stared at the silver embossed THANK YOU on the front for a few seconds. "You sent the cards," I said. "That's why they didn't have stamps."

"Clever girl. Just asking that question now, though? I almost ran them through the post just to make it perfect, but I needed them to come to you at set times. And who can trust the post office?"

"But Mrs. Greeves . . . ," I knew what had happened as soon as I'd said her name. "She sent the collage threat. It had a postmark."

Alice sneered a little and rolled her eyes. "She sent twelve of those stinky envelopes. I had to intercept them, which was a trial with all of you home from school."

My second sin smelled like the model glue because Alice had probably held them together, not because they were both from Greeves. I'd been stupid to think that meant something.

My stomach rolled and I squeezed my eyes shut against the nausea. "Why?"

Alice didn't answer, and when I looked up, she was back in her recliner, staring at the rafters of the barn. She was clearly not ready to answer my questions, leaving me just the one avenue of information.

I opened the card. This time the frame was a plain oval, and there was just a rough sketch of the head of the man that usually peeked in, but inside the frame was another frame—this one a window. In front of the window stood a woman who was clearly meant to be Mrs. Greeves. Just like she'd said, she stood outside our kitchen window and watched me hold a knife to my father's neck.

"That Greeves woman saw you." Alice spoke up to the rafters.

"I know."

288

"She heard from Constance Ross that you'd thrown the sword into the lake, then she saw you holding a knife to your father's neck and decided that meant you were the guilty one."

"I said I know. She told me herself. She's probably telling the police right now."

Alice stood and walked to the bars again. "She's not. You can thank me for that."

She had all my attention then, which seemed to be just what Alice wanted. "What do you mean?"

"She's dead." Alice watched me closely then, looking for my reaction when she added, "I did it for you."

"You killed her." I didn't know how she'd expected me to react, but I'd obviously disappointed her.

"I did it for you. She's been after you from the beginning. Haven't you put it together yet? She came there that night to *kill* you."

"But she didn't. She was dying on the floor, you didn't have—"

"And what if she survived?" Alice looked out through the doorway behind her. "I can't believe it took me this long to figure out who she was." She turned back to me. "As soon as you said what'd happened, I remembered that I'd seen her with Constance Ross at the police station. When I was arguing with Mallory about keeping you in custody, I saw her." Alice pointed at the white card that was still in my hands. "That Greeves woman was yelling at the officer who was trying to control Constance. So when you told me she'd attacked you, that's when I knew I had to get you away from London."

Alice was Y.

"She's been after you all this time, sending threats and calling in tips to the police. You said it's been her all along."

But if Alice was Y, that had to mean she killed Constance, which didn't make sense. "Did you kill Constance? And leave her on our stoop?!"

Alice seemed proud of herself as she explained, "Mallory already knew someone was after you. He would never believe you'd leave a body on your own stoop. I was giving him proof of what he already believed and getting rid of a statement that might have buried you. I did it for you!"

"Stop saying that!" I regretted yelling as soon as I did it. My head started to throb again with a steady rhythm. I sighed and dropped the card. There were a few smudges of dried blood on the back. The artist's, of course. It had to be. She'd killed Charles Ross before he could finish drawing my third sin. She killed his wife for daring to medicate herself. And she finished off Mrs. Greeves. Alice was a serial killer, just like my dad. And she was taking care of my brothers while I was locked in a cell in her horse barn.

That thought seemed to clear my head in a way hours of rest might not have been able.

"How did you find out about Constance and the drawings?"

"From one of my marks, of course. Or . . . ex-marks. I'm sorry to say he's no longer among us. You've met part of him, though."

Because his hand was in my rubbish bin. "Charles Ross was a mark."

Alice ran a hand across the bars. "He was the one who saw your father killing that girl in the park. He knew who the real killer was but didn't think he needed to get involved as a witness because your father was already in jail. But he couldn't convince Clara Greeves that your father was the true killer. And Clara had Crazy Constance all in an uproar, trying to force her to go to the police with what she knew about the sword. So Charles Ross came to me, hoping desperately to save his wife from having an episode."

"You killed them both?"

Alice shrugged. "I'm not normally a killer. I'm a player. Why actually do the deed when you can just move all the pieces into place and watch the game play out on its own? But this time I had to make an exception."

"People are not wooden pawns. You can't predict—"

"And yet, they are so very predictable. Aren't they?" She smiled and I remembered a time when I thought her smile was genuine. Now I wondered if it had ever been. "You, for instance. I didn't need to know where you were as long as I knew where Sherlock was."

Sherlock. I'd never reached the bandstand. He probably thought I'd refused him again. "He didn't help you. He wouldn't tell you anything."

Alice looked at the floor. "No, but we followed him to the park and that's when I noticed he was just staring at his phone, like he was watching something. I sent one of my boys in to ask him a question, and he saw the app on his phone. A tracking app."

"My GPS." I closed my eyes as my heart sank. He'd turned my GPS back on before he left the hotel room so he could watch to see whether I was coming for him or not.

"I thought you'd outwitted me when it was turned off the night before. But then all of a sudden, there you were again, and you were walking right toward us."

"Right into your trap." But if my GPS was on, that meant he could track me still.

A shred of hope must have somehow shone through my expression just then, because Alice smirked.

"We destroyed your phone," she said, her mockery returning in full force. "It was for your own good. Well, for my good. It gets you out of my way."

The fuzzy memory of my phone being stripped from my hand and crushed on the ground returned. I was so empty, every breath I took felt like it gusted through the dark cave that was my center. Every inhale was so loud. He couldn't stand to wait for me—couldn't take the not knowing. So he'd turned on my GPS to watch and see what I'd do. I wondered what Lock thought when he saw my stops and starts on the bridge, when he saw me finally coming toward him only to stop short and disappear. He'd think that was my decision.

One of my breaths snagged on a laugh that had no joy in it. Then another. Soon, I was laughing darkly to myself and holding my head in a vain attempt to keep the pain at bay.

"If only I'd actually walked away. Imagine that."

Alice's smile fell and she looked at me with a creepy sort of interest. Almost as if she was studying my reactions again.

"So you captured me," I said. "To what end? Why am I here?"

"Because you're nothing like your mother." Alice held the bars and leaned back like a little kid at a playground. "This wasn't in the original plan, of course. I was going to make you my partner, the way I'd been for your mom. I even tried to teach you. But, sadly, you aren't like Emily." She blew her bangs up off her forehead and pulled herself upright again.

"You said over and over that I was."

"Yes, which is why I sent you the cards. That was my test. Emily would have figured out what was going on ages before you did. But I suppose it's good that you turned out to be lesser. There can't be two of us. That won't do."

Two of us. I stared at Alice, wondering what in the world that meant.

"But you're not like her, are you?" She smiled. "You're like *him.*"

I knew immediately whom she meant. "I'm not!"

"Oh. Did I hit a sore spot?" Alice offered a mocking pout. "That moment in the hospital stairway I saw the truth. You actually put your hand around my neck. Do you remember doing that? Do you know how many times I watched your father do that to my Emily?"

My Emily. Her "two of us" comment made sense suddenly, especially if Emily Moriarty was whom she wanted to become. Her hero had left a giant gap in the lives of me and my brothers and I'd invited Alice to fill it. I'd ushered her right into the spot. But that couldn't be all of it. There had to be a bigger game to play for Alice. "If I'm so much like my dad, why would you want me around?"

"You'll find out soon enough."

"How foreboding, our Alice. I suppose you think I'll do something for you in the end."

"And you think you won't. As long as we're both clear on the starting point."

"Nothing is starting, Alice." I sat up too fast, which sent a rage of pain through my skull, but I covered it with the smile that most enraged my father. She was attempting to keep some kind of amused expression on her face, but it was clear to me how irritated she was that I wasn't cowed by her. "This is a lot of wasted effort." I stood, feeling stronger than I suspected I would. "So typical of a lowly con woman to go to so much trouble for very little return."

"What's your point?"

"Two things."

I slowly made my way across my tiny prison to the bars where she stood. She didn't back down and I didn't stop until we were practically face-to-face. It was foolish of her to underestimate me like she was.

"First, this," I gestured around my jail cell. "I'm sure this plan of yours will be full of lots of clever little fragments, but in the end it will mean nothing."

She laughed and stepped back from the bars, but too slowly. I jutted my arm through just in time to grab her by the hair and yank her head so hard against the metal bars, the thud rang for a few moments after impact. She whimpered and was forced to hang on to my cage to keep herself upright. I held tension on her hair to keep her in place, then leaned down so she could feel my lips at her ear when I said, "Second, and let the pain you're feeling now serve as the smallest proof that what I'm about to say is true—you're not smart enough to break me, Alice Stokes."

I heard footsteps coming and, with my hand still fisted in her hair, I let Alice's head sway away from the bars just enough so I could let go and drop her to the floor. I ignored the men who rushed to her aid. Ignored their panicked shuffling about and Alice's vague threats shouted through my new cage wall. I ignored everything and limped over to the cot to collapse, facing the back of my cell, so that no one could see the scattered tears that dripped down my cheeks.

I couldn't stop them. Maybe because I was all alone again to fight a battle I didn't want to fight. But I should've been used to that by now. Maybe because for all my supposed cleverness, I'd been ensnared by a second-rate copy of my mother. That was humiliating, to say the least. But staring at the wall of my new prison, I knew the exact reason for my tears.

I couldn't help but remember over and over the last thought I'd had before waking up to this new nightmare. I'd smiled just before they grabbed me, because I'd remembered something my Lock had said to me once. That we were our own army. That none could stand before us. In Regent's Park, for a brief shining moment, I'd thought he and I were finally going to become that. I'd thought maybe we'd belong to each other. At least for a while. That maybe he could keep me from becoming a monster while slaying one. But it was a stupid, stupid thought. Because as much as we wanted that fantasy to be our reality, even an attempt to make it happen ended only in disaster.

And so I cried for our army that would never be. I shed tears for the belonging I'd never know. Because Alice had declared war and I couldn't afford to have a liability like Sherlock Holmes if I were to win. I couldn't let him be my weakness like he'd been yesterday in the park. Never again. Because I had to win—for my brothers and myself. I couldn't let our lives be determined by anyone else.

So I made a set of promises to myself, that day in my horse-stall jail cell. I scratched a line into the wood behind my bed and promised that I would escape this cell as soon as possible. I scratched another line and promised that I would find a way to make my brothers safe again. Another line, deeper this time, as I promised that I would neutralize Alice and destroy my father.

I paused before I scratched my final line, and when I finally drew my fingernail down the grain of the wood, my vision blurred with fresh tears. I traced my finger down the divot I'd made, and then I promised that these would be the last tears I'd ever shed for Sherlock Holmes.

Acknowledgments

Writing this book was an adventure I might not have survived if it weren't for the following people who get my unending thanks:

To Laurie McLean, my amazing agent, who always manages to make me feel like a rock star, even when I'm a mess, and who cheers me up, even when she doesn't know I need it. You are an amazing partner and friend. I feel so lucky to be a small part of Team Fuse Lit.

To my patient and brilliant editor, Christian Trimmer, and to his lovely and insightful assistant, Catherine Laudone. Thank you so much for helping me dig deeper, and for giving me the time and space to make this the best it could be. And special thanks to all the S&S BFYR team, who have been so supportive in my debut year!

To my critique partners, Tracy Clark and Kristin Crowley Held, for fitting me into your schedules on super-quick deadlines and letting me argue with myself until I could find a path through. I love you both and I couldn't be more excited to finally see us all together on the same shelf.

To my Fearless Fifteeners, who have given the best advice and support possible, despite my monthly, K-pop-gif-filled rantings about cabins in the woods and bad bird poetry. You are all officially invited to my hermit lollipop commune. Thank you for being part of my tribe!

To Naomi Canale, Cynthia Mun, Terri Farley, Ellen Hopkins, Suzie Morgan Williams, and the rest of my NV SCBWI family. I would not have made it through this year without you! And to Zach Payne, Heather Riccio, and the rest of the Mentor Program crew, thank you so much for your patience and excitement. You guys are amazing. I can't wait to see your books on the shelves!

To Katie from Mundie Moms, Beth from Fangirlish, and all the other book bloggers, librarians, booksellers, and reviewers who continue to spread the word about Lock & Mori, I will never be able to adequately express how much I appreciate and adore you all.

And finally, to my endlessly supportive family. You somehow manage to keep our lives afloat while I flit off to events and working weekends, and all the other stuff that has taken me away from you this year. Thank you for tolerating all of it. I love you completely—even when I growl from my writing cave and stare at you like you're not in the room.